Acclaim for the novels of Julie Ortolon

"A fun, fast-paced, and fiery romance."
—Road to Romance

"Earnest and endearing, Ortolon's newest is a heart-warming and at times heartrending read."
—*Publishers Weekly*

"Entertaining and touching."   —*Booklist*

"Full of humor . . . very entertaining and well worth your time."   —Huntress Book Reviews

"Julie Ortolon takes her wonderfully colorful and appealing characters on an unexpected journey of discovery. Be prepared to laugh."   —Christina Skye

"So romantic it will make you melt!"
—Virginia Henley

"A smart and funny story."   —*Rendezvous*

"This is an author on the rise! An endearing, emotional, and romantic tale."   —*Romantic Times*

JUST PERFECT

Julie Ortolon

A SIGNET ECLIPSE BOOK

SIGNET ECLIPSE
Published by New American Library, a division of
Penguin Group (USA) Inc., 375 Hudson Street,
New York, New York 10014, USA
Penguin Group (Canada), 90 Eglinton Avenue East, Suite 700, Toronto,
Ontario M4P 2Y3, Canada (a division of Pearson Penguin Canada Inc.)
Penguin Books Ltd., 80 Strand, London WC2R 0RL, England
Penguin Ireland, 25 St. Stephen's Green, Dublin 2,
Ireland (a division of Penguin Books Ltd.)
Penguin Group (Australia), 250 Camberwell Road, Camberwell, Victoria 3124,
Australia (a division of Pearson Australia Group Pty. Ltd.)
Penguin Books India Pvt. Ltd., 11 Community Centre, Panchsheel Park,
New Delhi - 110 017, India
Penguin Group (NZ), cnr Airborne and Rosedale Roads, Albany,
Auckland 1310, New Zealand (a division of Pearson New Zealand Ltd.)
Penguin Books (South Africa) (Pty.) Ltd., 24 Sturdee Avenue,
Rosebank, Johannesburg 2196, South Africa

Penguin Books Ltd., Registered Offices:
80 Strand, London WC2R 0RL, England

First published by Signet Eclipse, an imprint of New American Library,
a division of Penguin Group (USA) Inc.

First Printing, October 2005
10 9 8 7 6 5 4 3 2 1

To Friends

For filling my days with laughter
For three-hour lunches (when we should be
writing)
For enabling my Chico's shopping addiction
For unquestioned support, sympathy, whining,
and wining
For champagne celebrations (anytime, any reason)
And for e-mailing in the face of deadlines!

A special thanks goes out with this book to:

Scott with Utah Search and Rescue for his patience
and expertise.
I hope I got everything right!

Author, friend, and ski junkie Cindi Myers for
answering all my questions and only laughing
a tiny bit at my ignorance.

And to Melinda for so many things, I don't know
where to begin. You were research assistant,
cheerleader, and my labor and delivery coach on
birthing this baby.

Cheers to all of you for making this book possible!

Chapter 1

Fear is a funny thing; without it, no one is truly brave.
—*How to Have a Perfect Life*

Christine couldn't believe she'd let her friends talk her into this. Standing in the plaza at the base of Silver Mountain, she felt her heart palpitate as she looked at the chairlift. It carried a steady stream of skiers up the mountain, all of them sitting calmly in the chairs—which were nothing more than narrow benches dangling a mile off the ground—chatting away as if gravity didn't even exist. As if the thought of slipping off that narrow seat and plummeting to the ground never entered any of their minds.

Growing up, she'd had a hard enough time riding the chairlift during her family's annual Christmas vacations to Colorado, but after doing her residency in a hospital emergency room, she had an all-too-vivid image in her head of exactly what the result of such a fall would look like.

How had she let Maddy and Amy talk her into this? Of course, sitting in a bookstore coffee shop with her friends last spring, the thought of facing her fear of heights hadn't seemed like that big a deal. Well, it had. Just not this big a deal.

She couldn't back down, though. The three of them had made a pact. Maddy had already fulfilled her challenge to face her fear of rejection and get her art in a gallery, but Amy had yet to face her fear of getting lost in order to travel on her own. If Christine backed down, Amy would be off the hook.

She had to do this.

For Amy, if not for herself.

And the best approach was to get it over with as quickly as possible—like ripping off an adhesive strip.

The one problem with that plan was her ski instructor was nowhere in sight. They'd told her at the ski school to look for a tall blond guy wearing a green jacket who'd meet her at the trail map. Granted, she'd arrived a few minutes late, but not that late.

Please, Lord, let him be late too, not already come and gone.

Rubbing her gloved hands against the cold, she turned away from the slopes to scan the crowded plaza. People moved in and out of the festively decorated shops and restaurants. Miles of garlands abounded, along with big red bows and holiday banners hanging from lampposts. Last night's snowfall dusted the roofs and windowsills of the tall lodge-style buildings.

But nowhere did she see a blond man in a green parka.

Growing desperate, she abandoned her post by the trail map and headed for the lift ticket window, walking awkwardly in her ski boots. Maybe someone there could help her.

"Excuse me," she said to the college-age girl behind one of the windows. "I'm looking for Alec Hunter. I don't know if you know him—"

"Crazy Alec?" The girl's face lit with a smile. "Of course I do."

Crazy Alec? Christine frowned as the girl craned her neck to search the plaza. What did she mean *Crazy* Alec? No, no, no, she didn't want Crazy Alec. She wanted Very Sane Safety Conscious Alec. The man at the ski school had said they were too shorthanded to spare one of their regular instructors for five days of private lessons, so he'd arranged for "a friend" to teach her. He hadn't mentioned anything about his friend being crazy. In fact, he'd made it sound like a great privilege that Alec Hunter had even agreed to work with her.

"There he is." The girl pointed. "That's him over there."

Christine turned but didn't see anyone who fit the description they'd given her. "I don't see him."

"Over there." The girl pointed again. "Talking to Lacy at the pub."

Christine looked again and finally spotted him. All this time, she'd been searching for a dark green parka, not an eye-popping fluorescent green. He stood at the edge of an outdoor eating area in front of St. Bernard's Pub talking to a very pretty brunette holding a serving tray. The woman shook her head and laughed at something he said.

"Thanks," Christine told the ticket booth worker and headed across the plaza to meet her instructor, her stomach somersaulting the whole way. Maybe she should cancel today's lesson and get a different instructor. But, no, she was here. He was here. And she wanted very much to get past the first trip up the mountain. Surely after that, it would get easier. *Please God, let it get easier.*

Her instructor stood in profile: tall and lanky with short golden hair that had been streaked lighter by the sun.

The waitress started to move away, but he grabbed her hand and placed his free hand over his heart. She shook her head even while smiling into his eyes. He dropped to one knee, holding her hand in both of his, pleading in earnest.

"Oh, all right!" The waitress relented as Christine drew close enough to hear. "But this is the last time."

"You're all heart, Lacy," he insisted. "And I'll pay you back tomorrow. I swear."

"You'll take a week to remember and you know it." The waitress laughed as she moved away.

"Alec Hunter?" Christine tipped her head to see his face.

Still down on one knee, he shifted toward her, revealing a boyishly handsome face with the bluest eyes she'd ever seen—brighter-than-the-sky blue—accented by long lashes a few shades darker than his hair. He didn't look crazy. He looked like a choir boy. A very mischievous choir boy, she amended as his eyes twinkled up at her. "That would be me."

"Oh good." She hoped. "I'm Christine Ashton."

"Hey, you made it." A grin flashed across his face as he stood, showing off sparkling white, perfectly straight teeth. Goodness, this guy could make a killing doing toothpaste commercials. "I was about to give up on you."

"Sorry." She blinked at his height. Being five ten, she was eye level with most men, but he topped her by several inches. "I had an emergency phone call."

"Ah." His inflection dismissed the word "emergency" completely.

Not that it was any of his business, but the call had been from the hospital back in Austin, where she'd recently finished her residency, with a question about a repeat patient. She couldn't very well tell them to please ask Mrs. Henderson to postpone any more myocardial infarctions until after her ski lesson.

Pushing the wry thought aside, she studied the man before her, judging him to be younger than her own age of thirty-three. Cute, but young. "I hope it won't offend you if I ask, but you are a qualified instructor, right?"

He flashed another killer grin. "If you're looking for someone to teach you how to ski, really ski, I'm your man."

Since that was indeed what she wanted, she refrained from questioning him further.

"Okay, Alec." Lacy returned. "Here you go."

Alec took the large to-go bag Lacy handed over. When the weight of it hit his hands, he knew he'd caught her in a generous mood. Good thing, since he was down to one power bar in his pocket and had forgotten his wallet. Again. "Thanks, darling. I owe you."

"Yes, you do. The receipt's inside. I expect a serious tip."

"Have I ever stiffed you?" He tried out a wounded-puppy look, which she ignored with a snort and flounced off. Unfazed, he turned to the woman Bruce had begged him to instruct. "You ready?"

An odd look of apprehension passed over her face as she glanced toward the chairlift. Then she straightened her shoulders. "As I'll ever be."

"Great. Where are your skis?"

"I left them in a rack near the lift."

"Me too." He headed across the plaza with her falling in step beside him, their boots clunking on the paving stones.

When they reached the racks to retrieve their gear, he couldn't help but raise a brow. Whoever this Christine Ashton was, she had money, no doubt about that. If the ice-blue-and-white skiwear with the distinctive Spyder logo splashed everywhere hadn't tipped him off, her gear would have. Everything from her helmet to her skis was all brand spanking new and probably cost more than three months of rent on his apartment. Bruce had sworn up and down she was an intermediate skier looking to improve her skill, but her gear gave him doubts. Seasoned skiers rarely had all new equipment at once.

Darn it, he thought as he clicked into his well-used Salomon Hots. He'd actually been looking forward to this, once he'd resigned himself to playing ski instructor. The way he'd finally figured it, a week of private lessons with a decent student meant he'd get in some non-work-related ski time while burning up some of those vacation and sick days the county manager was hounding him to take. Cool deal—if it was true.

If not, his buddy Bruce was going to owe him big-time for this.

His doubts grew as he watched her struggle with the bindings on her skis. There should be a law against people buying top-notch equipment they didn't know how to use just because they could afford it.

Although, even if she turned out to be a total novice, at least she offered some serious compensation in the eye-candy department. His brows rose when she bent to adjust her boots and her pants tightened about her long, slender thighs. Legs had always been his weakness. The rest of her wasn't bad either— even if she had a little too much of that ice-princess polish for his taste—but man, those legs promised to have his libido whimpering before the day was over. He felt the first pitiful whine coming on as she bent even farther forward. Her straight fall of white-blond hair slid over one shoulder in a slow, sexy glide. "You, um, need help with that?"

"No, I got it," she insisted, and finally managed to step into the bindings.

"Great." He cleared his throat. "Let's get in line."

She skied to the lift line with enough ease to reassure him that she had at least been on skis before. The line was fairly long, so he took off his gloves and opened the bag to see what Lacy had packed: ham-and-cheese sandwich, sour cream-and-onion potato chips, a can of cola to feed his sugar and caffeine addiction, and . . . He tilted the bag to see all the way to the bottom. Yes! A giant chocolate-chunk cookie. "I *love* that woman."

"I take it that was your girlfriend."

"Who, Lacy?" He scowled at the idea. "Heck no. She's engaged to one of the guys. Here, hold these, will ya?" He handed his poles to her, then pulled out the sandwich and went to work appeasing his overactive metabolism. He'd long since given up hope that it would slow down someday. Small wonder, though, with his daily exertion level.

By the time they'd reached the lift house, he'd inhaled the entire sack lunch. He pocketed the receipt as a reminder to pay Lacy back, and shot the bag and empty soda can into the trash.

"Thanks," he said as he took the poles back, which was when he noticed his student was breathing a little too fast and had gone from pampered-princess pale to about-to-faint pale. "Hey, you didn't just arrive today, did you?"

"No, yesterday." She breathed in and out. "Why do you ask?"

"You look like you're having a little trouble with the altitude."

"I'm fine."

"You know, one of the dumbest mistakes people make every year is to step off a plane, hop on a ski lift, and faint at the top of a mountain. If we need to postpone your first lesson—"

"I told you, I'm fine." A hint of snootiness chilled her words. "I know how to handle the altitude."

Yeah, famous last words of lowlanders everywhere. Before he could question her further, they were at the front of the line and the lift ops were waving them into position. Well, at least if she fainted, he had the training to deal with it.

The next chair came up behind them, scooped them off the ground, and carried them upward. He was just leaning back, settling in for a nice ride up the mountain on a clear, sunny day when he realized the woman beside him was clutching the armrest and chanting under her breath.

"Ohgod, ohgod, ohgod."

"Hey." He frowned at her. "You okay?"

"Actually, no, I'm not." She turned to him with frantic eyes. "I've changed my mind. I really don't want to do this. Get me off this thing!"

"There is no getting off once you're on."

"Then put the safety bar down! As in right now!"

"Okay, okay. Don't panic." He lowered the bar, which was a real nuisance with the foot rest banging on their skis, but one he'd gladly put up with if it calmed down the crazy woman. He looked over at her stark-white face. "Don't you dare pass out on me. Not up here."

"Did you have to say 'up here'?" Gripping the hand bar in front of them, she looked down, then snapped her eyes skyward with a groan. "Why am I doing this?"

"Good question. I thought you said you'd skied before."

"I have. But I gave it up because I hate riding on these stupid things. How can anyone stand this? I swear to God, I'm going to kill Maddy and Amy for making me do this!"

"Who?"

"My best friends. *Ex* best friends as of this exact moment."

"Look, it's okay." He reached over and massaged her shoulder. "You're not going to fall."

"I'm not worried about falling." She squeezed her eyes shut. "I'm worried about jumping!"

"Jumping?" He frowned at her. "Why on earth would you even think about jumping? We're at least fifty feet off the ground. You'd never survive."

"*I know!*"

"Well, then, don't do it!"

"I'm trying not to!"

"Why would you even want to?" His own panic level increased as he imagined the result.

"It's a common compulsion brought on by anxiety," she said. "The same compulsion that makes people think about driving off bridges, or straight into an oncoming eighteen-wheeler."

Holy Jesus, was she serious? "Remind me never to ride in a car with you."

"I don't get it on the highway. Just on ski lifts."

"Why?"

"I don't know!"

"All right, okay." He massaged her shoulder harder. "Try not to think about it."

The lift stopped, jarring the chair and making it swing. She let out a squeak, and her eyes squeezed shut. "Please don't let me jump. Please don't let me jump."

"Hey, hey, hey, let's do this." His heart hammering, he took hold of her nearest wrist. "Let go of the bar—"

"*Not on your life!*" She glared at him with murderous intent.

"Come on, trust me. Let go of the bar and move your hand to the back of the seat." He guided it for her. "There, like that, so you're facing me." He shifted his upper body to face her as well, trying to bang their skis together as little as possible. "Now look at me. Right here." He pointed to his eyes with two fingers. "You just keep your eyes locked on mine while we breathe. In . . . out . . . in . . . out . . ." Slowly her breathing steadied, but her grip remained tight on the seat back and safety rail. "Better?"

She nodded and continued to breathe. A gust of wind blew a spray of snow off the tops of the nearby pine trees, reminding him just how high they were off the ground.

"So tell me about your friends. Mandy and . . . ?"

"Maddy and Amy." She inhaled. "We have . . . a challenge going. We each have one year to conquer a fear that's been keeping us from doing something we've always wanted to do."

"And conquering your fear of the chairlift so you can ski is your challenge?"

"Not just so I can ski. So I can outski my big brother on the black runs. That's where you come in."

He lifted a brow. "How long has it been since you skied?"

"Fourteen years."

"How good is your brother?"

"Don't ask."

"That good, huh?"

"Yes, dang it! And I hate it." Color returned to her cheeks. "He beats me at everything. Skiing is the only thing I think I might be able to best him at. I know it sounds childish, but this means a lot to me. And I only have one week to get in shape before the rest of my family arrives for Christmas."

"The rest of your family?" he prompted to keep her talking.

"My parents, my brother and his wife and their two little boys. They spend every Christmas at my parents' condo in Central Village. Since I don't want them to know how much the chairlift frightens me, I haven't had Christmas with the family in years."

"Really?" He cocked a brow. "Me either. Although I'm sure for entirely different reasons. See, I've always thought family get-togethers are overrated. Especially during the holidays when everyone's even crazier than normal."

"Yes, but do you know how hard my brother, Robbie, would laugh if he knew why I never come for Christmas?"

The lift started moving again with a clanging of cables and a jolt of motion. She slammed her eyes closed.

"No, don't do that. Look at me." He waited for her to open her eyes. "Good. Just breathe and keep your eyes right here on mine." Man, she had great-looking eyes. A pale silver with only a hint of blue. The rest of her face was . . . classy. No other word for it. None of that "she wasn't classically beautiful, but there was something about her . . ." This woman *was* classically beautiful in every way, including the slender nose, high cheekbones, and the smooth line of her jaw. And then there was all that pale blond hair falling nearly to her waist, begging for a man's fingers to run through it.

His body stirred at the thought.

"So, um"—he cleared his throat—"tell me more about this challenge. Why did you and your friends come up with it?"

"Hmm?" She seemed to have lost the thread of their conversation while staring back into his eyes.

"The challenge." He moved the hand he had resting on the back of the bench to her wrist and worked his bare fingers under the cuff of her jacket to monitor her pulse. It was racing like a scared rabbit. If she passed out, would he be able to stop her from falling? "Tell me how it came about."

"Oh . . ." She relaxed a bit while he massaged her wrist. "The three of us were suitemates at UT. Actually, there were four of us back then. Three of us remained really close. Maddy, Amy, and me. The fourth was Jane Redding."

"From the morning show?" He raised a brow.

"Yes. Jane moved off to New York and became a hotshot news anchor, then went into motivational speaking."

"Didn't she write some book?"

"A self-help book for women titled *How to Have a Perfect Life.*"

"That's the one." He nodded. "I saw it at East Village Books and had to laugh. No offense to your friend, but nobody has a perfect life."

"I couldn't agree more, but that book is what started the whole thing. We all bought copies of it at Jane's book signing in Austin to be supportive of an old friend. But then we discovered that she'd used *us* as negative examples of women who let fear stand in the way of pursuing their dreams. Can you believe that?" Her pulse picked up again. "The bitch!"

"Excuse me?" Alec choked back a laugh at hearing profanity from someone who looked so refined.

"How dare she use us as examples in her book!"

"So what'd she say about you? That you let your fear of heights interfere with your dream of becoming an Olympic skier?"

"No." She gave a dignified snort, as if what she was about to say was ludicrous. "She said I was so afraid of parental disapproval that I put pleasing my father ahead of my own happiness."

"Is that true?"

"No, it's not true." Indignation sparkled in her eyes. "But what if it is? What is wrong with wanting to earn my father's approval? He happens to be a brilliant cardiologist. I respect his opinion, so of course I want to make him proud. That's not fear, and it doesn't mean I put my own happiness aside for him."

"How did all this turn into your ski challenge?"

"Oh." That reined her in some. "Well. It's a little complicated to get into while we're dangling a million miles above the ground."

"Don't think about that. Tell me about the challenge."

"Basically, we agreed that Jane was wrong about the big fears holding us back, but that we did have some smaller fears that were stopping us from doing things we wanted to do. So we came up with a separate challenge for each of us. Whoever hasn't met hers at the end of one year has to take the other two out for a really nice lunch and put up with ribbing for the rest of her life. Since my challenge is to go skiing, I thought as long as I'm going to do it, I'd really like to make my brother eat my powder in front of my dad. Just once in my life, I want to hear my father admit Robbie isn't perfect at everything. That there is this one thing, at least, that I can do better." Her gaze grew pleading. "Can you help me?"

"I guess we're about to find out, since . . . we're here."

"We are?" Christine turned forward to see the top of the lift right ahead. Before she had time to protest, Alec raised the safety bar.

Her whole body sang with relief as they hopped off the chair and skied down a gentle slope to an open area at the top of the run. She turned to take in the view.

The wide blue sky domed the Rocky Mountains while snow dusted the tall pine trees lining the slopes. Skiers and snowboarders swished down the mountain beneath the never-ending line of lift chairs. Wow. She looked at how high those chairs hung in the air—and felt triumphant.

"I did it!" A rush of gratitude made her want to throw her arms around Alec Hunter. Checking the impulse, she smiled instead. "Would it be entirely inappropriate if I kissed you?"

He chuckled. "Wouldn't bother me."

She let out an exuberant laugh. "Teach me what I need to know and maybe I just will."

Chapter 2

Alec really wished she hadn't made that joke about kissing him, because now he couldn't get the thought out of his head. They moved away from the crowded lift area so he could give her some basic instruction, but his brain had trouble focusing on skiing. That was a new phenomenon, since skiing was normally what he ate, drank, and slept.

He went through his safety-first speech by rote, then turned his attention to her equipment. "Okay, what you want to keep in mind is that your new skis are going to be very different from the ones you would have used fourteen years ago."

"Yes, the salesman mentioned that." Her face was a study in concentration, letting him know she had no trouble focusing. "Something about the shorter length and wider width taking less effort to make turns."

"Exactly. You won't need nearly as much body action. The motion is more of a shifting of weight, like this." He demonstrated while facing her. She copied his movements—which drew his gaze to her body. Even with her bundled in bulky skiwear, he could easily imagine the figure beneath: all long and lean and naked. That led to imagining how all her body parts would line up with all his body parts as he closed his mouth over hers for a slow, deep, soul-searing kiss that started with both parties standing and ended with them lying flat on their backs, sweaty, panting, and totally sated.

Okay, normal guy reaction to a good-looking woman, he assured himself, but he really needed to get his mind off kissing her.

"That's good." He nodded. "Only use less lip."

She stopped moving and stared at him. "Less *lip*?"

"What?" He stared back at those clear blue eyes of hers, pleasantly dazed—until his Freudian slip hit him. "I meant *hip*. Use less hip."

She gave him a dubious look that made him laugh at himself. Okay, so now she knew where his brain was, which was pretty dang amusing in an awkward sort of way.

"Tell ya what," he said, pushing against his poles to turn his back downhill. "Why don't we ski this first section nice and easy so you can get used to your skis, then run through some exercises?"

"You're going to ski backwards?"

"Sure. This way I can watch you better."

"Okay." She rolled her eyes as if he were a bit off in the head, then lowered the goggles from her helmet.

He watched her wobble through the first few turns. "You're sitting back too far. Get your shins against your boot fronts."

"I know, I know," she snapped, but her irritation seemed directed more at herself than at him.

"Shoulders front," he said and nodded in approval when she quickly corrected the fault in her form. After that, she fell into a smooth rhythm that had his brows arching.

Okay, so the woman did know how to ski, especially if her form hadn't suffered any more than this in a fourteen-year absence from the slopes.

"Let's kick it up a bit." He flipped around to face downhill and picked up their pace. He watched her carve a few turns with growing sureness. "We're coming up on some steeper terrain," he called out to her. "I want you to concentrate on keeping your weight forward. Don't back off."

She nodded and scowled at the slope, her expression so serious he wanted to laugh. Hadn't anyone told this woman that skiing was supposed to be fun? Before he could tell her as much, they topped a crest and she shot forward with a fearlessness that surprised him. Human instinct made a lot of skiers hold back, which, ironically, was the exact thing that made them lose control. After the way she'd flipped out on the lift, he'd expected her to be tentative on the slopes.

Nope. She went for it all out, bending at the knees to absorb the impact of the groomed snow against her skis.

He barreled after her, then slowed to match his pace to hers. As they skied nearly in tandem, he indulged himself watching her. Hot damn, if she could ski like this on day one, he'd have her skiing like a demon in no time.

She glanced over at him and the serious expression vanished as she smiled.

Something inside him clicked into place, an instant connection as he saw his own excitement in her eyes. He knew she felt the same thrill he did every time he skied—that elation that made him want to shout, "This is so cool!"

He loved every moment of flying down a mountainside: the bright sun flashing off the snow, the beauty of the trees passing in a blur, the crisp air hitting his cheeks.

He smiled back at her—

And she went down. Hard. Her body cartwheeling down the slope.

His heart lurched as he skidded to a stop as fast as he could, which still took him well beyond her. Turning, he found her facedown in the snow, arms sprawled, ski gear scattered both uphill and down. Fear kicked in when she didn't move. "Christine! Are you all right?"

To his surprise, she lifted her head and laughed like a loon. Her goggles were missing and snow clung to her cheeks and hair. "I'm great!"

He stared at her, amazed by the transformation that came over her face when she laughed so freely. He'd thought her beautiful before, in an aloof sort of way, but now, with her sprawled on the ground like a rag doll, she looked . . . happy. Which was even better than beautiful in his book. The only thing he liked more than really great legs was a really great laugh.

She worked her way to her hands and knees. "I can't believe it's been so long since I did this."

"What? Take a tumble?"

"No, ski." She sat back on her boots and shook like his dog, Buddy, after a bath. "This is so fun!"

"And people call me crazy," he muttered to himself, then glanced at the trail of equipment she'd created. "That's quite a yard sale!"

She looked about and laughed even harder. "See anything you wanna buy?"

"How much you want for that pole?"

"It's yours free, if you can find its mate."

"Hang on—" Fighting gravity, he sidestepped uphill in an effort to get closer as she crawled about to gather her gear.

Watching her, the thought popped into his head that he should ask her out. In fact, he wondered why the idea hadn't occurred to him the second he laid eyes on her. Okay, so maybe Bruce frowned on his instructors hitting on students, but Alec wasn't a regular instructor.

So here they were, attractive woman, friendly guy. No reason in the world he couldn't ask her to join him and the gang at St. Bernard's after their lesson.

He was still working his way toward her, warming to his idea, when a herd of teenagers on snowboards popped over a hill and headed straight toward her. "Look out!"

She let out a string of cuss words while he frantically waved his arms. The snowboarders swerved to miss them and flew by ten times faster than the ski patrol would tolerate. When they'd passed, he looked back to where Christine had huddled down with her arms wrapped about her head. "What was that you just said?"

"Nothing," she called back in exaggerated innocence.

"Something about duck, duck, duck, or sit?"

"Yeah." She finally had both her skis. "That was it. I was telling you to duck."

"You sure that wasn't 'fuck, fuck, fuck, oh shit!'?"

Planting a pole, she struggled to a standing position, then turned to face him. Above him on the hill, she easily stared down her nose at him with supreme haughtiness. "Do I look like a woman who would use the F word?"

"No." He smiled up at her. "You look like a princess . . . who would use the F word."

"Ha!" She tossed her long hair back and clicked into her skis. After a bit of searching, she located her second pole and gave him a really great view of legs and backside as she retrieved it.

Yep, he decided, no reason in the world not to ask her out.

When she had everything in order, she glided down to him, her cheeks flushed, her breathing shallow from exertion. "Okay, I'm ready to continue."

"I have a better idea. Why don't we take a little break? Let you catch your breath."

"No . . . I'm fine," she panted.

He smiled at her show of toughness. "So maybe I need to catch my breath."

"Yeah, right." She smirked at him and the urge to kiss her returned stronger than ever. The gorgeous rich babe he could resist, but not this woman who laughed when she fell and cussed like a sailor.

"Come on," he urged. "Just a short break."

"All right." She nodded.

"Where are you from?" he asked as they skied slowly toward a safe area near the trees.

"Austin."

"Really?" He stopped at the edge of the run. "We're practically neighbors. I grew up in Elgin."

"Oh yeah?" Her eyes brightened with interest, which he took as a green light. "I love Elgin sausage."

"Best in Texas," he boasted. "So what part of Austin?"

"Oh, um"—she shifted her eyes, the way people do right before they lie—"the Windsor/MoPac area."

"Ah." That drew him up a bit. Not a lie, but a toning down of the truth. A polite way to tell a poor hick from the sticks she'd grown up in Tarrytown, one of Austin's most exclusive neighborhoods. And the way she said it told him Christine Ashton wasn't "rich." She was "seriously rich." Women from that social stratosphere didn't go out with trailer trash. Not that he'd mentioned growing up in a mobile home, but women had some sort of built-in radar for that.

He considered ditching the idea of asking her out—for about one nanosecond—then shrugged. No guts no glory. "So, Austin, huh? Great nightlife."

"That's what I hear." She visibly relaxed and smiled back at him. Oh yeah, definite green light.

"Don't you get out and enjoy it?"

"Uh, no." Christine chuckled, thinking the only nightlife she ever saw was in the emergency ward at Breckenridge Hospital. The last thing she wanted to do, though, was talk about her residency while on vacation.

"Well now, that's a shame," Alec said. "Everyone should make the most of where they live." His gaze held hers in a way that made her forget what they were talking about. Although who cared about the words coming from his mouth when his eyes were saying, *You're gorgeous. I like you. Ya wanna get naked?*

Heat rushed into her cheeks as she returned his smile. *Maybe,* she told him with her eyes, even as a warning went off in her head. Every time she was instantly attracted to a man, he turned out to be a loser. After her most recent disastrous relationship, she'd promised Maddy and Amy she wouldn't date anyone who didn't get their stamp of approval first. Actually, she'd made them promise not to *let* her.

At times like this, though, when her hormones stood up and did the happy dance, that promise was really hard to remember.

Breaking eye contact, he took a deep breath, as if trying to cool down. "If you have your breath back, maybe we should continue."

"I'm ready if you are," she said with playful innuendo.

"I'm always ready." He gave her a wicked grin.

She laughed. Dang, he was cute! And funny. And *tall*. Please let Maddy and Amy give her the go-ahead when she told them about him. "What did you have in mind?"

"I'm thinking we should move to more even ground and work on your balance."

"Since you're the instructor, I'll put myself in your capable hands."

The hour and a half that followed turned into the sexiest ski lesson in history, Christine was sure. Between each exercise, Alec found an excuse to come up behind her, his skis straddling hers, so he could put his hands on her hips or shoulders and correct her form. His voice in her ear grew lower and rougher each time, until her whole body tingled with awareness. She even made it through two more rides on the chairlift—with him massaging her hands in a way that was very sweet, not to mention arousing.

At the end of their third run, he skied to a stop at the bottom. She slid in beside him.

"And that," he said, lifting his goggles, "concludes lesson number one."

"Already?" She pulled her glove down enough to see her watch. "Wow, time flies when you're having fun."

"Does it ever." He gave her another of his wicked looks that made her belly do the tango. "So, do you have plans for the rest of the day?"

Uh-oh. He was about to ask her out, but she couldn't say yes until he passed the Friend Test. Her libido argued to say yes now and get approval later. Her friends were so dang tough she hadn't had a date in months. Surely they'd like this guy, though.

No. Stay firm, Christine. Stay firm.

"I, um"—she cleared her throat—"thought I'd go back to the family condo, thaw out with a hot shower, and collapse on the sofa." That was the best plan. Especially since she had a ton of studying to do for her upcoming medical board certification exam.

"I have a better idea for thawing out." He crossed his arms over one of his poles, leaning his weight on it. "I'm planning to meet some buds at the pub. How does a warm brandy in front of a roaring fire sound?"

"Tempting . . ." *Very tempting.* "But no. I can't."

"Come on, just for a little while." He bent to remove his skis. "My friends are all expert skiers, sure to swap a few tips on conquering the black runs."

No fair. How was she supposed to resist that on top of a physical attraction that was pinging through her body? Hoping for distraction, she bent and removed her own skis. "I would love to, really, just not today. Can I take a rain check?"

"Absolutely." He straightened and didn't look the least discouraged, thank goodness. "Take that hot shower you mentioned and some ibuprofen for your muscles. Then get plenty of sleep and drink lots of water."

"You sound like a doctor."

"Just looking out for my student." He shouldered his skis and poles. "See you tomorrow. Same time, same place."

"I'll be there." Watching him stride away, she fought the urge to dance in place and shout *Yes!* Surely her dating drought was about to end.

After a quick shower, Christine pulled on worn jeans and a faded orange sweatshirt with her college logo—a white longhorn—emblazoned across the front. Her mind raced, trying to compose an e-mail to her friends that would win their approval as she hurried down the stairs that led from the loft outside the guest bedrooms to the condo's main room.

Like most of the building in Silver Mountain, the

street level was full of shops and restaurants with condos above. The wall of glass across from her opened onto a sundeck and offered a spectacular view of the mountains.

Her laptop waited on the coffee table, atop last night's pizza box. Coffee first, though, she thought, and veered toward the kitchen. The machine had finished brewing while she'd been in the shower, so she searched for a good-sized mug. Unfortunately, the cabinets held nothing but wimpy bone china cups with fragile handles. Resigned, she filled one, then carried it into the living area.

While the condo wasn't as formal as the Ashtons' main residence in Austin, the decor struck her as more appropriate for an English tearoom than a ski lodge, but that was her mother's style.

Stepping over the shoes she'd kicked off last night, she flipped a switch on the wall, which ignited the gas fireplace. Instant flames popped up through the fake logs, all of it carefully sealed behind glass. She thought of Alec Hunter at this very moment sitting before a real fireplace in a crowded pub, surrounded by friends and laughter, with the scent of wood smoke and fried food filling the air.

If the next few minutes went well, she'd be joining him tomorrow.

Determined, she sat on the sofa and opened her laptop. Now, what to say?

The time indicator on the screen read four fifteen Austin time, which made it three fifteen Mountain Time. Perfect. Since Maddy had moved to Santa Fe, they'd fallen into the habit of all three being online this time of day. Amy would still be at her desk managing her Traveling Nannies franchise, a business that placed temporary nannies with the vacationing wealthy and even some celebrities. Maddy was usually ready for a break from working on her art, and, until recently, Christine would just be waking up and getting ready for her night shift at the hospital.

E-mail might not make up for the girlfriend lunches and movie days they'd enjoyed during the ten years after graduating from UT, but it was the next best thing. After a little more thought, she decided to start with something that was sure to get a positive response. She typed *I did it!* into the subject line.

Message: *I rode the chairlift! Three times!*

Maddy was first to respond: *Woo-hoo! Now give us the details, woman.*

Amy was quick to follow: *I knew you could do it. I'm so proud of you.*

Christine worked on her response, wanting to get it just right before she hit send. She started with: *Actually, it wasn't as bad as I feared after the first ride. Mostly because of my ski instructor.*

There, that was a good opening. Now what else to say? She typed: *He's so cute!* Then groaned and hit the delete key to erase that line. Any time she started with a physical description, her chances of winning approval took an instant nosedive.

She pondered the screen, then flexed her fingers and tried again: *In fact, I really like this guy, and think you will too. His name's Alec Hunter, and he's very professional but not stuffy. Actually, I can't remember the last time I laughed so much in one afternoon. Mostly, though, he was wonderful on the lift, distracting me and keeping me calm. He's considerate and sensitive but also fun. And I'd like to go out with him, assuming you two approve, which I'm sure you will, because this one's really great.*

She reread the message a few times, wondering if she was laying it on too thick. Although everything she'd written was true. Bracing herself, she hit send.

And waited.

As the seconds ticked by, she pressed her palms together with her fingers against her lips.

Finally, Maddy's response came through: *When you say "professional" I hope you mean employed. Because yesterday you mentioned the instructor they'd lined up for you didn't work for the ski school. That he was doing this as some sort of favor for a friend. So what does he do?*

Damn! She cringed as she answered: *Actually, I'm not sure. I forgot to ask.*

Maddy: *Christine! Do we need to make out a list of minimum criteria?*

Angry at herself, because she'd probably flubbed it, Christine fired back: *Maybe you should just draw up an application for my potential dates to fill out.*

Maddy: *That's not a bad idea!*

Christine: *Absolutely not! And this is getting ridiculous. The only dates I've had in the past two years were with total duds who put me to sleep before we made it through dinner.*

Maddy: *That's because you always go to extremes. You either pick some starched shirt, then feel like you can't be yourself, or you pick up strays and want to take them home. While the second group are a lot more fun, they eat your food, borrow money, and leave you feeling used. I know you have a soft heart, that you want to heal every hurt, but men are not puppies, Christine. You don't take them in just because they're cute and homeless and you think you can fix all their problems. Can't you find someone who's between the two extremes? Someone who's fun AND responsible?*

"Apparently not," Christine grumbled to herself before inspiration struck: *How do we know Alec isn't both? Huh? Just because I forgot to ask if he had a job, doesn't mean he doesn't. Beside, I'm not looking to marry this guy. Jeez, I'm only going to be here three weeks. Come on, Mad, it's my vacation and I've been so good. Can't I have fun on my vacation? Sort of like going off a diet with one really great chocolate binge. Everyone needs to binge now and then. Even the diet books say so.*

Maddy: *They say to "treat yourself now and then," not binge! Otherwise you get sick to your stomach and hate yourself the next day.*

Christine: *I will not. I promise. And if I do, I won't blame y'all. I'm telling you, this guy is really cute and funny, and ohmigod, he's sexy.*

Maddy: *Amy! Talk to this woman, will you?*

Several seconds passed before Amy's calm and sensible response came through: *Actually, I agree with Christine. We don't know he's wrong for her until we get more information. I say we withhold judgment until after tomorrow's lesson when she's had time to find out more about him.*

Christine stuck her tongue out at Maddy's posts: *There, see? Mother Amy agrees with me.*

Amy: *However, Maddy's also right, Christine. I've been on enough diets to know binging isn't good for you. It just makes resisting temptation the next time that much harder. So promise, if you discover this man is a loser, you won't go out with him, okay? No matter how sexy he is.*

Christine: *Oh, all right! Man, you two are strict.*

Amy: *Only because we love you. When you get hurt, it hurts us too.*

Christine sagged with guilt: *I know. You're right. So, any advice on resisting temptation should the need arise?*

Maddy: *I have some. Actually, it's a variation of the advice you gave me when I arrived in Santa Fe and wanted to turn tail and head home. Keep your mind focused on why you're there: in your case, to conquer your fear of the lift and outski your brother on the slopes. Second, reread part of Jane's book. Not the part you told me to read, but the chapter about smart women who make dumb choices.*

Amy: *I'll second that advice.*

Christine: *Thanks, you two. I really do love you. Even when you are killjoys.*

With a sigh, Christine logged off, then looked at the stack of medical books she'd brought. She should probably study, but following Maddy's advice, she reached past them and grabbed Jane's book, *How to Have a Perfect Life.* As angry as she was at Jane for using the three of them as negative examples, she felt strangely drawn to the book. She found herself coming back to it over and over, searching for the little pearls of wisdom she occasionally found hidden among a lot of clichéd axioms.

Halfway through reading the chapter Maddy had suggested, she stared at the words as if seeing them for the first time. Not only had Jane used her as an example in the chapter on fear. She'd used her in this chapter too! It wasn't as obvious, but it was there in black and white.

Jane Redding had written Christine into every paragraph of the chapter titled "Smart Women, Dumb Choices."

Slamming the book closed, she tossed it aside. That did it! Maddy and Amy were right. She absolutely had to stop dating men who were either too stuffy or totally irresponsible.

Surely, though, there had to be a man out there somewhere who was just right for her. And hopefully he'd be as fun as Alec.

Chapter 3

Discipline is the foundation for self-respect.
—*How to Have a Perfect Life*

The following day, Alec stood in the outdoor food concession line, hoping to scarf a quick meal before his second lesson with Christine.

"So how goes it with Silver Mountain's newest ski instructor?" someone said behind him.

"Shut up." Alec laughed as he turned to find his friend Trent grinning broadly. Apparently his buddy Bruce had blabbed the news to half the resort that Alec Hunter had lowered himself to teach ski lessons. Now all the guys were dying to join in the ribbing. Not that he blamed them. When it came to making a living on the mountain, there was a definite pecking order with Alec at the top as the county search-and-rescue coordinator, then forest rangers and emergency personnel, followed by guys like Trent in ski patrol, with lowly ski instructors coming in barely above the lift operators.

A wide grin split Trent's face. "Will's fiancée tells me your student is hot."

Alec merely grinned at that obvious ploy for more data, which he had no intention of giving. He didn't need more ribbing or the competition. Especially since Trent had the kind of dark Italian good looks women went for instantly. Although, even born with the curse of being "cute," Alec had no problem holding his own.

Trent wiggled his brows. "Is Lacy right, or just jerking my chain?"

"Lacy. Dang, that reminds me." Alec glanced toward St. Bernard's Pub on the opposite end of the plaza. "Loan me twenty bucks, will ya?"

"Why?" Trent asked even as he reached for his wallet.

"Because I only have twenty on me. If I pay Lacy back for yesterday's lunch, I won't have enough to buy lunch today."

"Let me guess. You lost your ATM card again."

"Temporarily misplaced," Alec corrected.

"I swear, you have a black hole in your brain where all thoughts about money disappear."

"Maybe I'm just too busy thinking about more important things, like saving people from their own stupidity, to waste brain cells worrying about stuff that doesn't matter."

"You know, I don't get you. You can keep track of a million pieces of rescue gear, but you can never remember where you left your wallet and keys. That's just weird." Trent held a twenty upright between two fingers as a bribe. "Now tell me about your ski bunny."

"Nothing to tell." Alec snagged the bill out of Trent's hand.

"She as hot-looking as Lacy claims?"

"She's not too bad." He smiled to himself at that

understatement. With the way things had gone yesterday, he couldn't wait for today's lesson. The memory of how she'd returned every suggestive look with a sultry one of her own made his body eager for more.

"Why, you dog." Trent lowered his sunglasses to study Alec's face. "You're planning to show her some moves off the slopes, aren't you?"

Alec fixed him with his most intimidating look, which he suspected wasn't all that intimidating because it never worked. "Razz me about helping Bruce and I won't let you ride the all-terrain bike I'm buying with the money I'm making off these lessons."

"I thought you were going to stop spending your own money buying equipment for the county."

"I was, but . . . have you seen the new medical unit bikes?"

"Oh yeah." Trent patted his heart. "I read the article in *Emergency Magazine*, and drooled so much I had to change my shirt."

Reaching the front of the line, Alec ordered a double-meat cheeseburger, jumbo fries, large cola, and chocolate milk shake, then waited as Trent placed his order. When they had their trays, they searched for an empty table in the outdoor eating area, which offered a view of the slopes. With ski season picking up, they had to settle for a table that hadn't been bussed.

Alec shoved the clutter aside and dove into filling his empty stomach before his belly button touched his backbone. The rush of blood sugar to his brain made his eyes roll back in pleasure. God, maybe he would live after all, he decided as he swallowed a mouthful of salty French fries. "I didn't see a report on snowmobile traffic when I stopped by the fire station this morning. Have you noticed any tracks heading into the backcountry?"

Trent scowled at him. "I thought you were taking the week off."

"I am."

"You know, Hunter"—Trent lowered his burger—"I'm not sure you get the concept of taking a vacation. See now, most people go somewhere to relax and have fun."

"Yeah, they come to Silver Mountain." He swept an arm to include the whole resort, from the shops and restaurants with their festive holiday trim to the snow-covered mountains. "Lucky me, I'm already here."

"Well, at least refrain from going by the office every day."

"Can't do that. I have to drop off Buddy," he said, referring to his golden retriever, one of the best avalanche-rescue dogs in the country. "You know how he mopes when he doesn't get to work. The guys at the fire station offered to let him hang with them while I'm giving these lessons. Since my office is in the fire station, it's kind of hard to avoid going by."

"Right." Trent nodded skeptically. "You just dropped Buddy off and didn't stick around to do any work."

"Define work." At his friend's exasperated look, he relented. "Okay, so maybe I glanced over the Forest Service advisories."

"Uh-huh."

"Looks like we're getting a pretty good buildup already on Parks Peak."

"Yep." Trent calmly popped a French fry into his mouth.

"You gonna blast it?"

"If it snows again tonight, we'll blast it in the morning."

"You gonna use the new Avalauncher?"

"Yep."

"Need any help?"

"Nope."

"Because if you did—"

"Alec." Trent scowled. "You're on vacation."

"Man," he groused, "that's the trouble with vacations. You don't get to have any fun."

Trent chuckled. "You really are crazy, you know that?"

"I like what I do. So sue me."

"About Will's bachelor party on Friday," Trent said, changing the subject. "You got everything covered?"

"Hey, this isn't my first time up as best man. I know what I'm doing."

"If you'll remember, last time you got stuck with a whopper of a bar tab. If you need the groomsmen to pitch in some more when it's over, let me know. I'll suspend all their lift passes until they ante up."

"The only thing I need is—" He broke off when a tall blonde wearing a blue-and-white Spyder jacket stopped a few feet away. "Christine?"

She turned, holding a tray from the concession stand, and smiled when she saw him. She looked rested and glowing and somehow even more beautiful today than she had yesterday, which was saying a lot.

"Hey," she said. "I was just going to grab a bite to eat before our lesson, but I can't find a free table."

"Why don't you join us?" He eagerly cleared a place for her to set her tray.

"Thank you. That would be great." She sat down next to him.

Trent looked from her to him and raised one brow. " 'Not too bad'? Friend, you need glasses."

"What?" Christine blinked.

"Nothing." Alec kicked Trent under the table. "Chris, meet Trent. Trent, Chris."

"Christine," she corrected as she shook Trent's hand.

Alec cocked his head. "Why not Chris?"

"I don't know." She shrugged, as if the question had never occurred to her. "It's just always been Christine."

"How about Christi?" he suggested with a flirtatious grin.

"Definitely not." One of her throaty laughs spilled forth. Their eyes met and heat flared instantly, as it had yesterday. Rather than holding his gaze, though, she looked away and concentrated on unwrapping her turkey sandwich. A little frown marred her brow, as if she were trying to solve a problem. "So," she said to Trent, "you're with the ski patrol, I see. I've always thought that would be a fun job."

"It rocks." Trent puffed up at her attention, and Alec contemplated kicking him again. "Even if it's not as fun as what Alec does."

"Oh?" She turned to him with a strangely hopeful look. "What sort of work do you do?"

"Oh, Alec doesn't *work*," Trent was quick to put in. "He just plays all day. Isn't that right, dude?"

"When people let me," Alec grumbled.

"Ah." Christine kept her face impassive as disappointment filled her. Apparently her losing streak was holding firm and she'd picked another charming user, the kind of man who mooched off family and friends while "looking for work." She should have expected as much after the scene she'd witnessed yesterday, when he'd sweet-talked that waitress into buying his lunch. How did she let major clues like that slip past her in the beginning, when that was exactly the sort of thing that would drive her up a wall later?

Alec and his friend talked a bit more while she ate; then Trent stood to leave.

"Christine"—Trent held his hand out to her— "good meeting you. How long are you staying in Silver Mountain?"

"Three weeks."

"Cool. Perhaps I'll see you around."

"Perhaps." She looked at him more closely. He lacked Alec's height, but he had a roguish appeal. And at least this man was gainfully employed, she thought as he continued to hold her gaze and her hand. Maybe her friends would approve of him. Too bad the thought didn't give her the same zing as thinking about kissing Alec.

"Excuse me," Alec interrupted them with a pointed look at his friend. "Don't you have work to do? I heard a rumor about a poacher in the area."

"That's the forest ranger's job."

"As in the immediate area," Alec stressed.

"Oh." Trent turned sheepish as he dropped her hand. "Sorry. I'll um, just be going. And, Alec, I was serious about that bar tab. If you need help paying it, just let me know."

"Consider that twenty you just lent me a donation to the cause."

"Great. See ya at the party Friday night, then."

Christine turned to Alec as his friend walked away. He needed help paying his bar tab? Good grief, she really was a "user magnet," just like Maddy always said. At least he wasn't hitting her up for money, or a place to flop while he dried out, or help finding a job, or a million other things she had trouble refusing. And he wouldn't, because she wasn't getting involved with him. Absolutely not.

"You done?" He nodded toward the remains of the sandwich she'd left on her tray.

"Yes." She wiped her hands on a napkin.

"Great." He flashed a smile, and despite all the stern warnings from her brain, her heart fluttered. "I've been thinking about today's lesson. Since you did so well yesterday, what would you say to hitting the terrain park and catching some air?"

"Are you kidding?" Her mood instantly brightened. Alec Hunter might be a loser in the potential boyfriend department, but as a ski instructor, he was a definite winner. "I'd love that."

"Then let's go do it."

Over the course of the lesson, Christine had to remind herself constantly that Alec was off-limits. He was simply too much fun. And, oh man, could he ski! They spent the whole afternoon in the terrain park working on jumps. By the end of the session, her thighs screamed in agony, but her confidence soared at everything he'd taught her.

They finally left the park and stopped at the top of a run that would take them back down the mountain.

"Are you sure it's been fourteen years since you skied?" he asked as they caught their breath.

"Honest to God," she answered, laughing. Alec made her feel like laughing all the time, over every little thing.

He swiped his lips with lip balm as he surveyed the slope ahead of them. "Looks like we have this one practically to ourselves." His eyes danced with mischief as he looked at her. "Race ya to the bottom."

"Doesn't the ski patrol frown on that?"

"Only if you're reckless about it." He adjusted his goggles. "Besides, I have connections."

She shook her head at him, wishing he was a little less appealing. Although, even if she couldn't date him, she could still enjoy his company. "Okay"—she got into position—"you're on."

"One two three go!" he said without warning and pushed off, shooting out ahead of her.

"You cheater!" she called as she took off after him. He carved a quick series of turns with a powerful grace that filled her with admiration. Losing, however, was not something she accepted without a fight. She poured on the speed, ignoring the burn in her muscles. Cold air slapped her face as the trees flew by.

Try as she might, though, she never stood a chance. She skidded to a halt at the bottom of the run several seconds after him, breathing hard.

"Not bad, Chris." He nodded in approval as he lifted his goggles. "You almost made me work for it."

"Braggart," she accused good-naturedly as she removed her skis. People milled about them, either heading back for the lift lines, or calling it a day, as they were doing. "I would have caught you if you hadn't given yourself a head start."

"All's fair . . ." He grinned, refusing to admit she actually had made him work for it. He'd needed the exertion, though, to work off the arousal that had been building all afternoon. He couldn't decide what he wanted more, to get this woman naked, or simply sit and talk and get to know her better. Well, actually, he'd like to get naked, then get acquainted, but women always seemed to prefer the other order. He straightened from removing his skis. "How 'bout that rain check?"

"Rain check?" She went still.

"Yeah. Yesterday you were too tired, but you should be adjusting to the altitude. Want to go have a drink in front of that roaring fire I mentioned?"

"Ah. Well. Hmm."

He watched her struggle with her answer, sensing that she wanted to say yes. "Come on. Put your feet up on the hearth, sip a hot buttered rum."

"I'd prefer coffee this early in the day."

"Really? A woman after my own heart. If Harvey's tending bar, he makes a wicked pot of joe."

"I can't. Really. I have things to do."

"One cup. Just to thaw out." He watched temptation battle restraint in her eyes. "Relax. Unwind."

A frown wrinkled her brow. "I shouldn't."

Ah-ha! "Can't" had changed to "shouldn't." He smiled at her. "I'll give you a foot massage."

"In a bar?" Her eyes widened.

"We could go to my place if you'd rather." He wiggled his brows.

"I'm afraid I have to pass."

"On the coffee or the massage?"

"On all the above." Regret tinged her voice. "I really do have things to do. Okay?"

Ah, but she wanted to say yes. He could see it in every line of her face as her eyes pleaded him not to tempt her any more. Yeah, right. Like he was going to give up when she clearly wanted him as much as he wanted her.

Encouraged, he leaned close and took on a German accent. "It is futile to resist. I will only wear you down with my charm."

She struggled with a smile as she laid a gloved hand over his chest, as if afraid he'd try to kiss her. "Ah, but see, I'm allergic to charming men. Which is why I've been inoculated against them."

"With the new charm vaccine?" *Tsk*ing, he laid his hand over hers. "I hate to tell you, but the serum is a failure. It wears off, and the minute it does, you're doubly susceptible. Better to just give in now and enjoy the allergic reaction."

"I can't." She stepped away, shaking her head. "I'm sorry. I have things to do, and I'm determined to be good."

"But being bad is so much more fun."

"I know!"

"Then come to the pub."

Her expression turned exasperated, which told him he'd lost. For today. "I'll see you tomorrow," she said and shouldered her skis.

"If you change your mind, I'll be at St. Bernard's," he called as she headed for the locker room behind the ticket window. A smile split his face. Yep, she liked him, no doubt about it. He just had to get her to admit it.

Shouldering his own skis, he headed in the opposite direction, whistling as he went.

Chapter 4

Aiming too high is better than settling for too low.
—How to Have a Perfect Life

Christine wasn't sure if she should be buoyant with pride for resisting temptation, or depressed because here she sat for the second evening in a row, alone, when she could be at a pub sipping a "wicked cup of joe" before a roaring fire with a man who made her laugh.

Going with depressed, she opened her laptop.

Subject: *I hope you two are happy.*

Message: *Turns out you were right. I picked another user. I honestly don't know how this always happens. Do I have a sign across my chest that says "I love losers"? The deal is, I really like this guy—in spite of the fact that he's unemployed and seems to spend a lot of time hanging out at a bar with "the guys." What is wrong with me!*

Amy: *Oh, Christine, I'm sorry. I was really hoping you'd have better news to report.*

Maddy: *Me too, C. Don't lose heart, though. I firmly believe we all have a perfect match out there, but as Jane said, you have to know what you want and refuse to settle for less.*

Christine typed, *I just want someone to love me*, then stopped. How sad did that sound? She hit the delete key to erase that line, and tried again: *Thanks, guys. I don't know what I'd do without you.*

The following day, Christine was on her best behavior. She squelched a spurt of joy when she saw Alec waiting for her by the trail map, ignored the hitch in her breathing each time he smiled, resisted the urge to return his flirting, and completely denied the tingling in her belly when he touched her. Their time together flew by as it had the day before, and at the end of the lesson, she gave herself a mental pat on the back as she removed her skies.

She was being so good, she deserved a medal.

"Well"—she straightened with a polite smile— "thank you for another great lesson."

"No problem." He shouldered his skies. "You're progressing really fast."

"I hope so. Just a few more days to go before big brother gets here. So I'll see you tomorrow?"

"Actually, if you're heading for your condo, I'll walk with you, since I'm heading into Central Village as well."

"Oh." That drew her up short. "Don't you need to change your boots?"

"I left my stuff in the locker room." Which he hadn't done before, so he'd obviously planned this out ahead of time.

As they crossed the plaza, she did a quick mental scramble for a way out of walking with him through the village. On the slopes, they had the lesson to keep things safe, and the constraints of trying to talk while skiing. Walking side by side offered no barrier to talking.

He kept the conversation neutral, though, reviewing what they'd worked on that day as they racked their skies and entered the unisex locker room. The colorful clutter of clothes and gear littered the benches as skiers changed in and out of street cloths. Since everyone wore long johns, there wasn't much point in retreating to the separate men's and women's rest rooms. Plus, most people were, like them, merely changing boots, which took only a minute.

Christine attached the carrying handle to her snow-caked ski boots while Alec left his gear in the locker he'd rented. When they stepped back out into the cold, she contemplated telling him she wasn't going back to the condo, that she was headed down to East Village on an errand.

"Here, I'll get those," he said, retrieving her skis.

"What about yours?"

"I'll get them later. Ready?" He lifted a challenging brow as if he'd read her mind about the phony errand. He also had a firm hold on her skis. What was she supposed to do—wrestle them away from him?

Besides, she was being silly. What harm would come from simply walking with him for a few minutes? It wasn't like she planned to invite him inside when they reached the condo so they could neck on her parents' sofa. Desire leapt in her belly at the idea. She ruthlessly pushed it back down.

"All right." She nodded toward the skis. "Thanks."

"Lead the way." His smile had warmth sliding

through her as they headed up one of the pedestrian malls.

What are you doing? her conscience demanded. *You should have told him no.*

Oh, shut up, another part of her argued back. *I'm just walking with him.*

She had a sudden image of herself strolling along the mall with miniature versions of herself on each shoulder, one dressed as an angel, the other wearing a red merry widow, carrying a pitchfork and sporting horns. The fact that the devil version looked exactly like the tattoo on her bottom probably said a lot about which one she listened to most often.

Not today, though, she promised the angel. *Today, I'm going to be good.*

For distraction, she took in the shops along either side. Santas and elves abounded in the display windows. "They certainly go all out for the holidays here."

He looked about. "They do all the holidays up right. It's one of the things I love about living here."

"You don't become immune to it after a while?"

"Never."

They continued past vacationers shopping for Christmas gifts and souvenirs. The scent of cookies baking wafted from a nearby pastry shop. Outdoor heaters allowed the shop to be open across the front and bathed them in warmth as they passed.

"Hey, Alec!" the attractive redhead behind the counter called.

"Hi, Bree," he called back with a friendly wave, then looked at Christine. "Want a cookie? My treat."

Her stomach rumbled, but she shook her head.

Stopping for a cookie would just prolong their walk. "No, but thank you."

"I'll catch ya later, Bree," Alec called.

"I'll be here." The redhead's flirtatious voice followed them as they moved past the pool of warmth.

Christine denied a little spurt of jealousy. She should be used to having people call Alec by name and wave. Half the residents of Silver Mountain seemed to know him. His popularity made sense, though. Moochers had to be charismatic to get by.

A few paces later, he nudged her with his shoulder. "This is where you're supposed to say, 'So, Alec, tell me about yourself. How did a guy from Elgin wind up living in Silver Mountain?'"

"Actually, a lot of Texans have transplanted to Colorado."

"True. And with good reason." He gestured toward the festive, crowded mall.

Enormous flowerpots filled with poinsettias separated the benches that ran down the middle. Strings of white lights zigzagged overhead at the first-story roof line, while snow decorated the floors above like icing on gingerbread. At night the lights gave the village a fairy-tale feel, but even during the day, Silver Mountain enchanted her.

"Can you think of a better place to live?" Alec asked.

No, she couldn't. With a frown, she quashed that thought. "I like living in Austin," she insisted. "Live music, lots of parks and hiking trails. It's a great place to live."

"Yeah, but no mountains."

"There's more to life than skiing."

"You're right." He nodded gravely. "You're absolutely right. There's also snowboarding."

She laughed. "You're hopeless."

"I know." His pretense at seriousness vanished.

She cocked her head, studying him. What was it about Alec Hunter that drew her so strongly even when she fought it? It had to be more than just the golden good looks and all that wonderful height. Maybe it was the eyes. They were always filled with so much . . . *life*. "So how did you wind up living in Colorado?"

"I came to Breckenridge on a student ski trip when I was in high school. The mountains hooked me the instant I saw them, even before I clicked into my first pair of rentals and hit the slopes. Elgin had nothing to hold me, so the day after I graduated, I stuffed my clothes in a backpack, hitched my way up here, and never went back."

"Don't you have family in Elgin?"

He chuckled. "Actually, I'm not sure about that."

"What do you mean?" She sent him a puzzled look.

"My theory is the stork dropped me accidentally while flying over a trailer house full of lunatics. Of course, this theory would hold up better if we didn't all look so much alike. Other than that, I have nothing in common with anyone in my family. Every time I call home to touch base, I'm reminded how much I flat don't fit in with them."

"I know how you feel," she said without thinking, then frowned at her own words. What had made her

say that? She had a lot in common with her father
and brother. They were all three doctors, weren't
they?

"Hey," he said brightly, "maybe we had the same
stork and he dropped you at the wrong house too."

"Maybe." She chuckled.

"See? And here I bet you've been thinking we have
nothing in common, since you obviously come from
money and I so obviously don't."

"Well, that's offensive." She stopped to stare at
him. "Do you really think I'd refuse to go out with
you because of that?"

"I don't know." For once, he looked completely
serious. "You tell me."

"For the record, money is irrelevant to me and
hardly the measure of someone's worth. What's inside
a person, their ethics and convictions, is what matters."

The smile came back, a slow, flirtatious curling of
his lips as his gaze held hers. "Then I'd say we have
something else in common, since I feel the same way."

Her heart started the meltdown it did every time
he looked at her that way. And darn it, she'd forgotten to list responsibility as one of the things that mattered. Her longest relationship had been with an
English lit major who'd turned going for his PhD into
a lifelong pursuit. For all she knew, he still hadn't
graduated or written the novel he'd talked about.
That debacle had taught her that people could have
all kinds of lofty ideas yet be too lazy to follow
through on any of them.

Her temper simmered at the memory as they left
the mall and entered the central plaza. The sound of
Christmas carols over a loudspeaker drew her atten-

tion to the skating rink. The kaleidoscope of children skating to "Jingle Bell Rock" presented such a picturesque scene, her anger evaporated.

As she watched, two young boys raced in and out from between slower skaters, taunting each other as only young boys can. An older girl in tights and a skirted leotard made a turning leap and landed in a one-footed pose as she glided over the ice.

"Hey, Alec." A young woman with a little girl on her hip waved at him from the rink's sideline.

"Hi, Linda." He waved back. "Are you going to teach Colleen to skate this year?"

The woman laughed while her daughter studied the skaters with a dimpled frown. "We're still trying to decide."

"Friend of yours?" Christine asked as they crossed toward another pedestrian lane.

"Linda's married to one of the guys," he answered, referring to the group of friends who apparently hung out at the pub every day for happy hour.

Christine glanced over her shoulder at the pretty young woman with the little girl. Linda didn't look like the type of woman to put up with a shiftless husband. Another smart woman who made dumb choices?

"Speaking of things you can do here that you can't do in Texas," Alec said when he saw her looking back at the rink. "When's the last time you went skating?"

"We have skating rinks in Texas."

"Not like that you don't. Do you skate?"

"Sort of." She chuckled. "At least I used to. I'd probably fall on my face if I tried now."

"Want to find out? We can drop off your stuff, then go back and give it a go. That is, if you don't mind skating with munchkins, which actually makes it more fun if you ask me."

Her heart gave a little sigh of longing as she looked back over her shoulder. Ice skating with children sounded like a blast. Especially since kids were her secret weakness. They didn't make her turn all maternal like they did Amy; they made her want to *be* a kid again. Only this time, be a real kid who could get dirty without getting lectured, who could play loud music and have slumber parties and eat junk food.

Dang it, how did Alec always know how to tempt her?

"I"—she jerked herself back from saying yes—"can't."

"Come on, if you've forgotten, I'll teach you."

She imagined Alec holding her hands as he pulled her around the rink, catching her against him when she started to fall, both of them laughing themselves silly, and her heart whimpered a little louder. "Really, I can't."

"Okay, let's skip the skating and grab something to eat. You're bound to need refueling after all that skiing."

"I thought you were heading somewhere."

He gave her a get-real look. "Yeah, to walk you home. So how 'bout some nachos?"

"I'd love to, but I have some things I need to do."

"Let me guess." He smirked. "You have to wash your hair?"

She frowned at the irritation that had edged into

his voice. "Actually, I always e-mail my friends this time of day."

"Now *that's* original!" His laughter lacked its usual level of humor.

"Do you have a problem with that?" They reached the building that held her parents' condo. The street-level entryway, wedged between a gift shop and a restaurant, led them into a small lobby. They both stomped snow from their boots.

"You know, I probably shouldn't say this, but haven't women ever heard of the word no?" he asked while she pushed the button for the elevator. "It works really well. See, I say, 'Go out with me.' And you say, 'No.' End of discussion, because it doesn't give me an opening to ask again."

The doors slid open and they stepped onto the elevator. She punched the button for the second floor as Alec continued his rant.

"When a woman says 'I can't because I have to fill-in-the-blank,' then the man will just keep asking, sometimes as no more than a game to see how many grandmothers you're going to kill off before you finally admit you're flat out not interested—which, in this case, you are." With them standing so close, he easily reached out and cupped her chin in his gloved hand.

Twin bolts of panic and excitement shot through her at the unexpected contact. Would he try to kiss her right here? Would she stop him if he did? Her breath caught as she stared up into his eyes.

Those eyes warmed as he stared back. "What you should say is, 'Yes, Alec, I'd love to spend the rest of the day with you.'"

Her heart leapt into her throat as he moved closer. She dropped her gaze to his lips. *Just one small taste,* her naughty side argued. *What would one little taste hurt?*

Lifting her gaze back to his eyes, she started to lean forward in acceptance.

The doors slid open, jarring her back to her senses. What was she doing? She all but jumped into the hall. That had been a narrow escape, she thought as she fumbled for her keys. "Has it occurred to you that maybe women are trying to be nice and spare men's feelings when we make excuses? And that men should take the hint and stop asking?"

"Nope." He followed her down the short hall.

"Alec . . ." she sighed, hoping he couldn't tell her insides were shaking. At her parents' door, she turned to face him, outwardly calm—she hoped. "How about this? I think you're very attractive and appealing in a number of ways, but you're simply not my type."

"That's still not no." He set the ends of her skis on the carpeted floor and regarded her levelly. "Besides, you're not my type either."

"What?" She blinked in surprise.

"Yeah, see, I like simple women. Boring, dull, easy to understand. Gorgeous, complicated women?" He shook his head. "They don't do it for me. However, I'm willing to give you a shot for one date, see how things go."

A frown pulled at her brows. "Are you trying to charm me again?"

"That depends." He planted a hand to the wall beside her head. She flattened her back against the doorjamb when he leaned in. He looked down into her eyes with their lips mere inches apart. "Is it working?"

"Absolutely not." Her cool voice belied the heat coursing through her.

His gaze moved over her face before a knowing smile turned up his lips. "That's only because the charm vaccine hasn't warn off yet." He backed off, making her sag in relief—and disappointment. "Just you wait. When it does, you won't be able to resist me."

That's what I'm afraid of! She turned and managed to fit the key in the lock and slip inside the open door. Turning back, she gave him her haughtiest look. "We'll see." She started to close the door in his face.

"Uh, Chris?" he said.

"What?" She scowled at his broad grin.

"You forgot these." He tilted the skis toward her.

"Oh." Her face flaming, she took the skis and pulled them inside. "Thank you."

"Anytime." His grin turned seductive.

She closed the door and sagged against it. Now *that* had been a close call. Three lessons down. Two more to go. Surely she was tough enough to resist him for two days.

Chapter 5

Once you know what you want, never give up.
                    —How to Have a Perfect Life

"Where'd I lose control?" Alec asked Trent. "That's what I want to know."

"Excuse me?" Trent said over the live music coming from the small bandstand.

For the bachelor party, they'd reserved a big table in the corner of St. Bernard's Pub—the favorite hangout for search-and-rescue volunteers, ski patrol, and emergency workers. Which was why Alec dropped by every afternoon for his happy-hour pot of coffee. If a man wanted to know what was happening on the mountain, the fireplace pit in the center of the pub was the place to find out. He could kick back in one of the armchairs around the open-sided hearth, warm the bottoms of his boots, and catch up on everyone's latest adventure.

On a Friday night, though, the atmosphere went from laid back to high gear. Vacationers and locals filled every table and kept the waitstaff scurrying for food and drinks.

The band ended an old honky-tonk standard followed by applause from the couples crowding the dance floor. As the sound died down, Alec leaned closer to Trent so the whole table wouldn't hear his romantic woes. "I'm telling you, I just don't get it."

"Get what?" Trent frowned at him. "What are we talking about?"

"Christine," Alec said in exasperation.

"Huh?" Confusion lined Trent's face. "I thought we were talking about Will and Lacy moving to Ohio after the wedding."

"No, that was way back in the conversation. Although I still can't wrap my mind around the idea." He looked toward the opposite end of the table, where some of the guys were toasting Will, who'd been grinning like a fool for the past hour. The groom-to-be was either deliriously happy about marrying Lacy tomorrow afternoon, or on his way to getting ripped. Hopefully it wasn't the latter because Alec had promised Lacy that Will wouldn't be hungover for the wedding. "Why would any sane person move from Silver Mountain to *Ohio*?"

"Because that's what people do when they get married," Trent explained slowly, as if talking to a moron. "They settle down, buy a house, and raise kids."

"But why do they have to do it someplace boring? Why can't people 'settle down' somewhere fun?"

"Because, unlike Jeff and Linda, most people can't afford to buy a house and raise kids in a ski resort."

"Okay, yeah, whatever." Alec waved all that aside. "Let's get back to the subject at hand."

"What subject?"

"Christine! Jeez man, keep up." Apparently Will wasn't the only one who'd had too much beer. "I was so sure she'd go out with me, but I've tried everything I can think of for the past five days, and she's said no every time. I don't understand. Where'd I lose control?"

"Wait. Hang on." Trent gave his head a quick shake to clear it. "We're talking about understanding women, and you want to know where you lost control? Dude, let me clue you in here. You can't lose something you never had."

"Come on, man, I need advice. We had our last ski lesson today. So how do I even see her now to ask her out? Loiter outside her condo?"

"Might work. Yo, Steve!" Trent called to the sheriff, who sat on the other side of Aaron and Jeff, two of Alec's best-trained volunteers. "If Alec starts stalking a woman, will you promise not to arrest him?"

"Jesus, Trent." Alec ducked his head as eight interested faces turned toward him. "Shut up."

"That depends," Steve called back. "Is she someone I'd want to ask out?"

Trent grinned. "Tall, blond, mile-long legs, sexy smile, and killer eyes."

"I'd arrest him in a heartbeat," Steve assured.

"Who's this?" Brian and Eric, two of the younger volunteers, asked in unison.

"Nobody." Alec glared at them, then Trent. "I'm trying to be serious here—"

"You serious?" Trent guffawed and tossed back more beer.

"I really like this woman. She's smart. She's funny. She looks so classy, but she's really down to earth. And she likes me too. I'm not imagining it."

"Hunter, *all* the women like you. Which is why we

get together on a regular basis to plot your demise. Isn't that right, Bruce?"

"Huh? What?" Bruce, who sat across from Trent, turned toward them.

"Nothing." Alec waved him off. The last thing he needed was for Bruce to hear that he was hitting on a ski student. When Bruce's attention was elsewhere he turned back to Trent. "If I'm so popular, why won't she go out with me?"

"You haven't landed on the right thing," Trent said.

"Right thing?"

"Her idea of a perfect date," Trent explained. "Something so irresistible she can't say no, even if she'd rather go with anyone but you."

Alec lowered his voice as the band slid into a softer number. "I don't want her to go out with me because I have tickets to some sold-out concert. I want her to go out with me because she's, you know, dazzled by my personality."

"Just get her to go out with you, then dazzle her."

Normally that wouldn't worry Alec. As Trent said, women liked him. True, most of them started out thinking of him as "the fun, cute guy," but he'd learned to work that to his advantage. Besides, he liked relationships to be as much about friendship and fun as truly great sex.

"I just don't get it," he repeated. "Why is she so bent on rejecting me?"

"Maybe you should ask her." Trent nodded toward the door.

"What?" Alec turned and his heart lurched when

he saw Christine standing just inside the door. Shaking off snow, she pulled back the hood of her parka.

Could she possibly have come looking for him? She knew this was his favorite hangout.

The thought sent something shooting through his system like an electrical current. He'd never felt such excitement just from seeing a woman. Attraction, yes. Lust, definitely. But not this . . . this . . . whatever it was she stirred up inside him.

Then she shrugged out of her coat, revealing a soft gray sweater that cupped a pair of nice-sized breasts on a long, narrow torso, and the funny feeling in his chest migrated due south. Okay, so maybe some of what she stirred up was lust. Understandable, though, since imagining what she looked like beneath her ski jacket didn't compare to actually finding out.

After hanging her coat on a row of hooks, she glanced about the dimly lit pub, taking in the antique ski gear hanging from the rafters, the crowded area around the fire pit, and the Victorian-era bar that lined the wall opposite her. The look that came over her face reminded him of a kid entering an amusement park.

Then her gaze landed on him, and she froze.

Disappointment cut deep since that was not the reaction he was hoping for. Making thing worse, she hesitated when the hostess spoke to her. Surely she wasn't going to leave just because he was here. Had he bungled things that badly? But how? What had he done?

Finally she turned to the hostess, shook her head no to a menu, and gestured to the bar. He tracked her progress as she maneuvered through the tables, his mind racing for what to do next, how to approach her.

She found an empty stool, a rarity at St. Bernard's on a Friday night, and placed an order with the bartender.

"Wow, who's *that*?" Eric asked.

Alec turned to find the kid half out of his chair as every male in the bachelor party strained to see who had snagged his attention. Even Buddy, who'd been dozing under the table, lifted his head with a questioning whine.

Oh great, Alec thought with an inward groan, this was all he needed. Knowing his friends, he knew what was coming.

Steve, who was late thirties, divorced, and reasonably good-looking, raised a brow. "My guess would be the woman Alec is stalking. Damn, Trent, you weren't kidding."

Across from him, Lt. Kreiger, the retired Navy pilot who flew the rescue helicopter, raised his mug in salute. "Now that, my friends, is what I call a long cool drink of water."

Bruce sent Alec a look of accusation. "You're dating the ski student I asked you to teach?"

"Actually, he's not dating her," Trent was helpful enough to inform the whole table. "That's why he's stalking her."

"I'm not stalking her," Alec tried to get in, but Brian ran right over him.

"No way! Man, I can't believe it. Bruce asked me first, and I turned him down."

"Well, see"—Bruce turned his attention to the red-headed kid—"that's what you get for turning your back on a friend in need."

"You could have told me she was hot," Brian complained.

"I didn't know it when I asked you," Bruce argued back. "Do you think she called up and said, 'I need a private ski instructor, and by the way, I'm tall, blond, and gorgeous'?"

Alec tuned his friends out and went back to watching Christine as she accepted a frosty mug of beer from the bartender. All he had to do was think of an "irresistible" date, then go over there and ask her out. While he was racking his brain, some guy he didn't recognize turned on the stool next to her and struck up a conversation. Alec scowled when Christine smiled at the stranger rather than giving him the brush-off. No, no, no! Dang it! Now he had to go over there, beat the crap out of some tourist— which wouldn't please the sheriff—then ask her out.

The stranger said something that made Christine laugh.

Alec downed the last of his beer in one big gulp and shot to his feet. "Hey, looks like we need another pitcher. Y'all hang tight, I'll be right back."

Christine knew the instant Alec headed over. Her skin tingled in anticipation even before she glanced in the ornate mirror above the bar to find his reflection coming toward her. She mentally kicked herself for staying. The second she realized he was here, she should have left. Had she honestly thought he wouldn't approach her?

No, if she were being honest, she'd admit she'd

hoped he would. She'd been so proud of herself earlier when they had parted at the end of her last lesson—until she was alone and realized that was it; she'd successfully resisted him for five straight days. Game over. She had won.

How thoroughly depressing.

No more lessons meant no more seeing him every day.

But now, here he was coming toward her and her whole body perked up. Her gaze ran eagerly over his image in the mirror. She'd formed the impression that he was on the skinny side, but from the way the brick-red pullover hugged his torso, she realized there were muscles on that tall, lanky frame! Some really nice muscles that let him move as agilely here as he did on the slopes.

"So where are you from?" the stockbroker from Kansas said.

Before she could answer, Alec slipped between them to lean against the bar facing her. He smiled so broadly, she couldn't hold back answering it with a smile of her own.

"Hey, funny seeing you here," he said as if just noticing her. "I thought you didn't like bars."

"I never said that. In fact"—she looked around—"this place is great."

"You picked a good night since Michael Hearne is playing." He gestured toward the four-piece band on the stage that had a guitar, fiddle, stand-up bass, and drums. "He's Bill Hearne's nephew."

"Who?" She frowned as the fiddle player and singer sawed their way through a torch-and-twang number she'd never heard before.

"Bill Hearne," he said. "You know, Bill and Bonny Hearne?"

"Am I supposed to know them?"

He gaped at her. "I thought you said you were from Austin."

"I also said I don't get out much to enjoy the music scene."

"They don't actually play there anymore, but dang, Chris, they're legends!"

"Sorry." She shrugged.

He gave his head a sad shake. "Well, stick around the mountains long enough, you'll hear all the good bar bands."

"Uh, excuse me?" The stockbroker tapped Alec's shoulder. "We were in the middle of a conversation."

Alec turned to him, all smiles and good cheer. "Hey, thanks for keeping Chris here company while she was waiting for me. Can I get you a drink? Harvey!" He called to the bartender. "Set me up with another pitcher and get this dude a drink on me."

Christine hid a smile at his audacity.

Mr. Hi-I'm-Bob-from-Kansas looked from Alec to her then back to Alec, who'd straightened to his full height. A look passed between them that she couldn't read, but Bob seemed to understand it completely. He held up a hand, palm out. "No problem. I didn't know she was meeting a date."

"He's not my date," she tried to explain, but the man had already turned to scan the crowd for a fresh target.

"Honey, you wound me." Alec pressed a hand to his chest, his look so sincere, she considered forgiving him for running off Bob, who would easily have won the Maddy and Amy Stamp of Approval. "And after you came here looking for me."

Exasperation dampened her amusement. "I came here assuming you'd be gone since you usually come here for happy hour and it's now nine o'clock. What do you do, live here?"

"Actually, I do. Well, not here, here." He pointed at the spot where he stood. "I live upstairs."

"So you spend your entire evening here?"

"Normally, no. Tonight's special. I'm throwing a party."

"Let me guess. For 'the guys'?" She looked toward the table where he'd been sitting to get a look at the infamous gang of men. She found every one of them staring back at her, openly checking her out. Trent and Bruce she recognized, but the rest were an odd mix that ranged in age from two college-age kids on up to a stern-looking older man with a military buzz cut.

"Unfortunately, it's a bachelor party," Alec said. "Or I'd ask you to join us."

"The waitress's fiancé?" She looked closer. "So who's the lucky groom?"

"The guy at the head of the table with the goofy-looking grin."

"Hmm." She considered the sandy-haired man with the pleasant face. "Cute."

"Taken."

"So I gathered." *The good ones always are,* she added to herself.

"Yeah, they're getting married tomorrow, with me as best man. Why they had to pick the same weekend as the big snowboarding competition, I have no idea. Talk about a test of friendship."

"The what competition?" Her attention was piqued.

"Snowboarding. On Jibber's Run. Are you going?"

"I hadn't heard about it."

"You're kidding." His eyes widened. "Not only do you hibernate in Austin, you hibernate here too."

"Pretty much," she admitted.

"What a waste. If you do nothing else while you're here, you should go to the competition this weekend and see some airdogs in action." His face lit up. "Hey, why don't we go together on Sunday? I can get you into the VIP stands."

How did he always know how to tempt her? "Actually, my family's flying in tomorrow, so what I do Sunday depends on them."

"Bring them along. That'll give me a chance to meet this hotshot brother of yours."

Before she could come up with a reason to turn him down, a golden retriever came through the tables, trotting toward them. "Oh my goodness," she exclaimed as the dog sat at Alec's feet and let loose one sharp bark. Even knowing Colorado was a pet-friendly state, seeing a dog in a pub surprised her. "Who's this?"

"Who, this mangy mutt? This is Buddy." Alec ruffled the dog's ears, bringing forth a canine grin. "What'd they do, boy, send you to fetch me?"

Buddy barked again, then grabbed Alec's pant leg and started tugging.

"In a minute." Alec tried to brush the dog away. Buddy tugged harder, nearly jerking Alec off his feet. "Come on, Buddy, be a pal. Can't you see I'm making time with a beautiful woman here? You're cramping my style."

Christine laughed at that. She'd always wanted a dog, and what could be better than a big, friendly golden retriever?

"Jeez, all right!" Alec made a grab for the pitcher of beer, nearly sloshing its contents as Buddy kept tugging. "Apparently I have to go. But you stay put. I'll find a way to sneak back."

She felt instantly deflated as he left, the way she had that afternoon. She knew continuing the game of flirt and resist was asking for trouble, but hadn't she proved she could hold her own? As long as she didn't do something stupid, like fall for him, she could still talk to him, couldn't she?

As she watched him take his seat, the men leaned forward in a huddle around the table, apparently demanding details as they glanced back and forth between him and her. Too bad it was a bachelor party and she couldn't join them.

Actually, her saner half argued, it was probably a good thing she couldn't join them. A few minutes of flirting with Alec was one thing, but sitting with him would be too much like a date, which could lead to who knew what.

Trent rose unexpectedly and cupped his hands to his mouth. "Christine!" he called over the music. Then waved for her to come over.

Uh-oh. Now what should she do?

Going over there was a really bad idea. But if she refused, she'd embarrass Alec in front of his friends— a fate worse than death for most men. She couldn't do that to him, could she? Even Maddy and Amy would agree with that. She had no choice, she assured herself as she slipped off the bar stool, none at all.

Chapter 6

In order to win, first you have to stay in the game.
—*How to Have a Perfect Life*

Yes! Alec nearly shouted aloud when Christine headed over. *Thank you, Trent.*

He rose as she neared the table. "Sorry," he said, not the least bit sorry. "They insisted. Really. I had nothing to do with this."

"I thought this was a bachelor party." She smiled at the men. "I hate to intrude."

"You're not," Will assured her, his speech slightly slurred. "As long as you're not a stripper who'll get me in trouble with Lacy, there's no problem." He squinted at her. "You're not a stripper, are you?"

"Shut up, Will." Alec scowled at him. "Does she look like a stripper?" Of course they all had to give her body serious consideration after that. "Never mind. Let's see, introductions." He pointed around the table, calling out names. The men all waved a greeting in return, except for Brian, who asked if she still needed lessons.

Grabbing an empty chair from a nearby table, Alec set it next to his own and held it for her. He sat facing her, his thighs straddling her chair. "Ignore them," he told her. "They're all idiots. I have no idea why I hang out with them."

"Ah, come on, you know you love us, man," Eric said with enough fake emotion to have Brian snickering. "Ouch!" Eric jumped. "Who kicked me?"

"Oh, was that your shin?" Lt. Kreiger glared at him in one of his attempts to teach the "young pups" manners.

Alec propped an elbow on the table and shielded his face from his friends so he could speak to only her. "Meeting these jokers probably isn't going to help my cause, is it?"

"Probably not." She smiled as she said it, though, and looked right into his eyes. "But then the cause was already lost."

"No it wasn't." He resisted the urge to trace her cheek with his fingertip. "Never give up, that's my motto. Besides, you were weakening. I could feel it."

"Maybe." Color rose in her cheeks as she sipped her beer. He smiled in satisfaction.

"So, Will," Steve said, "any second thoughts about locking on the old ball and chain?"

"Absolutely none," Will answered, grinning broadly.

"I don't know. I'm with Alec on this one," Brian said. "I can't believe you're moving to Ohio to work for your dad's insurance agency. I wouldn't do that for any woman."

"But that's just it." Will leaned forward, serious now. "When it's for the right woman, it's not a sacrifice. For me, Lacy's the right woman."

"Yeah, that's what I thought about Judy," Steve grumbled. "Until she busted my damn nuts in the divorce." The minute the words left his mouth, he flashed a sheepish look at Christine. "Pardon, ma'am."

"No problem," she assured him, looking amused.

Considering the language that frequently came out of her mouth, Alec found Steve's embarrassment pretty amusing too.

"Don't listen to him," Kreiger said in his gravelly voice. "I had thirty-six years with Mai Tien before I lost her to cancer. When it works, it's the best thing that can happen to a man."

"There, see?" Will toasted Kreiger with his beer. "And you're right. When I'm with Lacy, it's as if . . . everything inside me settles into place. I've never been so comfortable around anyone. Not even you guys. I can actually see myself growing old with her. And that's what I want, to grow old with her. To have kids and grandkids and a mortgage on a house. I just love her like crazy and can't wait for her to be my wife."

"Oh man." Eric buried his face in his hands. He looked like a skinny scarecrow with straw-colored hair sticking up in every direction. "Somebody cut him off. He's had way too much to drink."

"Isn't that what you're supposed to do at these things?" Brian grabbed the pitcher to refill his mug.

"Well then, give me another one." Eric held his mug out. "I need it if I have to sit here and listen while he gets sappy."

"Just you wait." Will nodded sagely. "It'll happen to you."

"Not me!" Eric insisted.

"What about you, Alec?" Brian called from his end of the table. "You ever getting married?"

Alec stared at him, unable to believe he'd ask a no-win question like that in front of a woman.

"What, Peter Pan marry?" Eric laughed uproariously. "No way. That would require growing up."

Christine arched a brow at him. "Peter Pan?"

"Stupid nickname." He felt his face heat.

"Oh?" She looked intrigued.

"Yeah, um . . ." He cleared his throat, thinking maybe he shouldn't thank Trent for inviting her over. "Lacy called me that once when she was mad at Will. You know, Peter Pan and his Lost Boys." He gestured to his friends. "The 'Lost Boys' here found it so hilarious, it sort of stuck."

"Actually"—Steve smiled—"Peter wouldn't have to grow up to get married. He'd just have to find a Wendy who didn't mind him spending all his money on expensive toys. A habit of which I highly approve."

"You would." Alec scowled at the sheriff, whose budget had to cover search and rescue. "Since it saves you from having to buy them."

"Exactly." Steve grinned.

Alec saw Christine's eyebrow go up even more and knew he was sinking fast. Fortunately, the band struck up a lively tune, giving him inspiration. "I assume you know how to dance even if you don't get out much."

"The two-step?" She looked to the dance floor, where a crowd of regulars were spinning and scooting in a counterclockwise pattern. "I'm a little rusty."

"I'll refresh your memory." He stood and held his hand out to her. "If you boys will excuse us."

Her hand slipped into his. He pulled her to her feet, then bent near Trent's ear. "Do me a favor and don't let Will drink any more beer after this one. Get him a soft drink or something."

"Got it." Trent nodded.

Alec led Christine onto the dance floor.

"So those are 'the guys,' huh?" she said.

"That's them." He pulled her to him with one of his hands holding one of hers, the other at the small of her back. "Best buds in the world. Or so I thought until a few minutes ago."

She laughed. "Ah, come on, it's a guy thing, isn't it, to give your friends a hard time when they're trying to impress a date?"

"Are you my date?" He pulled her closer, their faces mere inches apart.

"No." Her humor fled, but her eyes looked steadily into his.

His gaze dropped to her lips, then lifted back to her eyes as he guided her in a standard two-step. "That's becoming your favorite word."

"You taught it to me."

"How about I teach you something else?" He made a tight turn that brought her body more snugly against his. One of her legs moved between his thighs. "Very good," he said. "Are you going to be as quick a study on the dance floor as you are on the slopes?"

She shook back her hair, playfully arrogant. "That depends on how well you lead. Because if you don't, I will."

"Oh, yeah?"

"An annoying habit of mine. Or so I've been told. But I always figure, if you're going to dance, then dance. Don't just shuffle around the floor."

"I couldn't agree more." He flashed a grin, then spun her out to arm's length and reeled her back to his side so they both faced front. "Except the steps are a little different here than they are back home. So pay attention." He showed her one of the patterns. She watched his boots, picking it up quickly.

"Very good," he said. After the next set of steps, he twirled her about, passed her behind his back, then brought her back in against his chest. "You are a quick study."

"And you know how to lead." She smiled up at him, her face glowing.

"See, another reason you should go out with me."

"Shut up and dance."

"Yes, ma'am."

The night sped by, and as happened too often when she was with Alec, Christine forgot he was off-limits. They laughed their way through several songs, stopping back at the table now and then to catch their breaths and so Alec didn't ignore his friends. Then they headed back to the dance floor.

Toward midnight, the band slid into a slow waltz.

"Finally," Alec sighed as he pulled her close, fitting their bodies together. "I thought they'd never slow things down."

She stiffened for a heartbeat, remembering her vow to resist this man. Although, it was only a dance. What harm would come from just dancing? She relaxed against him and rested her head on his shoulder.

Then their bodies lined up, hip to hip, as they swayed to the dreamy tune, and she remembered. *Oh yeah, that's what harm comes from dancing.* A slight bulge pressed against her belly as he guided her across the dark dance floor. The lyrics told of deep longing and endless yearning. Their thighs brushed, and she knew exactly what the song writer meant. She should ease back, she told herself. Get a little space between them. And she would.

In a second.

"I've always liked this song." His hand moved lower on her back, urging her even closer. Then that hand slipped beneath her sweater. The warmth of his palm had liquid heat pooling in her loins.

Okay, she really needed to move away.

In a second.

His fingers traced tantalizing circles, setting off tremors and making her want to arch like a cat into the caress. "You're right about the band. They're, mmm, very good."

"Very." The sleepy roughness of his voice sent a shiver of need through her. "Now, aren't you glad you came?"

"Actually, I am."

"Good." He rocked back on a turn, bringing one of his thighs between hers. It pressed briefly against the seam of her jeans and the sensual contact set off sparks of pleasure, making her want to rub wantonly all over him.

Okay, this was getting way out of hand. She absolutely had to ease away.

In just one more second.

His cheek rubbed against her hair as he whispered in her ear. "Come with me."

"Hmm?" With her mind hazed with arousal, her first thought was come as in orgasm. He wanted her to come with him? Right here? That made her lean back enough to see his face, even though her hips remained pressed to his, with the now not-so-subtle bulge prodding her belly. *"W-what?"*

"On Sunday." He frowned at her shocked expression. "The snowboard competition. Come with me."

"Oh." She laughed. "I thought—Never mind."

"What?"

"Nothing. And no. I can't. I told you, my family will be here."

"Meet me there anyway, in front of the VIP stands. I'll leave passes for all of you at the gate."

"Alec, really, I . . . I can't."

"Why not? Wait a second." His eyes shifted, then widened. "You're not married, are you?"

"No. I'm not married."

"Involved?"

"No."

"Dying from a rare disease?"

"No."

"Embarrassed to tell me you're bi, you were once a man, you have an STD?"

"No!" She laughed.

"Then meet me Sunday."

"No." Her humor turned to exasperation.

"Why not? I'm serious. There has to be a reason."

She narrowed her eyes. "I thought you said the word 'no' worked."

"I lied. Well, no actually, I forgot to clarify that you have to mean it when you say it, and you don't."

"Yes, I do!"

"Christine—" He looked incredulous. "I'm not blind. I'm not stupid. I know you're attracted to me. So give me one good reason why you won't go out with me."

"Maybe I'm not attracted in that way."

"Right." He glanced about, then made three quick turns that took them off the dance floor. Darkness engulfed them. A quick look about told her they were at the base of the steps leading to the stage. A curtain shielded them from the people in the pub. In the next instant, she found her back pressed to a wall. Alec's mouth started toward hers.

"Wait!" Panic had both her hands flat against his chest and her voice coming out as a squeak. "What are you doing?"

"Kissing you. Or rather, I'm about to."

She opened her mouth to say no, but somehow the word got stuck. She stared up at him in the shadow, the noise of the bar muffled. Dim light glinted in his eyes as he stared back at her, his gaze intent. She dropped her gaze to his mouth. How many times had she wanted to feel those beautifully masculine lips moving on hers?

She looked back at his eyes. "One kiss."

His head started down again.

"Wait!"

He lifted his head, his expression saying: *What now?*

"No hands," she said, and whipped her hands off his chest to tuck them between her back and the wall.

The incredulous exasperation that flashed into his eyes would have been funny if her heart wasn't fluttering up into her throat.

Very slowly, very deliberately, he moved his hands from her hips to plant them one at a time against the wall to either side of her head.

And then his mouth covered hers.

Oh my God was her last coherent thought as she slipped into the liquid wonder of his kiss. His lips molded and moved, leading her as he had on the dance floor. His head slanted for a better angle as his tongue slipped inside, coaxed, teased, and tangled her up with need.

A whimper escaped her as she followed, returning every lick and taste, hungry for more, and more, and more. If she had only this one kiss, she wanted it to last forever. He seemed bent on the same goal, pouring everything he had into the play of mouths, until her body started melting down the wall.

When the kiss ended, she let out a long, heartfelt sigh. Then opened her eyes. Slowly.

She found him smiling down at her with a look of utter male satisfaction.

Apparently, she'd slumped several inches down the wall.

"Ah, well." She cleared her throat and willed strength into her wobbly knees. Somehow she managed to straighten. "Yes. That was . . ." She cleared her throat again.

"Eloquently put." He stepped back and offered her his hand.

She took it. Gratefully.

When he started walking, she followed numbly,

vaguely aware that the pub wasn't as crowded as it had been earlier. The band appeared to be quitting for the night. Rather than go to the table, he walked her to the front door, retrieved her coat, and helped her put it on.

Stepping out into the cold, he pulled the hood into place, then cupped her face and gave her another kiss, this one sweet and all too brief.

She frowned in disappointment when he lifted his head.

"I'll see you Sunday."

And then he stepped back inside.

She stood in confusion, staring at the closed door of the pub. When her senses snapped back into place, she wanted to stamp her foot. "No," she said. "No, no, no. I mean it."

Chapter 7

Your gene pool might be where you're born, but you don't have to live there.

—How to Have a Perfect Life

Christine welcomed the noisy chaos of four adults and two children arriving and unpacking as her family descended on the condo. It kept her from thinking about Alec and that devastating kiss at the pub.

Almost.

Actually, she had trouble thinking about anything except that kiss, but her family provided at least some distraction.

"I can't believe it's been so long since I spent Christmas with you guys," she said at breakfast Sunday morning.

"Well, there was the little matter of your residency," her mother pointed out with a gracious smile as she sprinkled artificial sweetener on her bran cereal.

Sitting at the round, glass-top dining table, Christine marveled at her mother's beauty. How did a woman just shy of sixty manage to look so lovely, young, and perfectly put together all the time? People told her she'd inherited her mother's looks and her father's brains, but frankly she didn't see it on either count. Next to Barbara Ashton she was a gangly giraffe.

As for the brains, she came in last in the family there as well. She watched her brother as he read the Denver paper. Like their father, Robbie wasn't so much handsome as impressive, with sharp, angular features, but both men were off-the-charts intelligent.

"I was so glad when Robbie told me you were joining us this year," Natalie, Robbie's wife, said as she managed to feed their baby in the high chair, their two-year-old, and herself at the same time. As a refreshing contrast to so much tall blondness, Natalie had a petite build, dark hair, and big brown eyes. "There's nothing more important than being with family during the holidays, especially for children."

Baby Jonathan let out a screech and clapped his chubby, messy hands.

"Agreed." Christine nodded, and congratulated herself on going a whole five minutes without thinking about Alec.

"Hey, check this out." Robbie folded the newspaper inside out. "There's a snowboard competition going on today. Anyone interested in going?"

Christine froze.

"To watch snowboarding?" Robert Senior raised a disapproving brow. He sat with his legs crossed in a manner that Christine had always considered the epitome of masculine elegance. Lifting a sharp knife, he cut his grapefruit into precise sections, as he had every morning for as long as she could remember. A half a grapefruit and a bowl of bran cereal was what the Ashtons eat. Every. Single. Morning. "I'm afraid I don't quite understand the attraction to snowboarding. In my day, people skied. They didn't skateboard down the mountain like a bunch of wild hoodlums."

Praying her father would override Robbie's suggestion, she poked at her own cereal and longed for a Danish.

"They still ski." Robbie laid the paper next to his bowl. "And snowboarding isn't just for teenage boys anymore. In fact, I've been thinking about learning."

"You have?" their father asked—and just like that, suddenly snowboarding was acceptable. Figures. Christine made a face at two-year-old Charles that made him giggle. "Where is this competition?"

"On Jibber's Run," Robbie answered. "It starts at ten. Maybe afterward, we could look into renting boards for tomorrow and giving it a try."

Oh, no. Christine put down her spoon. First, she did *not* want to go anywhere near Jibber's Run where Alec would be waiting for her to join him. And second, she had *not* spent a week honing her skiing skills just to have her brother take up snowboarding. If the pattern of their lives held true, he'd be great at it from day one, and she'd be scrambling to keep up.

"Excuse me." She raised a hand. "I thought we were going to ski tomorrow."

Robbie shrugged. "We'll be here two weeks. There's plenty of time to do both. Natalie?" He turned to his wife. "Any interest in seeing a snowboard competition?"

Natalie looked up from the baby food she was coaxing Jonathan to eat. "Oh, I'd love to, but what about the boys? I haven't had time to contact the babysitting service."

"Mom'll watch the boys. Won't you, Mom?"

Barbara Ashton stiffened slightly. "Actually . . . I've arranged for the decorator to come by and put up our holiday decorations."

"Great." Robbie beamed at her, ignoring the subtle no. "Since you'll be here all day, it won't be any trouble for you to watch the boys. Hey, they can help you hang ornaments on the tree." He tickled his older son's tummy. "How's that sound, Chuckie? You want to help Grammy decorate?"

The boy screeched with glee.

Christine glanced over just in time to see the horror that flashed through her mother's eyes at that suggestion. Allow a rambunctious toddler near her professionally decorated, twelve-foot-tall artificial tree?

Christine had yet to see this monstrosity, but Natalie had regaled her with enough stories to have her cringing at the thought. She looked at her sister-in-law, expecting her to beg for a real tree—which she knew Natalie desperately wanted for her boys. Instead, Natalie just kept coaxing the baby to eat, not saying a word.

She looked at her brother next. He looked right back at her, his expression amused and challenging. Dammit. Neither one of them planned to bring it up.

Steeling herself for battle, she bravely took up the standard. "Speaking of trees . . . since this is my first Christmas with the family in so long, I was hoping for a real tree."

"Don't be silly." Her mother waved the thought aside. "Real trees are much too messy."

"They're worth it, though," Christine countered. "Especially for children."

Her mother sent her a chilly look. "They never look as nice and we already have a tree."

"Yes, but—"

"Must you always argue?" Her mother gave the sigh of disappointment that never failed to make Christine feel twelve again.

"I'm sorry." She straightened her posture the way she'd been taught during all those interminable charm classes she'd endured during middle school. "It was just a thought."

From the corner of her eye, she saw her brother calmly pick up his paper. A little kernel of resentment burrowed inside her. If Robbie had asked for a real tree, their father would have sided with him, and their mother would have relented.

Trying not to sulk, she gave up on the disgusting bran cereal and turned to her coffee. Dang it, though, she wanted a real tree. Something gaudy and fun like the trees Maddy had always squeezed into the corner of their dorm room and Amy and Jane had helped them decorate. Then they'd all sat around it drinking hot chocolate with peppermint schnapps and singing Christmas carols until their dorm mom came by and told them lights out. Why couldn't family Christmases be like that?

The silence that had descended over breakfast broke when Jonathan shrieked and tossed a glob of yellow baby food at Natalie. The blob landed with a splat on Natalie's white Escada blouse.

Christine stared as Natalie gasped in surprise. Even knowing Natalie, she half expected her sister-in-law to throw a fit over having such an expensive designer shirt ruined with baby food.

Recovering, Natalie merely laughed. "Oh, you little rascal, you." She leaned forward to rub her nose against the baby's, making him giggle. "But you're still messier than me."

"I'm a rascal too." The toddler splashed his spoon in his cereal bowl. Barbara pressed a manicured fingertip to her forehead as if staving off a migraine.

"You certainly are!" Natalie exclaimed as she stood and lifted the baby from the high chair. "You're my big rascal."

The boy beamed and splashed his spoon even more.

"You shouldn't encourage them to misbehave," Barbara sighed, the same way she had over Christine's tree suggestion.

Natalie, however, seemed immune. "If we're going out, I need to change my blouse, and most likely this little stinker needs a change too." She lifted the baby and sniffed. "*Phew!* Somebody needs a big change. Honey, will you watch Charles? See if you can get him to eat at least a little of his cereal."

"You bet," Robbie assured with a smile.

"Thanks, sweetie." Natalie kissed the top of her husband's head before carrying the baby up the stairs.

"Okay, big guy." Robbie pulled the boy into his lap. "It's just you and me now. No Mom here to save you. So what's it going to be? Cereal, or . . . tickle torture?"

"Cereal's icky!"

Christine stifled a laugh and the urge to give the kid a high five of agreement. Sure bran was good for you, but yuck!

"Are you going to eat it?" Robbie raised a menacing eyebrow.

"No!" the boy declared with the vehemence only a two-year-old can lend the word.

"Torture it is!" Robbie announced and attacked the boy's tummy. The boy shrieked and squirmed and laughed until tears came to his eyes.

Watching them amazed Christine. Ashtons were not known to be demonstrative, yet she'd seen her brother roll on the floor and behave like a kid himself more than once.

"Okay!" Charles finally screamed. "I give!"

Robbie stopped, but held his hand at the ready. "You mean it? You'll eat your cereal?"

"Yes." The boy sighed, catching his breath. Red blotches decorated his chubby cheeks as he sat up on his dad's lap. He summoned an impressive pout, though, as he accepted the spoon. "It tastes like poo!"

Christine snorted coffee out of her nose and quickly smothered the laugh with her linen napkin. "Sorry. I must have swallowed wrong."

"So, Christine," her brother said with his son in his lap, dutifully eating. "Do you want to go with us to watch the snowboarding, or stay here and help Mom?"

She weighed her options. Go watch some airdogs in action, or help her already-irritated mother supervise the precise decorating of a fake tree. Even with the threat of running into Alec, going to the competition won hands down.

"You know"—she smiled—"I believe I'll go with you."

Her brother smiled back. "Somehow I thought you might."

*   *   *

"I love that hat on you," Natalie said, fluffing the white faux fur that completely hid Christine's hair and partially shielded her face. "You look like a snow queen."

"I feel ridiculous." Christine glanced nervously about the crowded area in front of the entrance to the stands, wishing the men would hurry up with buying the tickets.

"Then why did you ask to borrow it?" Natalie asked in a hurt voice.

"Hmm?" Turning back, Christine nearly kicked herself. "I—I remembered how good it looked on you and wanted to try it. You always carry this stuff off so well, and I just . . . don't."

"That's not true." Natalie stepped back to admire the long coat that matched the hat. "I think you look glamorous."

"Well thank you, for the compliment and the loan." She gathered the big collar together, like a spy in a trench coat, and made another quick scan for Alec. So far, so good. "Now back to the tree issue. I still say we should have a real one."

Natalie sighed. "You won't get an argument from me. Robbie and I totally agree."

"Then why didn't you say something this morning? Never mind, I know why *you* didn't speak up, but what's Robbie's excuse?"

Natalie fussed with the faux fox she'd chosen to wear. "As he sees it, your mother has few enough things in life that make her happy, so what's the harm in letting her obsess over decorating all the time. I mean, come on, she's been married to your father for forty years. Maybe that's how they stay together."

"What are you talking about? My parent's have a good marriage." She caught a flash of fluorescent green jacket and her heart did a little flip. Peeking over the collar of the coat, she found Alec looking about as he talked to one of the gate attendants.

The memory of their kiss washed over her, followed by hundreds of others that drove home how much she enjoyed being with him. How alive he made her feel. And there he was, looking for her, probably wondering if she was going to show up.

She longed to raise her hand, call his name, and watch his face light up when he saw her.

Instead, she pretended to tuck her hair beneath the hat so her hand would hide her face. What were she and Natalie talking about? Oh, yes, her parents. "I admit, they aren't overtly affectionate, but it's not like they have big marital problems or anything. They never even fight."

Natalie pursed her lips. "It's hard to fight when you rarely talk."

"Mom's just a bit reserved."

"Christine, it's not just your mom. Look, I don't mean to be critical, but . . . Oh, to heck with it. Robert Senior is one of the most self-absorbed, egotistical, chauvinistic men I have ever met."

Christine's jaw dropped. "He's also a loyal husband and a good provider. I don't hear Mom complaining."

Natalie raised a brow in disagreement.

"Okay, so she gets in her subtle digs," Christine admitted. "What they have works for them."

"Oddly enough, it does," Natalie agreed. "Robbie's point, though, is that if having the condo professionally decorated for Christmas every year makes her happy, let her have it. It's better than having her stew for two weeks, looking for little passive-aggressive ways to get back at all of us."

"So you're just going to let your sons grow up with fake Christmas trees?"

"No." A devious grin played about Natalie's lips. "We're going to wait until your parents are in bed, then sneak a real tree into the loft so the boys can cover it with every kitschy ornament we can find. By the time Barbara discovers it, it will be too late."

"Oh, I love that plan." Christine's spirits lifted with childlike pleasure. "Can I help decorate? Please."

"Only if you wear your pj's and agree to drink copious amounts of hot cocoa."

"With marshmallows?"

"Of course."

"You're on!" Christine hugged her sister-in-law. "I'm so glad you married my brother."

Natalie hugged her back. "I'm rather glad I did too."

When Christine straightened, she saw the same happiness shining in Natalie's eyes that she'd seen shining in Maddy's every time she looked at her fiancé, Joe.

That's what I want. That right there. The kind of love that fills you up until it spills right out.

If only she could have it with someone fun, like Alec.

Rattled by the thought, she glanced over her shoulder, but the sudden appearance of her brother and father blocked her view of the gate.

"The conquering warriors return!" Robbie proclaimed holding up two tickets. "We scored big-time. VIP seats, right behind the announcers' stand."

Christine's eyes bulged. "No. That's impossible."

"Impressive, huh?" Her brother wiggled his eyebrows at his wife. "I'll expect a suitable reward later."

Natalie giggled when he nuzzled her neck, whispering in her ear.

Robert Senior handed Christine her ticket. "Shall we find our seats?"

"Lead the way," Robbie suggested, tucking Natalie into his side.

Christine held her breath as she turned, prepared to duck behind her father's back. Alec, though, had vanished, probably heading for the area before the announcers' booth, where he'd told her to meet him. Okay, all she had to do was make it past him and reach her seat, then employ some hunker and hide maneuvers.

When they rounded the stands, she breathed a sigh of relief. Alec was nowhere in sight. Then they started up the steps just to the side of the announcers' booth, and she tripped at what she saw.

Alec wasn't in front of the booth. He was inside it! He sat beside the announcer wearing a microphone headset.

Her disguise was such that if she hadn't stopped to gape, he probably wouldn't have given her a second glance. No such luck. He saw her trip, did a quick double take, then squinted with uncertainty.

Before she could duck her head, her brother plowed into her back, nearly knocking her over.

"Oops, sorry," he said, steadying them both.

"Who's that?" Natalie asked.

"Hmm, what?" Christine tried to shield her face.

"That man waving to get your attention?" Natalie pointed straight at Alec.

Seeing no choice, she turned to face Alec. He smiled broadly seeing it really was her. But what was he doing in the announcers' booth? At her questioning look, he tapped his watch, held up five fingers, then made an OK sign. Oh, please don't let that mean he'd join her in five minutes.

"He's cute," Natalie said.

"Who is he?" Robbie asked, equally curious.

"He's, um, my ski instructor."

"Ski instructor?" Robbie's curiosity turned to a narrow-eyed frown. "You're dating a ski instructor?"

Christine cringed. When it came to disapproving of her boyfriends, her brother was as bad as Maddy and Amy. At least her father had continued up and couldn't hear the exchange.

"No, I'm not dating him," she insisted, hoping to avoid the brotherly lecture of "Why can't you find someone appropriate to date? Someone suitable, like I did?" As if she needed a reminder that her brother even *dated* better than she did. "Actually, I hired him to teach me how to kick your ass on the slopes tomorrow."

Robbie laughed. "Fat chance, little sister."

"You two," Natalie scolded, the way she did when they met at the country club tennis courts. "Why does everything have to be a competition between you?"

"It's not." Robbie grinned. "Since I always win, it's more a lesson in humility than a competition."

"Robbie!" Natalie punched her husband in the arm. "Don't be so mean."

"Isn't that what big brothers are for?" He laughed.

"Laugh now," Christine taunted as she stomped up the risers. "We'll see who's laughing tomorrow."

The exchange distracted her from thoughts of Alec, until they were settled in their seats and she heard the words coming over the loudspeaker.

". . . pleased to have Alec Hunter here with us today, one of the best jibbers in Colorado. Alec, you're normally one of the top finalists; I was surprised to see you weren't competing this year."

"I had a personal obligation that kept me from entering."

"I'm sure some of the competitors here this weekend were sorry to hear that," the announcer joked. "Tell us about the course and any top picks you have for this year's winner."

Christine sat transfixed, listening to his voice while she watched him from behind. Part of her winced at his liberal use of what she called "dude speak," the jargon unique to snowboarders and trick skiers. And yet, in spite of the lingo, his natural charisma came through. If only he would do something with all that charm and obvious intelligence to make him a good dating choice.

Maybe she could encourage him to do something more with his life than snowboard and ski.

Realizing what she was thinking, she mentally rolled her eyes. This was exactly what got her into trouble, thinking she could help some guy fix his life.

Although . . . with Alec, she didn't have time to run the full cycle from infatuation to frustration. She had only two more weeks in Silver Mountain. That was hardly time to really get to know him, much less set out to change him.

Two more weeks.

Now that she thought about it, that really wasn't enough time to do much of anything other than enjoy each other's company. After that, she'd be back in Austin, a thousand miles from temptation. Even if she got involved with Alec here, the physical distance would keep her from doing anything stupid, like let him waste several months of her life and whatever money she lent him before he dumped her for nagging him.

What harm could come from enjoying his company for the next two weeks?

You're justifying, Christine, said a tiny voice in the back of her head that sounded suspiciously like Maddy.

Besides, Amy's voice added, *feeling good about yourself has to come from inside you, not from dating emotionally needy men.*

Oh, all right! I won't date him, she mentally groused. *Although for the record, Alec isn't emotionally needy. He's just undermotivated.*

And fun loving. And happy. Gawd, she wished she had a life like that: carefree and filled with friends. She had Maddy and Amy, who loved her completely, but most people found her too intimidating to befriend for reasons she'd never understood.

She wasn't sure anything intimidated Alec Hunter. Or discouraged him. The memory of their dance and the kiss in the dark made her smile—until she realized the announcer was thanking him for his time. The next thing she knew, he was leaving the booth and heading up the bleachers straight toward her. She mentally scrambled for what to say. What if he tried to join them?

Glancing frantically about, she gave thanks that the seats to either side of her family were taken. Even if he stopped to say hi, he wouldn't be able to join them.

Or so she thought.

To her horror, Alec maneuvered down the line, greeting several spectators by name, exchanging handshakes, and asking half a row of people to get up and move down a seat. Of course they did. No problem. Anything for good ol' Alec.

Honestly, the man could sell ice to Eskimos.

"Hey, Chris," he said when he reached her. "I see you got the passes I left at the gate."

"Actually, we bought tickets."

"You didn't have to do that. So is this your family?"

"Uhhhh." Her mind went blank.

"Hi, Alec Hunter." He leaned across her to offer his hand to her brother. "You must be Robbie."

"Pleased to meet you." Robbie shook his hand. "This is my wife, Natalie, and my father, Dr. Robert Ashton, Sr."

"Hello." Natalie greeted him with a friendly smile. Robert Senior barely grunted, then turned his attention back to the course as they waited for the action to begin.

"I hear you're Christine's ski instructor," Robbie said as Alec took a seat next to her.

Alec laughed at that, showing off those gorgeous white teeth of his; then his eyes went to her face with a long, admiring look. "Something like that."

Please God, don't let him say anything else. Please! She clasped her hands between her knees, jiggling slightly as if trying to stay warm. In truth, she was sweating inside Natalie's coat and the strong mountain sun wasn't helping.

"I also take it you know something about snowboarding," Robbie said. "I don't suppose you teach lessons on that as well."

"I might." Alec sent her a flirtatious look. "For the right price."

"How much?" her brother asked.

"Hmm?" Alec tore his attention away from her. "Oh, I didn't mean money. If I did it, it would be as a favor to Chris."

"Oh really." Robbie gave her a searching look. " 'Chris'?"

"Look." She straightened. "I think the first contestant is heading down."

Both men turned their attention to the slope. The next several minutes passed with all of them watching the snowboarders do aerial stunts that Alec proclaimed to be "huge" or "awesome" unless the boarder "biffed" or "bailed." Alec and Robbie leaned forward almost constantly, talking around her, while

Alec explained the language as much as the action. Hearing her brother pick up the lingo should have made her laugh, but all she could do was cringe. She'd heard Alec use boarding terms before, but never like this. Why did it have to be in front of her family?

She tried to tune both men out, but felt Alec's puzzled gaze land on her several times. Finally, he looked right at her. "Chris, how about going with me to the concession stand?"

"I'm fine," she insisted, knowing if she went with him, Robbie's suspicions about them dating would return. "I don't need anything."

"Or we could talk right here."

"Talk?" Panic shot through her. "About what?"

He leaned closer and lowered his voice. "About why you'd meet me here, then freeze me out."

"I'll go with you to the concession stand!"

Chapter 8

Alec stared as Christine shot to her feet, then scrambled past him and half a row of knees to get to the steps. After a look at her brother, who'd gone from cordial to confused, he rose and followed. She stayed ahead of him, clambering down the steps until she reached the bottom and ducked in front of the announcers' stand, where they'd be hidden from her family.

"Hey, where's the fire?" he asked.

She turned to face him, looking flushed. "I did not come here to meet you."

"What?" He frowned.

She crossed her arms, refusing to meet his eyes. "I came with my family."

"But this is right where we agreed to meet."

"That's why I wore all this—this stupid fur." Frustration flashed in her eyes. "I was hoping you wouldn't recognize me."

"I don't understand." Although he was starting to and hurt nudged against confusion. She looked like royalty standing there in a fussy coat and hat that didn't look at all like the expensive but no-nonsense clothes she usually wore. If he hadn't looked right at her earlier, he probably wouldn't have recognized her. "Once again, I don't get it. I know you're attracted to me."

"I am." Her gray eyes pleaded with him. "I like you, Alec. I really do. But I can't go out with you. Can we please just leave it at that?"

"No, we can't leave it at that. I want to know why."

She glanced nervously at the stands, as if to be sure her family couldn't see them.

He followed her gaze, and understanding smacked him in the face. "You think I'm not good enough for you? So much for your claim that money doesn't matter."

"No!" Color flooded in her cheeks, convincing him otherwise. "Do you really think I'm that kind of snob?"

"I didn't before, but now I don't know." His mind did a fast replay of the whole week, how she'd rejected him at every turn, then shown up at the pub, danced with him, flirted with him, and given him that brain-spinning kiss. "What happened Friday night? Did you finally get bored and decide to do a little slumming before the family arrived?"

Her jaw dropped before she snapped it closed and spoke through gritted teeth. "I was not slumming."

"Then why am I good enough to hang out with in a crowded bar, but in front of your family, I'm something to scrape off your designer boots. Which look ridiculous, by the way. Who wears city boots to walk on a ski slope?"

"They're not mine," she growled as anger sparked

in her eyes. "They're my sister-in-law's, and they *feel* ridiculous!"

"Then why are you wearing them?" His voice rose along with his temper. He had a long fuse, but she'd definitely lit it. "Oh yeah, so that I wouldn't recognize you. Well, good job, because I don't! For the past half hour I've been wanting to ask who this person is in Chris's body."

"My name is Christine."

"It certainly is." He looked her up and down. "How could I have been this wrong about you? I thought you were different from the rich vacationers who think they're above us working-class stiffs or the women who think the words ski pro and gigolo are synonymous. I guess I should be thankful you aren't one of the latter, because frankly, it's the more insulting of the two."

"I'm not either one of those things."

"Oh yeah? Prove it." He stepped closer, lowering his voice. "If I'm wrong, give me the real reason you won't go out with me."

She stared up at him, and he thought she wouldn't answer, but then she nodded. "Okay, you want to know? I'll tell you. It's because you're an unemployed ski bum. I don't care how much a man makes as long as he makes *something*!"

"I'm—I'm what?" He pressed a gloved hand to his forehead trying to make sense of her words. "What did you say?"

"I have a terrible weakness for immature, irresponsible men. I'm going to break that habit, though. I don't care how much I'm attracted to you or how much fun you are. I'm not going to do this to myself anymore."

"You think I'm unemployed?" The accusation spurred his anger higher because it lumped him into the same group as his lazy bum of a father. She thought he wasn't any better than that? "You came up with this theory how, exactly? Without even asking me?"

"I did ask! And Trent said you didn't work. Plus, you spend all your time skiing or hanging out in that pub, drinking with your friends. Is this the schedule of a responsible, working adult?"

He shook his head in amazement. "This coming from a woman who takes three-week vacations in her rich daddy's condo and wears clothes that could bankrupt a small country. What do you know about working? Have you ever had to work for anything?"

"Talk about unfair assumptions," she nearly sputtered. "You know nothing about me."

"Ditto, babe."

"For your information—"

The crowd rose with a gasp. Alec looked to the stands and saw a sea of horrified faces. Whipping around to face the slope, he saw a snowboarder rolling in the snow, clutching his leg.

The announcer's voice rose over the sound of the crowd. "Oh, that's a bad one, folks."

"Stay here," Alec snapped at Christine and took off at a dead run for a break in the barrier between the stands and the course. One of the workers tried to step in his path. "Let me through!"

Realizing it was either that or get plowed over, the

worker stepped aside. Alec raced toward the downed boarder who was thrashing about, screaming.

Dropping to his knees, Alec grabbed the guy's shoulder and tried to hold him still.

"I'm a paramedic. Will you let me help you?"

"My leg! Shit! My leg!"

Alec glanced at the thigh and silently cursed. The fractured femur hadn't broken through the pant leg, but he'd bet money it had broken through skin. And he couldn't do squat until he had verbal permission or the guy passed out.

"Hey! Listen!" He pressed the boarder down. "I'm a paramedic—"

Christine dropped to her knees on the other side of the boarder. "You're a what?"

The surprise on her face would have been comical if he'd had time to enjoy it. Ignoring her, he turned back to the boarder, getting his first good look at the kid's face. Jeez, he was young. "Will you let me help you?"

"Yes! Shit!" The face contorted in agony.

"Try to be still," Alec ordered and ripped off his ski gloves before reaching for the surgical gloves in his jacket.

Christine surprised him by pulling a similar pair out of her purse and snapping them on like a pro. He looked from her hands to her face.

"Surprise." She smiled. "I'm an ER doctor."

"You're a *doctor*?" The notion seemed ludicrous with her kneeling in the snow in a white fur coat and matching hat haloing her supermodel face.

The boarder screamed, jarring Alec's attention back into place.

Christine bent forward, pressing her fingers to the patient's throat. "What's your name?"

A stream of obscenities spilled forth.

"Hold him still," Christine ordered and pulled a pair of scissors from her purse. "This is going to be messy."

Alec pressed the kid's shoulders down with one forearm and reach for his radio. While he called in the situation, she cut the pants from hip to knee. Yep, she was right. It was messy. Blood gushed out, staining the snow about her and turning the fur coat red.

"This is 14B32 to dispatch," he said to Doris back at the station, then gave her a quick rundown. "I'm going to need a trauma kit, spine board, and traction splint."

"Ski patrol heard the accident over the loud-speaker and is already on the way," the ever-efficient Doris told him. "Do you want an ambulance or life flight?"

"Stand by." He glanced at Christine as she worked to remove the boot without injuring the leg further. "You want life flight?"

"Do we have a head injury?"

Alec lifted the kid's goggles onto the helmet. "Hey, dude, can you tell me your name?"

"God, it hurts!" The kid squeezed his eyes shut.

"Yeah, I know. Hang in there. Help's on the way. You're going to be fine." He cradled the kid's head in both hands and used his thumbs to lift his eyelids. "What's your name?"

"I . . ." The kid's eyes shifted back and forth, searching for the answer. "Tim."

"You got a last name, Tim?"

"O'Neil." He groped for his leg again.

"Where you from?"

"Bailey." A few choice obscenities followed.

Alec worked to keep him still. "What's your phone number?"

"It's uh, it's uh, shit!" The kid screamed as Christine pulled the boot free.

Alec glanced over his shoulder. "Pupils are even and responsive. Mild disorientation. Could just be the pain. You got circulation below the break?"

"Strong and steady," Christine confirmed. "Where's the nearest hospital?"

"Over the pass. Thirty minutes by ambulance if the roads are clear."

"That's too far with the way he's bleeding. Call for life flight."

"You got it." He radioed in her request as Trent skied up towing a toboggan.

"Hey, man." Alec nodded as Trent grabbed supplies and hurried over. "Good of you to join the party."

"Wouldn't miss it." Trent set the oxygen tank within Alec's reach. Getting the tube set took some doing with Tim writhing about.

"I need an IV with a large bore needle and a C collar," Alec said out of habit, then looked at Christine. "Sorry. I'm used to running the show. Do you want to set the IV yourself?"

"Be my guest." She'd moved back up the leg to stabilize the break before Tim did more damage with his thrashing about. Blood covered her hands and the cuffs of her white fur coat. "I'm kinda busy."

At Trent's questioning look, Alec laughed. "Turns out Chris is a doc."

"No shit?" Trent sent her an incredulous look.

"No shit." Alec fastened a C collar around the neck, noting Tim's struggles had grown weaker. Pulling off one of the kid's gloves, he inserted the IV needle in the back of the hand. "Hey, Tim, how you doing?"

"I've been better," he answered weakly.

"You on any meds?" Alec leaned forward to recheck the eyes. "Prescriptions? Over the counter?"

"No."

"Anything illegal?"

"No."

Alec gave him a hard look. "I can't help you if you're not straight with me."

"I'm not wonked, man!" Tim's breathing grew ragged. "I'm clean."

"How about allergies to drugs?"

"I don't . . . think so. Jesus!"

"Okay, then. You're doing good." He patted the kid's shoulder. From the corner of his eye, he saw Trent grab the traction splint. "Listen, Tim, we're going to splint your leg. It's going to hurt like crazy while we're doing it, but as soon as the splint is in place, you'll feel a lot better. Do you understand?"

The kid nodded, gritting his teeth.

Alec forced a reassuring smile. "You hang in there, scream all you want, and we'll try to be fast, okay?"

Tim squeezed his eyes shut as tears leaked out.

Alec turned to Christine. Working around doctors had taught him to tiptoe over egos. "Hey, um, Trent and I are used to doing this together. You mind trading places with me?"

"What?" Christine glanced up. Blinked. "Oh." Looking from Alec to Trent, she saw them waiting for her to move. With a laugh, she leaned back. "Not at all."

She shifted to monitor—and distract—the patient. "Hey, Tim, how long have you been snowboarding?"

"Long time." His face scrunched up.

"Two years? Three?"

"Four. Shit!"

She glanced over her shoulder and saw Trent supporting the leg while Alec strapped the splint into position. Turning back to Tim, she took hold of both his wrists and pressed them to his chest. "You hang on. They'll be as fast as they can."

"Here we go," Alec warned.

Tim let loose a bloodcurdling scream as the splint pulled the lower leg away from the body to realign the bone. She leaned all her weight into holding him down.

"You got him?" Alec called over the yelling.

"Sort of!" She ducked as fists came flying toward her face.

"Done!" Alec announced.

Tim's struggles stopped so abruptly, she tumbled on top of him. Sitting back, she saw he'd gone limp. "He's unconscious. Airway clear. Breathing good." She pressed her fingers to his neck and felt a steady pulse. "Pulse good. Check for circulation and reflex."

Alec pressed his fingers to the pulse point at the ankle, then ran his finger up the bottom of the foot. "We're good."

A shadow fell across her and she looked up to see her father standing over her. He pointed at the IV bag. "As much as he's bleeding, you need to be forcing liquid."

"I got it, Dad," she growled since she'd already been reaching for the bag to squeeze it.

"Need any help?" her brother asked. "Not that I'm into inviting lawsuits."

"No, I don't need help." Jesus, had they completely forgotten she was a trauma specialist? She looked to Trent. "I need a blanket."

"Got it!" Trent hurried to the toboggan.

A thumping beat sounded overhead. She looked up to see life flight sweeping over the crest of the mountain, then circling overhead.

A voice sounded on Alec's radio. He held it to his ear to hear over the noise of the helicopter, then lowered it to shout, "They can't land here! We need to move downhill!"

Crap! Christine thought. "Let's get him on a spine board." As much as Tim had been thrashing about, that was probably overly precautious, but better safe than sorry when transporting a patient.

While her brother and father watched, they strapped Tim to the board and lifted him into the toboggan. Christine climbed on, straddling Tim with her knees. The first IV was already empty, so she tossed it aside and started a second, all the while watching Tim for any signs of gagging or respiratory distress.

"You ready?" Trent called, clicking back into his skis.

"Yes. Let's go!" She steadied herself with her free hand.

With Trent towing in front and Alec on the rear rope to keep control, they slid down the course toward level ground at the bottom. She spared a glance at her father and brother and gave thanks when they didn't try to follow. The last thing she needed was them hovering over her, telling her how to do her job.

At the bottom of the course, a worker rushed forward to take the rope from Trent and pull the toboggan through a barrier. Other workers cleared a path through the curious bystanders.

Christine barely registered the crowd as they continued toward an open area where the helicopter had landed. Tim opened his eyes as the toboggan came to a halt, relieving her fear of a coma.

"Hey, there." She smiled down at him. "How ya feeling?"

"A little sick," he moaned.

"Do you know your name?"

"Tim O'Neil."

"Great."

The helo crew appeared beside her, helping her off.

"Tim, these men are going to get you to the hospital." She gave his hand a reassuring squeeze. "You're going to be fine. Okay?"

He nodded weakly.

She rattled off the patient's status as the life flight crew took over. Within seconds, Tim was loaded inside and the helicopter was lifting off.

She stood between Trent and Alec, watching it sweep up and circle back over the mountain. As the thumping sound of the blades faded, she realized her heart was pumping to the same hard beat.

"Well." She exhaled in a rush. "That's certainly one way to get your adrenaline going."

"No joke." Alec laughed, then looked at her. "Now what were we discussing before Tim interrupted?"

Looking back at him, at his sunlit hair against the blue sky, at his wide smile and laughing eyes, suddenly she felt lighter than air. "I um, believe it was something about you being an unemployed ski bum and me being a rich bitch who's never worked a day in her life."

"Ah yes." His smile grew broader. "I remember now."

"Alec unemployed?" Trent laughed. "Crazy Alec who works twenty-four seven, and would whether they paid him or not?"

Her mind spun with all this new data. "Is that why they call you crazy? Because you're a workaholic?"

He turned sheepish, although his smile never faded. "Well that and the, um, no-fear thing."

"What 'no-fear' thing?"

"Yeah, Hunter," Trent put in, even though they were too busy looking at each other to spare him a glance. "Tell her how you lecture us on safety, yet who's the first one to make a risky helo jump, rappel down a cliff during a rock slide, or belly crawl across a snowbank that's about to give?"

"That's my job," he said.

She shook her head in confusion. "Don't paramedics usually leave that sort of stuff to trained search-and-rescue volunteers?"

"Hmmm." He finally broke eye contact long enough to look at the blood-soaked gloves covering his hands. "Why don't we duck into the restroom and get cleaned up; then I'll drive you back to the village. We can talk on the way."

"Absolutely." She sent him a glowing smile.

Chapter 9

Stay open to surprises.

—*How to Have a Perfect Life*

Alec tried not to fidget as he waited for Christine to join him at the gate, but that smile she'd given him had his pulse jumping. She'd looked ready to kiss him right there in front of Trent and a crowd of onlookers.

That had to be a good sign.

Unless she'd simply been caught up in a post-rescue rush.

Anyone who worked emergencies knew all about the endorphin high. And when you mixed men and women together, bumping into each other as they worked, was it any wonder that sex became a common release? Adrenaline was a really great aphrodisiac. One that currently had his body primed and ready to go.

No doubt it had effected Christine too, but he really hoped that it wasn't the only thing behind the look she had given him. What if it was, though? What if she'd merely been temporarily juiced and it all wore off while she was in the women's room?

She might come out and go right back to pushing him away.

Finally, she appeared, coming through the crowd, tall and graceful with her long coat flowing about her.

Her very ruined coat.

She stopped before him and held her arms out to the side, looking down. She'd rinsed her gloves but left them on; a wise choice with all that blood hopelessly soaked into the fur.

"I guess I forgot I wasn't wearing scrubs." When she looked up, he saw amusement dancing in her eyes. "Not that it would have made any difference. What was I going to say? 'Excuse me, Tim, would you mind not bleeding while I find something more suitable to wear'?"

The fist in his chest relaxed a bit at seeing that the wall hadn't gone back up. *This* was the woman he'd been steadily falling for over the past week: a contradiction between the polished surface and the irreverent humor bubbling beneath. He wanted to take her face in his hands and kiss her hard on the mouth.

Instead, he nodded toward the parking lot. "Come on, I have an extra coat in the truck."

She followed him through the sea of SUVs and Outbacks with ski racks. He pointed his remote key toward a four-wheel drive, dark green pickup with crew cab, lights on top, and the word "Rescue" splashed in silver across the side.

"Wow, is this your truck?" Her eyes lit. "Talk about a man's wet dream on wheels."

He barked with laughter over her choice of words. "It comes with the job."

"Which is what, exactly?"

Pride expanded his chest. "I'm the county coordinator for search and rescue."

"Oh, really?" She raised a brow. "Impressive."

He opened the passenger door and greeted an enthusiastic Buddy, who took several sniffs and knew there was a rescue afoot. The dog barked and wiggled, waiting for Alec to put on his red vest, which was his cue to go into work mode.

"Sorry boy. Fun's over." Buddy whimpered when Alec didn't reach for the vest. "Oh, now don't pout. I can't stand it when you pout. How about I take you on a pretend rescue later, eh?" Buddy barked with glee at that idea. "There, that's my boy." Alec ruffled the fur.

With Buddy placated, he reached back into the crew cab and grabbed the firefighter's coat he wore whenever the need arose and held it out to Chris. "Here, try this."

Removing her ruined coat and protective gloves, she folded everything inside out and tossed it in the bed of the pickup. The hat came next. The instant she ripped it off, her blond hair tumbled down around her. She gave her head a good shake, tossing her hair back and forth.

His brain blanked at the sight of all that glorious hair whipping about her.

Next time he kissed her, she could forget the no-hands rule. He wanted his hands buried in that hair while his mouth feasted on hers.

When she presented her back, he slipped the coat up her arms, then indulged himself by helping pull her hair free of the collar. It felt like silk that slid sensuously through his fingers.

Too soon, she stepped away and faced him. "So how do I look?"

He raised a brow, caught off guard by an intense punch of arousal. The coat engulfed her. He had no idea why that turned him on, but his body heartily approved of seeing his coat covering her.

"Looks good." He nodded, warning himself to keep things light. He wasn't after a post-rescue bout of hot sex. He wanted to talk to her, sort things out, and score a date. "You could start a whole new fashion trend."

"Rescue gear on the runway in Milan?" She sent him an impish smile. "Now there's a thought."

Not trusting himself to speak, he went around to the driver's side and climbed in. She was already in the cab, accepting sloppy kisses from his dog.

"Come on, Buddy, show some pride." He shooed the dog farther into the backseat.

"Ooh." Christine pouted, then turned to face him, studying him for a minute before she smiled. "So. You're a paramedic *and* you do search and rescue? Isn't that unusual? I thought search-and-rescue volunteers, or in your case workers, had to be available twenty-four hours a day, which generally cuts out those of us in other emergency fields."

"Which is why I'm certified as a paramedic, but I've never worked as one." He started the truck and headed across the parking lot. "For me, it's always been search and rescue, and I've been working my tail off for years to land a paid position."

"When did that happen?"

"Two years ago. Before that, I did everything from work in ski shops to bus tables, usually working two jobs at a time and living with three other guys in cramped apartments just to be close enough to the mountains to answer a call." He smiled at her. "Kinda blows your theory of me as an unemployed ski bum, huh?"

She smiled. "Kinda."

He studied her before turning onto the road that led around the back of the village. "So you're an ER doc."

"Kinda blows your pampered rich girl theory, huh?"

"The pampered part, anyway. I don't think there's any getting around the rich girl part."

"Is that a problem for you?"

He thought about it. "Just so I'm clear, how rich are we talking?"

She took a deep breath and let it out slowly. "My family is 'comfortable.'"

He whistled. "Anyone who downplays it that much is megarich."

"I thought we agreed that money is irrelevant. I think that's especially true when it's family money, not something a person earned."

"Is that why you became a doctor? Sitting around spending your daddy's money lacked integrity?"

She pursed her lips. "Actually, that would be my granddaddy's money, from my mother's side of the family. He founded a brokerage firm. My father is a pauper by comparison."

"I thought he was a surgeon."

She nodded. "He's the chief of cardiology at St. James Hospital in Austin."

"Now you're scaring me."

"I am not," she teased, then seemed to reconsider. "Am I? Does money matter to you?"

"I like to think not, but what you're talking about is a little intimidating."

"Why?" She tipped her head, studying him.

He released a dry laugh. "Okay, just so we're both clear upfront, I come from poor, Chris. I'm talking white trash, dirt poor. You know all those Jeff Foxworthy jokes about 'You might be a redneck if . . .'? They pretty much describe my family. And I may have scraped some of the trash off my boots when I stuck out my thumb and hitched my way out of there, but the poor part isn't going to change. I barely make subsistence wages working for the county, and what money I do make, I spend buying equipment. So I can't lavish you with fancy dinners, but I can show you one heck of a good time if you like outdoor sports."

"Doesn't the county buy your equipment?"

"Most of it, but never enough." He pulled into the parking lot for Central Village. "In fact, that's why I took a week of vacation time to give you ski lessons. I wanted to buy one of those new, specially equipped all-terrain bikes for summer rescues."

"I've seen those." She nodded with interest. "They're like an ambulance on two wheels."

"Yeah, really cool, huh?" His eyes danced like a kid describing a new toy—and everything fell into place.

"That's what your friends meant Friday night when they said you spent all your money buying toys?"

"Guilty." He pulled into an empty space and set the brake.

"And what Trent meant when he said you don't work, you just play all day."

"I seriously like what I do." He shifted on the bench seat to face her. "It's got to be the best job on the planet, even if it doesn't pay squat."

"I can relate. There's no greater thrill than working ER. Well, at least I didn't think so. But today . . . that was quite a rush."

"That was nothing. You should go on a backcountry rescue."

"Really?" Her heart beat faster at the idea. Or maybe from sitting in a truck with Alec and knowing he wasn't off-limits. "Would you take me?"

He narrowed his eyes. "If I say yes, will you go out with me?"

"That depends."

"On . . . ?"

She bit her lip. He'd obliterated her main obstacle to dating him, but there was still one left. "How old are you?"

He sighed. "It's the face, isn't it? Do you know I still get carded, which the guys think is flippin' hilarious."

"You don't look *that* young. I mean, you aren't, are you?"

"I'm twenty-nine."

She sagged in relief. "That's only four years' difference. I can live with that." Which left no reason why she couldn't spend every minute of the next two weeks with Alec. Grinning, she crooked a finger at him. "Come here."

His eyes lit with understanding. Ripping off his

seat belt, he leaned over, moving in for a kiss. Before his lips met hers, though, he pulled back. "Wait a sec. You're only twenty-five? How'd you get to be a doctor so young?"

She laughed. "No. Four years the other way. I'm thirty three." She traced his jaw with her fingertip. "But you win major points for thinking the opposite."

"An older woman." He smiled slowly. "Cool."

"Hey." She scowled.

He wiggled his brows. "I can be your boy toy."

"I thought that was insulting."

"Only if that's all it's about." He reached down and unfastened her seat belt with an audible click. "I'd like this to be about more."

"Good." She wrapped her arms about his neck. "Because I don't want a boy toy. I want a man."

"Then I'll be your man." He lowered his mouth over hers.

She sank willingly into the heat of his kiss, as joy and arousal unfurled inside her. One of his hands slipped inside the coat, and she arched in response, needing his hands on her body as desperately as she needed the taste of his mouth, the scent of his skin.

Ravenous need built as they fumbled to touch through bulky clothes, struggling for more body contact in spite of the confines of the truck.

One of his hands buried in her hair as the other swept down her leg. She felt herself being lifted and turned. Afraid he'd end the kiss, she held his face in both her hands and kissed him back with her whole mouth. She wound up straddling his lap in the middle of the bench seat as their tongues tangled.

Moaning, she indulged herself fully as he cupped

her bottom and brought her snuggly up against him.
The instant his hard arousal connected with her aching center, she broke the kiss, arching back with a
gasp of delight.

His mouth trailed down her neck, then lower,
where too much clothing covered her breasts.

Hearing his growl of frustration, she tried to shrug
out of the coat at least. A loud blast split the air when
her elbow hit the horn. Buddy planted his paws on
the back of the seat, wagging his tail as he came to
see what was going on.

Laughing, Christine leaned against the dashboard.

Alec's laugh sounded strained as he looked at her.
"A public parking lot in broad daylight probably
isn't the best place for this."

"Probably not." She glanced around, relieved to
see no one nearby. Turning back to Alec, she gave
him a naughty grin. "I think we can safely say my
charm vaccine wore off."

Laughing, he pulled her to him for a hug. "You
know what?"

"What?"

He leaned back enough to see her face. "I like you."

The words filled her with a rush of happiness unlike anything she'd ever felt before. He liked her. It
was so simple, yet so wonderful. He liked her. Just
like that. Without asking for anything from her.
Without her having to earn it. He liked her.

A smile spread through her. "I like you too."

"Good thing. Since you're going to be seeing a lot
of me. Although"—he looked at his watch—"right
now I need to drop by the station, check on Tim,
and fill out a report on what happened."

"Oh." That deflated her. "I should let you go."

"I'll walk you home." He patted her bottom.

"You don't have to." She moved back to her side of the bench seat.

He cocked a brow at her. "You think I'm going to give up the chance to kiss you again at your parents' door?"

"Well, there is that."

"Come on, Buddy," he called as he got out of the truck. The two of them came around to her side and Alec looked in the bed. "Sorry about your coat."

"It's not a big deal," Christine assured him. "Natalie refuses to wear real fur, so it wasn't as expensive as it looks. If she's upset, I'll buy her a new one."

He took her hand as they entered the pedestrian area. "Are you going to go skiing with me tomorrow? Not as a lesson. Just to spend time together."

"Are you still on vacation?"

"No, but part of my job is monitoring tracks into the backcountry. That takes skiing a lot of black diamond trails and even going out-of-bounds." He gestured to the mountains that stood like giant sentinels over the village. "I can take you places others rarely see. Places where the snow is pure powder and the views will take your breath away."

"You really know how to tempt a girl."

"So, how about it?" He grinned suggestively. "Wanna go out-of-bounds with me?"

"Oh, you are bad."

"I get the feeling you like bad."

She did. That was part of her problem. "I'm supposed to go skiing with my dad and brother in the morning."

"Ah yes, the big challenge. Tell you what. You can meet me in the afternoon and let me know how it goes."

"On one condition." They'd reached the condo entrance and she led the way into the warm lobby. "Teach me how to snowboard before my brother learns how."

"You got it."

"And kiss me good-bye here."

"That's two conditions, and I'd rather neck on the elevator."

"No. And definitely no to necking outside my parents' door." She shrugged out of the firefighter coat and handed it to him. "I have visions of us getting carried away, rolling all over the floor in the hall, and Mom opening the door to see what all the racket is."

"You're a big girl." He pulled her against him. "What with you being the ripe old age of thirty-three, surely she knows you neck with boys."

"Watch it." She poked his ribs. "If you want any kiss, you'll lay off the age jokes."

"My lips are sealed. For anything but this."

She melted against him as he kissed her. By the time he finished, her head was spinning nicely. She barely managed to nod in agreement when he told her when and where to meet him the following day.

Then she drifted upstairs to e-mail Maddy and Amy. She couldn't wait to tell them everything that had happened.

"Daddy!" Little Charles jumped to his feet and ran full tilt for the door.

Lying on her back amid a jumble of toys, Christine

turned her head to watch Robbie and the others return from the snowboarding competition.

"Hey, Chuckie!" Robbie scooped up his son and tossed him in the air, much to the toddler's delight. Noisy kisses and laughter followed.

Christine smiled at the scene. Falling in love had done wonders for her formerly uptight brother.

"Don't I get a kiss?" Natalie asked while Robert Senior hung up all their coats in the entry closet.

Robbie tipped Charles sideways so the boy could give his mother a smacking kiss. Then, with his son on his hip, he led the way into the living area. He nodded gravely at the tree. "So this is this year's tree."

"This is it." Christine rose with Jonathan in her arms.

They all gathered in a semicircle, staring at the towering piece of artificial foliage that stood before the wall of windows with the mountains in the background. Dozens of white swans made from real feathers circled the branches, tailing yards of iridescent ribbon. Thousands of tiny white lights shone off hand-blown glass ornaments from Marino, Italy, in shades of pink, lavender, silver, and gold. Frosty glitter covered plum-colored balls and Waterford icicles dripped like diamonds.

"Yep." Robbie nodded. "That's a tree all right."

"It's pretty!" Charles exclaimed, his eyes dancing with reflective light. Christine had to admit, it really was beautiful. Even so, she would take one of Maddy's trees covered in makeshift ornaments any day.

"I presume there's a theme." Robert Senior tilted his head, considering it the way he would an abstract painting. "Barbara always has a theme."

"I believe she and the decorator called it a 'sugar-plum confection,'" Christine informed them.

"Hmm." Her father pinched his lower lip. "Well, if she's happy with it."

"Speaking of confections . . ." Natalie sniffed the air. "Do I smell something baking?"

"Candles." Christine wrinkled her nose. "The decorator lit sugar cookie-scented candles before she left. They're driving me and the boys crazy with hunger and sent Mom to bed with a migraine. I blew them all out, but my stomach is still demanding 'cookies'!" she said in her best Cookie Monster imitation.

Jonathan clapped at her funny voice, so of course she had to tickle him. What a darling boy he was.

"Well"—Natalie took the baby from his aunt—"we'll just have to do something about that, now, won't we?"

"You know how to make sugar cookies?" Christine asked hopefully.

"Get real." Natalie rolled her eyes. "I'll call that little grocer in East Village and have them deliver some packages of premade dough and squeeze tubes of colored icing. It's not from scratch, but it is fun. We can have a cookie decorating party."

"Works for me," Christine decided.

"Would anyone care for a drink?" Robert Senior asked as he moved to the wet bar near the fireplace.

Christine and Robbie both said yes while Natalie headed for the kitchen with both the boys to fix their afternoon snack.

"That was quite a show you put on today," Robbie said to Christine as they settled on the sofa.

"Did the crowd enjoy it?" she asked.

"I don't know about that, but I did," Robbie said. "I must hand it to you, sis, you know your stuff."

"Did you think I didn't?"

"Don't get touchy. I'm giving you a compliment."

"He's right." Their father handed her a glass of white wine, assuming that's what she wanted, since that's "what women drank." "I was quite impressed."

Christine blinked. Had she heard right? A compliment from her father? "T-thank you."

Her mind reeled as her father took a seat, crossing his legs and sipping his Scotch. She could count on one hand the times her father had praised her. Well, "praise" was probably a strong word. Given her "a nod of approval" would be more accurate. For him to be "impressed" left her speechless.

Her brother settled back with his glass of Scotch. "Are you still set on working ER?"

"Absolutely." She straightened. "I really do love it."

Robbie looked at their father. "Dad, isn't St. James hunting for a good trauma specialist? They should consider Christine."

"You know, you're right." Robert Senior nodded. "I hadn't even thought of that."

No, of course not. Why would he automatically think of his daughter just because the hospital on whose board he served happened to be looking for someone with her qualifications?

He looked at her. "Would a position at St. James interest you?"

To work at her father's hospital, among his closest

colleagues? To have a chance to earn their respect? To really prove herself once and for all? She'd sell her soul!

She schooled her features into a bland expression. "I'd consider it. What are they offering?"

"I'm not sure. I do know they want someone with experience." He sipped from his glass. "If you like, I could offer my recommendation."

Her eyes stung unexpectedly. "You'd do that?"

"As I said, I was quite impressed with you today. Besides, you *are* an Ashton." He toasted her.

A shaky feeling assailed her, so intense she couldn't even return the toast. "Thank you." She took a quick sip and set the glass on the coffee table, worried she'd drop it. "If you'll excuse me, I think I'll go see if Natalie needs help."

She fled the room before she did anything completely embarrassing, like burst into tears. Her father, Dr. Robert Ashton Sr., was going to recommend her for a post at St. James Hospital.

This was everything she'd ever wanted!

Okay, so Robbie had been the one to prod their father by making the suggestion, but still, their father had offered to lend her the same support he'd given Robbie.

Joy so sweet it hurt expanded inside her.

For a second, she didn't even care whether she outskied Robbie on the slopes tomorrow. This victory was enough. Then she laughed that notion off. After a lifetime of eating her brother's dust, she hoped she trounced him!

Chapter 10

They say patience is a virtue, but action gets things done.
—*How to Have a Perfect Life*

Christine was late. Alec checked his watch, then scanned the rest area near the Union Park lift house. A good-sized crowd stood in line, waiting for a chair, while others sat at the picnic tables taking a break. But still no sign of Christine, which puzzled him. She'd been late a few times for her lessons, but never half an hour late. Was she confused about where they'd agreed to meet? She had looked more than a little dazed when he'd told her.

The memory of how she'd looked after he'd kissed her made him even more eager to see her again. Where was she?

Buddy let out an impatient whine. Once he had on his red vest, he was used to working, not standing around doing nothing.

"I know, boy." Alec absently scratched the dog's head, wondering if he was being stood up. Maybe he should ski down to the trail map, see if she was waiting for him there. But what if he passed her?

The radio he always carried while on duty crackled, and Trent's voice came out. "Ski patrol to 14B32. Alec, you there?"

Frowning, he pulled the radio out of his coat pocket. The last thing he wanted right now was a call that would have him skiing off to rescue some idiot who'd ignored the out-of-bounds markers, leaving Christine to think he'd stood her up. "This is 14B32, copy."

"Ski patrol to 14B32. We have a situation at the Free Flyer lift house that needs your attention. Over."

Situation? What the heck was a "situation"? "Copy ski patrol. I'm a little tied up. Is it something you can handle? Over."

"No, I really think you need to handle this one personally. Over."

"Can you give me more information? Over."

"We have a skier by the name of Christine Ashton suffering from a case of acute panic disorder—"

"Copy that. I'll be right there. Over."

Buddy jumped into action when Alec pushed off, running at his side. They made it from the Union Park rest area to the Free Flyer lift house in record time. Alec skidded to a halt, but didn't see any sign of Trent or Christine. "Hey," he shouted to one of the lift ops. "I hear you have a problem?"

"Over there." The liftie pointed to an area near the edge of the slope.

At first, all he saw was Trent standing with his back to him, but as he skied closer, he saw Christine sitting on a boulder. She had a bottle of water clasped in both hands as she stared straight ahead.

Trent looked over as he approached. "That was quick."

Ignoring Trent, he removed his skies and knelt before Christine. Her breathing was entirely too fast
and shallow.

"Hey, there," he said softly. "What's up?"

"I can't get on the lift." She blinked rapidly, but
her eyes remained dry. "I can't do it."

"It's okay. You don't have to." Pulling off his right
glove, he slipped his fingers under the cuff of her
jacket to take her pulse. The rapid beat alarmed him.
"We'll just sit here for a while, okay?"

She nodded, swallowing hard as she battled back
tears. Buddy nudged her hand with his nose, his
brow wrinkled with worry.

Alec glanced over his shoulder. "What happened?"

"She froze up at the front of the lift line," Trent
explained. "Started hyperventilating and clutching
her chest. The ops thought she was having a heart
attack and called me. Chris insisted it was just panic
and would stop in a second, but it doesn't seem to
be stopping. And I have no idea what triggered it."

"She has a thing about heights." Alec turned back
to her. "You've been doing so great, though. What
happened?"

The tears she'd been fighting welled up, filling her
eyes. "You were always with me before. You weren't
with me today."

"Oh, baby." His heart clenched as he slipped onto
the boulder beside her and pulled her into his arms.

"I'm sorry." She ducked her head against his chest.
With her helmet off, her hair brushed against his
chin. "This is so embarrassing."

Alec looked at Trent. "Hey, look, I got it, man."

"She's all yours." Trent picked up his backpack

and skied off, apparently grateful for the chance to escape. Alec almost smiled at Trent's haste. They'd been through a lot of tight situations together, risking their lives to save others, but give them a crying woman, and Trent turned jittery every time.

Alec rubbed Christine's back through her parka, hoping to soothe her as Buddy laid down at her feet. "So, tell me what happened. Did you do okay this morning with your brother and father?"

"At first I did." She straightened and dried her face with her gloves. The wind and cold had chapped her cheeks. "Like you said, I've been doing really well, so I thought I was over this. On the first lift ride, I didn't even hesitate. We all jumped on a chair together, and I thought, Okay, this is great. No panic at all. But then, I don't know, halfway up . . ." Her breathing turned ragged again.

"Here, drink some water." He coaxed the bottle up, and waited for her to drink. "Better?"

She nodded. "Halfway up, Robbie started teasing me the way he always does."

"How's that?"

"Saying things like, 'So you really think you can out ski me, huh? Maybe we should do some jumps and have Dad score us.' And I told him, 'Yes, let's do that.' But then my dad sighed and said, 'Can't I just proclaim Robbie the winner now and enjoy the rest of the day without these useless challenges? We all know he'll win anyway.' "

"What?" Alec shook his head in surprise. The father she loved so greatly and respected so much would say something that cruel? "Ouch."

"Yes! Thank you!" Some color returned to her face.

"How does Dad not see how insulting it is when he says things like that?"

"So what happened?"

"Robbie and I insisted that we do the challenge. So we went to Miner's Basin."

"Good choice." Alec nodded. That area had lots of places to catch some air. "How'd you do?"

"I annihilated him, Alec." Her eyes sparkled now, but with excitement, not tears. "I kicked his ass. You should have seen me. I was unstoppable."

"Of course you were." And good for you, he thought. "You nearly blew me away on that run."

Her shoulders slumped. "Yeah, well Dad proclaimed it a practice run. He said the first one didn't count because I've been here a week, and Robbie just got here. So we did it again, and again, and again. I kicked Robbie's butt every time. I shredded that run and boosted some insane air off a few kickers, while Robbie took at least five face plants trying to match me. Yet, every time, Dad found some reason why that run didn't count."

"That's totally wacked." Anger joined his disbelief.

"Exactly," she agreed. "So we'd get back on the lift to go up again, and each time, I don't know, the ride up got harder and harder. I could feel the panic squeezing in on me, but I was *not* going to show it. No way. I was going to ride that lift, and make that run however"—she took a deep breath—"however many times it took my father to admit that I was better than Robbie at something.

"I know I'm not as smart at him. I know he's a neurologist and I'm a lowly ER doc. I know he was valedictorian and I wasn't. I know I'll never be as good as him in most things, but Goddamm it, in this one thing, I *am* better! I am!"

He stared at her, his heart aching. "Did your dad finally admit it?"

"No." She snorted in disgust. "It was Robbie who'd finally had enough. He said he was exhausted from the altitude and tired of me beating him. So *he* proclaimed me the winner. That was like"—she searched for words to describe it—"one of the greatest moments in my life! My brother actually said, 'You win. Congratulations, sis. You finally did it.' "

"And what did your father say?"

"Basically, he shrugged it off, turned to Robbie and said, 'Let's go get lunch.' Then they skied off without me."

"What?" Alec frowned "They just left you there?"

"They knew I'd agreed to meet you, and I needed to get going, but yes, they left me standing there."

"What jerks!" He struggled against the urge to track both men down and punch them. "What'd you do?"

"I skied over here to get in the lift line and go meet you. I was so angry, though, I was shaking. And then suddenly, I was at the front of the line, and I—I don't know what h-happened. I just—" Her eyes welled again. "I couldn't get on the lift."

"It's okay." He pulled her to him and held her tight, wishing there was something more he could do.

That was all Christine needed, though, to have someone hold her. Slowly, the fist squeezing her chest began to relax.

"Hey," Alec said, rubbing her back. "Why don't I

take you home? You can rest for a while; then when I get off work, we'll go scare up some fun."

"No, I don't want to do that." She sighed, her head resting on his shoulder. "If I do, Robbie will know I'm upset, and he'll feel sorry for me. I really hate that. All this stuff goes right over my father's head; he never gets it at all, but Robbie does. It doesn't stop him from wiping up the tennis court with my ego, but he does get it. He just thinks I should let it go. Easy for him to say. He never had to work for attention." Lifting her head, she looked at him. "Why are families so complicated? How can you love and resent the same people?"

"I don't know. But I understand how you feel."

"I wish . . ."

"What?"

A lump rose unexpectedly in her throat. "I wish my parents loved me as much as they love Robbie."

"Oh, Chris." He pulled her back into his arms.

She squeezed her eyes shut, hating the tears that leaked out. What a way to start her first date with Alec, by crying all over him. Determined to get her emotions under control, she straightened. "You know what they say, though. If wishes were wings, frogs wouldn't bump their asses on the ground when they tried to fly."

He laughed. "I thought it was: If wishes were horses, then beggars would ride."

"That's because you're nicer than me. And more charming."

"That's me. Mr. Charming." His quick smile helped lighten the mood. "And I think you're very nice."

She dried her face. "You also don't cuss as much as me."

"Now, before you start thinking that makes me a Goody Two-shoes, I have a good explanation."

"What?"

"See, it goes like this. Everyone's allotted so many cuss words when they're born. I realized early on that my dad and brother were burning through their quota really fast. So, I decided to be generous and let them have some of mine."

"See? Charming." She smiled at him. "And very sweet."

"No, not sweet." He shuddered. "I'll go with charming. Charming is good. But not sweet, and not cute."

"But you are."

"No. Ack. Puke. *Pluwie!*" He rolled sideways, pretending to gag in the snow.

"Will you stop?" Laughing, she shoved at his shoulder.

He turned and grabbed her hand. "Only if you kiss me."

"Why should I?" She tipped her face up, thinking how wonderful he looked with sunlight in his hair. And how quickly he'd turned her tears to laughter.

He cupped her cheek as his eyes went from playful to intense. "Because I haven't been able to think about anything else since I met you."

Her heart fluttered from desire now, not panic, as he traced her bottom lip with his thumb. "There are people all around."

"They're too busy skiing to care. Kiss me."

"Yes," she sighed, and closed her eyes as his head descended.

There was nothing "sweet" or "cute" about the way Alec kissed. His mouth claimed hers, bringing her whole body alive until she ached to be skin to skin so he could replace all the hurt inside of her with pleasure.

Moaning, she wrapped her arms around his neck and kissed him back.

"Dispatch to 14B32, do you copy?" a gravelly female voice squawked.

Startled, Christine jumped back and looked about, but no one was there.

"Dang!" Alec fumbled with his coat. "Hold that thought." He gave her a quick peck on the lips and pulled out a radio. "This is 14B32, copy."

She laughed as she pressed a hand to her racing heart.

"We have a report of an avalanche in Cutter's Basin," the woman's voice explained. "The witness reports three snowmobilers buried. One victim has been located alive but unconscious. The other two are still buried. Over."

"Copy." Alec straightened, scanning the horizon as he spoke into the radio. Sensing excitement, Buddy danced in place, ready to go. "Notify Lt. Kreiger to pick me up at the Cutter's Basin trail head and page out whoever you can reach. Over." He lowered the radio. "Looks like I gotta go. Will you be all right? I can call Trent to come back."

"Actually, do you need any help?"

"On an avalanche rescue? Honey, I'll take every digger I can get! Are you up to it, though?"

"I'm very up to it." Excitement erased her other rioting emotions as she strapped on her helmet.

"Okay then." He lowered his goggles. "Let's do it!"

Chapter 11

"A *helicopter*?" Christine shouted over the sound of the blades as a bulky relic descended practically on top of her. Unlike Alec's truck, there was no shiny paint or lettering to proclaim it official county property. It looked like a military castoff that had been salvaged from a junkyard. Panic rose from her chest into her throat, making her voice go up an octave. "You didn't tell me I had to ride in a helicopter."

"Duck your head!" Alec's hand clamped down on the top of her helmet and forced her to bend over as the craft touched down. Wind from the blades buffeted her back. The door slid open and she saw the two younger guys from the bachelor party.

"Come on!" Alec shouted over the noise. "Get in!"

One of the guys grabbed her skis while the other grabbed her arm. With Alec and Buddy coming in behind her, she didn't have much choice. Before she knew it, she was sitting inside with her back against the side wall of the craft. Her heart lurched when the craft lifted off with the speed of an express elevator, leaving her stomach behind.

She'd flown many times in her life, but always on nice big commercial airplanes. Never in anything this small, skimming the tops of trees through a windy mountain valley.

Closing her eyes, she monitored her anxiety level. Would it go into a full-fledged attack for the second time in one day, or abate?

Breathing slowly, she listened to Alec talking to the pilot, the squawking of his radio, the whirling of the helo's engine and blades. So far, so good. She could do this. She *would* do this. Although, she'd really like her stomach to catch up with her body.

"Hey, you need boots?" Someone nudged her shoulder.

"What?" She opened her eyes to find the kid with bright orange hair looking at her. If she remembered right, he was Brian, and the tall, skinny blond checking the contents of backpacks behind him was Eric.

"Boots." Brian pointed at her feet. "You can't help much wearing those."

"Oh. Right." She saw Alec in the copilot's seat unbuckling his ski boots.

"Okay, copy," Alec said into his radio. "Request one life flight and have a second standing by. We're two minutes ETA. Over." He looked back at her. "You okay?"

"Never better." She forced a smile, refusing to let anxiety win. He gave her a big thumbs-up.

"Here you go." Brian set a pair of soft boots down next to her. "These might fit."

"Thank you." She focused on changing her boots as the helicopter continued to climb.

"There!" Alec pointed out the front window. "Put us down there."

"You got it," Kreiger said.

Christine stifled a moan as the craft banked in a wide arch and headed downward. With a gentle thump they were on the ground. The instant Eric opened the door, Buddy shot through it, barking with impatience.

"Okay, let's go. Let's go!" Alec clapped his hands, herding them.

Christine clambered from the helicopter onto a huge expanse of glaring white.

"Over here!" a woman screamed, though the wind made her voice sound distant and thin. "Please, help me!"

Squinting against the sunlight, she saw a woman in a bright yellow parka kneeling next to something blue that was buried in the snow.

Alec thrust a backpack into Christine's arms. Then, grabbing a spine board and oxygen tank, he took off toward the woman with Brian and Eric carrying shovels and poles and packs. Christine followed, stunned by the hard-packed ice beneath her feet. She didn't know what she'd expected from an avalanche field—loose, unstable snow perhaps—but this was like running on frozen concrete that had been broken up with a jackhammer.

Behind them, she heard the helicopter take off to pick up more volunteers.

Alec reached the woman first and dropped to his knees as she wept hysterically, clutching her left arm.

The blue object turned out to be the parka of a second woman with only her head and one arm exposed.

"What's your name?" Alec asked the woman in yellow, even as he focused on the other woman, lifting her eyelids, checking for a pulse.

"J-jenny," the woman managed. "I couldn't dig her out! Help her!"

"She's alive." Alec announced. "Brian, Eric, dig her out."

Christine opened her pack to check what supplies she'd been given as Alec questioned Jenny. "Who are we looking for? Where were they when this hit?"

"Paul and Theresa's husband, Ted. They were up higher. Over there." She tried to point, but winced in pain.

Alec turned on a hand-sized tracker. "Are they wearing transmitters?"

"Ted is. Paul forgot to pack ours."

Alec let out a rare curse and stood. "Okay, Buddy, are you ready, boy?" His voice turned bright and playful. "You wanna go to work?" Buddy barked and quivered with joy. "Okay, *search*!"

The dog took off in the direction Alec pointed. Alec followed, carrying a shovel and metal rods to probe the ice.

"Where are you hurt?" Christine asked Jenny, doing a quick visual assessment. The patient looked about mid-thirties, dark hair, fair skin, slightly overweight, but in overall good health.

"Everywhere," Jenny choked out. "My shoulder mostly."

Christine felt inside the parka and found a broken

collarbone. The arm clutched to the woman's chest had a possible radial or ulna fracture. No acute abdominal pain to suggest internal damage. The only other injury was a badly wrenched knee. Nothing life threatening, and nothing that couldn't wait.

"You're going to be fine," Christine assured her and draped a blanket over her shoulders. "Just keep still while we help your friend, okay?"

Jenny nodded, crying softly.

Christine shifted so she could take over for Brian, who was holding Theresa's head steady while Eric dug.

"I'll go help Hunter," Brian said, and took off with a shovel.

Looking down into the battered face, Christine cringed in empathy. This woman hadn't been as lucky as her friend. Definite head and probable neck trauma, and no telling how many broken bones and internal injuries they'd find. But she was breathing, and she had a pulse.

"Is Theresa okay?" Jenny stared at her friend.

Christine summoned a calm smile. "A life flight's on the way. We'll have her to a hospital in no time."

"I can't believe this happened," Jenny sniffed. "Paul and Ted can be so stupid when they're drinking. They kept making runs straight up the slope to see who could leave the highest mark. They know how dangerous that is. I asked them to stop, and when they ignored me, I decided to leave.

"I was nearly to the trees when I heard Theresa coming after me, to leave as well or ask me to stay, I don't know. Before she reached me, I heard this rumble. Then everything went crazy. The whole mountain just . . . gave way. It happened so fast! One second Paul and Ted were there, and then—and then—this wall of snow crashed into them and headed straight for us. We tried to get out of the way, but it swallowed Theresa, then knocked me into the trees.

"When it stopped, I saw Theresa's arm sticking out, and managed to uncover her face and call for help." She looked around. "I don't see my husband, though. I don't see him! Why were they being such jerks? I swear to God, if he's dead, I'm going to kill him!" Realizing what she'd said, she burst into fresh sobs.

Several yards away, Buddy barked. Christine glanced up to see the dog digging frantically. Alec and Brian joined in with shovels.

"Oh God!" Jenny started to rise. "Who did they find? Is it Paul? Is he alive?"

"Wait!" Christine grabbed her good arm. "Stay still. I don't want you moving around until I've examined you better."

"Good dog!" Alec's voice carried over the snow. "Let's find another. Come on, Buddy, *search*!"

Buddy set off on his quest, tail wagging, his vest bright red against the snow. Brian stayed behind digging out whomever they'd found.

The thumping of a helicopter sounded overhead. Christine looked up to see a life flight zooming over the treetops. This was getting to be a daily occurrence, she thought. The instant they landed, the medical crew rushed out to help, one man coming toward her, the other heading for Brian.

"Hey, you again," the EMT said, smiling at Christine. "What'd'ya have for us this time?"

Christine listed what she knew about Theresa's condition. Within minutes, they had Theresa on a spine board with oxygen and an IV going.

"At this altitude, we can take only one or two at a time," the EMT said. "Hunter called for another life flight, though, so it's on its way."

"Then he's alive?" Christine nodded toward the man Brian was digging out.

"Yes."

"Oh, thank God," Jenny wept.

"Okay." Christine considered Theresa's condition. "See how close they are to having him ready to go and how critical his condition is. If it's going to take more than five minutes, or he's fairly stable, go with this one."

"Got it. What about her?" He nodded to Jenny.

"I need to set her shoulder, so she can wait for the second chopper. This one needs to go now, though."

While the men carried Theresa to the helicopter, Christine turned back to Jenny.

"Let's take another look at you." Digging through the backpack, she found everything she needed and gave thanks that Alec knew his stuff. She was setting Jenny's shoulder when the life flight took off, which was either good news on the other victim's condition, or they were having trouble digging him out. She looked over, watching Brian and Eric work at a slow, careful pace. *Please, God, don't let that mean they're dealing with a broken spine.*

The second life flight appeared. Like before, the crew rushed out to help.

"Can she walk?" the EMT asked when he reached her.

"Not on that knee." Christine finished securing the splint on the forearm. "When you reach the hospital, make sure she goes straight to X-ray."

"Will do." He knelt and lifted Jenny in his arms.

"Wait," Jenny protested when they headed for the helicopter. "Take me over there. I need to see if that's my husband."

Christine tried to calm her. There was no way she would let this woman see what was over there until she'd seen it herself. "We need you to wait in the helicopter."

"No!" the woman protested louder as the EMT carried her away.

Christine gathered the medical gear and went to join Brian and Eric and the other EMT. They already had the man on a spine board. Brian shifted aside to give her room. The victim, who was conscious but disoriented, looked like he'd been dumped from the back of a cement mixer, his face a bloody, pummeled mess.

"What do we have?" She checked the eyes and pulse, worry mounting.

While the EMT listed the injuries, which included a possible broken spine and dangerously low responsiveness, Christine wondered if this were Ted or Paul. The EMT finished by saying he'd alerted the hospital to have a surgeon waiting in the OR.

If the patient made it that far. "I'm a doctor. Is there any way I can ride in with you?"

"At this altitude?" The EMT shook his head. "Not unless the other patient stays behind."

"What about the other man?" She looked around and saw Alec and Buddy searching at the far edge of the avalanche field. She could clearly see the definition between the solidified snow and the loose powder surrounding it. How pretty this slope must have been when Jenny and the others arrived. Clear blue sky, fresh snow. A snowmobiler's dream. Add alcohol and stupidity and it turns into a nightmare.

"Any sign of him?"

"Not yet." Brian checked his watch and let out a string of curses.

"What?" Christine asked, alarmed by his distress.

"The dude's a goner." Brian kept working. "Goddamn it!"

"Are you sure?" Christine asked.

Brian nodded. "Even if he survived the impact, and avoided slamming into a boulder or a tree, too much time has elapsed. Unless he got lucky and fell into an air pocket."

"That can happen, though, right?"

"Sometimes." Brian looked up at her with eyes that had seen too many lifeless bodies for someone so young. "Chances are, he suffocated about ten minutes ago."

The news squeezed Christine's chest. Did losing patients ever get easier? She hadn't even met this one, but either Jenny or Theresa had just lost a husband.

"Okay, we're ready," the EMT announced. "Let's take this slow."

Brian and Eric nodded, and on the count of three, they lifted the stokes basket. Christine followed beside them, fighting frustration. Normally she'd be charging beside this man's stretcher toward the OR, snapping out orders. On the side of a mountain, though, there was nothing she could do that hadn't already been done.

"Is it Paul?" Jenny called from inside the helicopter as they loaded the basket. Seeing the man's battered face, she burst into tears.

"Is it?" Christine asked her.

"No!" Jenny sobbed uncontrollably. "It's Ted! Is he alive?"

"He is." *For now*, Christine thought, praying he remained that way. If he made it to the hospital, she gave him about a fifty-fifty chance.

"Where's Paul?" Jenny asked. "Have they found him?"

"They're still looking," Christine told her, refusing to repeat what Brian had said. Jenny's husband could still be alive.

Brian and Eric went back to gather their supplies and resume the search.

The pilot leaned back, calling to the medical crew as they worked on Ted. "Are we ready?"

"Almost," one of the EMTs answered, then looked at Christine. "Stand clear!"

"Wait!" Jenny shouted. "Not without my husband. Please—" The door closed on her words. An EMT took Jenny in his arms, where she collapsed against him, crying.

Christine stepped back, aching for Jenny as the helo lifted off. When it vanished over the trees, Alec joined her.

"Any sign of Paul?" she asked.

He shook his head. One look in his eyes told her he believed the same thing Brian did.

Dammit! Christine struggled to maintain professional detachment and failed. Being a doctor didn't make her immune to emotion, and premature death was the enemy she spent her life trying to beat back.

In the absence of the helo, the wind became more pronounced. It held a vicious bite as it blew across the ice. Buddy whined, pressing his body up against Alec's leg.

"I know, boy." Alec patted the dog's head, averting his eyes from Christine. "He thinks he failed."

Her heart clutched as she realized Alec was talking about himself as well. "He didn't, though. He found one of the buried men alive."

"Yeah." He continued petting Buddy. "This is usually when someone says three out of four's not bad."

She nodded in understanding. "Four out of four would be better."

He turned away and stood with his back to her, scanning the field as the wind battered his parka. "Four out of four would be a lot better."

She wrapped her arms around him from behind and pressed her cheek between his shoulder blades.

"Why wasn't he wearing a transmitter?" Alec demanded in a burst of anger. "If he'd forgotten to pack them, he should have rented some."

"Alec, no." She moved around in front of him and took his face in her hands. "Don't play the 'if only' game, because you'll start with 'if only he'd done this,' and end with 'if only I'd done that.' Don't do this to yourself."

"You're right." He exhaled in a rush. "I know this. Heck, I give this speech to the volunteers all the time. It still . . . you know."

"Yes, I know." She sighed in empathy. "So now what?"

The thumping of helicopter blades drew her attention skyward in time to see Kreiger returning.

"Now," Alec sighed, "we switch from rescue mode to search mode."

Chapter 12

A few hours later, Christine had a whole new appreciation for the men and women of search and rescue. She'd always admired their dedication and willingness to work long hours under adverse conditions. Nothing drove that home, though, quite like screaming leg muscles and raw hands.

"How you holding up?" Alec asked, joining her at the base they'd set up around the helicopter. The craft protected them from the wind, which had picked up as the day wore on.

"To be honest, I could use a three-hour session with a masseuse and a soak in a hot tub." She reached for a thermos and poured them each a cup of hot coffee.

"That can be arranged." He smiled as he accepted the coffee, then patted the floor of the helicopter. "Up, Buddy. Let me check your paws, boy."

Buddy leapt into the helo, looking tuckered out. He panted while Alec checked each paw and sprayed them with a fresh coat of cooking spray to keep the ice from sticking.

While Alec tended to his dog, Christine watched the search effort. The volunteers had formed a line at the bottom of the avalanche field and were steadily working their way upward, probing the ice with metal rods. The field had set up so hard, they'd actually broken several rods. The steep slant and uneven ground made the work grueling and time-consuming.

Christine looked down at her tattered ski gloves. "I've worn out my gloves."

"That's why we carry spares." He leaned his hips against the floor of the helo and joined her in watching the others. Handlers with two other dogs worked higher up on the field, where they'd found one of the snowmobiles.

"How long do you estimate this could take?" she asked.

"Minutes, hours, days." He lifted his sunglasses to rub his eyes. He looked exhausted, and she realized this was the first break he'd taken since the others arrived. "Longest avalanche rescue I've been on was when I was still a volunteer. We spent five days recovering twelve bodies. The space was cramped though, not open like this. The coordinator at the time had us set up base on the actual field, which is a big no-no, but we didn't have much choice. Turns out our food table was sitting on top of three bodies."

"Really?" Her lip curled at the thought.

"Yeah." He reached back and ruffled Buddy's ears. "This guy kept trying to tell us, but the coordinator said he was poorly trained and begging for scraps. I didn't argue, even though I wanted to. Avy dogs are trained to ignore food and sniff for scents like sunscreen. Buddy and I were a new team, though, so I kept my mouth shut. Turns out Buddy was right. Weren't you, boy?"

Buddy gave Alec's face a few sloppy kisses. Christine smiled as she watched the show of mutual devotion.

"Okay, that's enough. No tongue in the mouth." Alec shook his finger at the dog. "Only Chris gets to do that. Got it?" Buddy stared at Alec with worshipful eyes while Alec stroked his fur. "That rescue taught me to trust him more. Unless there are rabbits involved, like earlier."

"Rabbits?"

"We were working the far edge, over by the cliff, and we scared up a snowshoe rabbit. That's Buddy's big weakness."

Buddy pricked his ears at the word "rabbit," then barked and danced in place.

"See? He's obsessed." Alec shook his head. "We've been working on it, and I thought he was getting better, but nope. One glimpse of a rabbit, and he was ready to go charging off, completely away from the search area."

"Are you sure it was the rabbit that had him barking?"

"Hmm?" Alec looked at her.

She raised a brow. "Weren't you just saying you should trust him more?"

"But . . . that doesn't make sense." He looked toward the cliff edge several yards away. The avalanche field stopped well before the edge. Logic dictated that anyone caught in the avalanche would be buried in the field. When it came to nature, though, anything was possible. Even the illogical.

"Oh, man!" He straightened. Buddy came to attention instantly. Alec pointed toward the cliff. "Okay, Buddy, *search*!"

The dog took off like a shot. His red vest and golden fur were a vivid streak of color against the white snow. By the time Alec caught up, Buddy was standing at the cliff edge, barking down into the ravine. The wind howled up from the canyon, kicking up sprays of ice.

"Stay back." He held his hand up when Christine came up behind him. "The last thing we need is to start another slide."

"Well, be careful," she said, staying at the edge of the hard-packed ice.

He inched up behind Buddy, testing the snow as he went. The canyon was deep, with jagged cliffs stair stepping down to a river far below. He'd pulled more than one unfortunate rock climber out of this area. Retrieving a body in winter would be even more challenging.

Reaching the edge, he leaned out, spotting a snowmobile first at the bottom of the ravine. Leaning farther, he found an outcropping of rock barely fifteen feet down and there on it's ledge was the fourth victim lying in a twisted heap.

"Well, what do you know." Turning, he split the air with a whistle, then waved. The volunteers stopped and looked his way. "I found him!"

"Is he alive?" Christine asked as he moved back to the edge of the packed ice field.

"Can't tell. Maybe," he said as everyone hurried over. Excitement and worry shone on several faces as others repeated Christine's question.

"Everyone stay back," he warned. "I don't trust the snow here. Our man is on a cliff, not too far down. Aaron, Jeff." He singled out his two best rock climbers. "Let's get geared up."

"What can I do?" Christine asked as he started back toward the helicopter.

"Pray," he suggested, squeezing her arm as he moved past her.

She nodded, frustrated that she couldn't do more, but not stupid enough to get in the way. The ER was her world; this was Alec's.

The men returned with ropes and a stokes basket. She stood back, chewing her tattered glove as Alec and Aaron went over the side. Jeff stayed up top to help guide the basket down. With the wind screaming through the ravine, the men had to shout to communicate. Even then, she could hear only Jeff.

After several agonizing moments, Jeff turned to the group, a broad smile breaking over his face. "Looks like we need another life flight."

The group cheered and hugged.

Relief flooded Christine as she held her hands to her mouth and gave silent thanks. If only she could be down there, working with the patient, not standing on the sidelines. Although, picturing Alec dangling from a rope off the side of a mountain, she decided maybe not. She consoled herself by petting Buddy. "You did good, boy. You did very good."

He panted in agreement, then went back to staring in the direction Alec had gone.

A life flight arrived just as the stokes litter carrying Jenny's husband made it to the top. Aaron and Jeff helped Alec get it up and onto safe ground.

Christine hurried over. "What's his condition?"

"Hypothermia and a lot of broken bones, but he's alive." Alec wiped his forehead, breathing hard. "All things considered, this is one lucky son of a gun."

The life flight crew stepped in, and Christine moved out of the way. She watched as they loaded the basket onto the helicopter, then they lifted up and headed for home.

She stood a moment, her hands shielding the sun from her eyes. Alec joined her, watching the helicopter disappear.

"Four out of four," he said. "Do we rock, or what?"

"You, sir, definitely rock!" Laughing, she threw her arms around him. He lifted her off her feet and twirled her about. Setting her down, he turned to the others. "To the pub! First round on me!"

Another cheer went up.

As they headed for the helicopter, arm in arm, she smiled up at him, filled with admiration.

He tipped his head to study her face. "What's that look about?"

"I was just thinking, you really know how to show a girl a good time on a first date."

Laughing, he hugged her to him.

St. Bernard's Pub burst into applause the minute Alec stepped through the door. Christine blinked in surprise as whistles split the air.

"Thank ya, thank ya." Alec waved at the crowd

standing around the fire pit, doing his best Elvis impersonation. "Thank ya verra much."

"Get a lot of standing ovations, do you?" she asked as the volunteers filed past them, shedding coats and gloves.

"A few. You?"

"Never." She stripped off her coat, then shivered from the cold coming through the door.

"Well, that's a shame. Of course, you probably don't work with an audience."

"Audience?"

"These guys listen to the emergency frequencies the way some people follow baseball on the radio." He pulled her to him and rubbed her arm to warm her.

"Good job, Hunter." Steve came over to slap Alec on the back. He wore his sheriff's uniform today, with a gun on one hip and a radio on the other.

Christine looked about as the two men talked and saw four firefighters and two forests rangers along with men and women in street clothes. Vacationers at the tables looked on with open curiosity as the new arrivals received high fives.

Steve turned to her, holding out his hand. "Thanks for taking time out of your vacation to lend a hand. Word from the life flight crew is you make a good field doc."

"Thank you." She accepted the handshake.

"She's not bad." Alec tightened the arm he had draped over her shoulder.

"Not bad?" She jabbed him in the ribs with an elbow.

He gave a satisfying grunt, then led her into the

pit. "Who wants beer?" Voices and hands rose all around. He turned to her. "How about you? Is beer okay? Or would you like something else?"

"Beer." She nodded, welcoming the warmth from the open hearth. Bright flames crackled from the logs as smoke scented the air. "Most definitely."

"Harvey!" Alec called to the bartender. "Put three pitchers on my tab. After that, these guys are on their own."

"You got it." The bartender started filling pitchers from the tap.

"Any news from the hospital?" Alec asked Steve as he took one of the big chairs.

Christine let out a startled shriek when Alec pulled her down to sit with him. The wide chair easily held them both, although it was a tight fit. He moved her legs to drape over one of his thighs and looped his arms about her waist. She thought about protesting for half a second, then settled her back against the rolled arm of the chair.

"So far, the news has been mostly good." Steve took a seat on the stone hearth, his back to the fire while Buddy sprawled on the floor for a well-deserved break. "The woman with the concussion has regained consciousness and is listed as stable. The first man you pulled out is out of OR but in intensive care."

"What about paralysis to his legs?" Christine asked as the waitress arrived with mugs and pitchers.

Steve waved off beer since he had a cup of coffee. "Nothing definite."

"And Paul?" Christine accepted a mug of beer. "The last man?"

"He's still in OR but expected to pull through fine," Steve said.

"Thank goodness." Christine relaxed. "I can only imagine his wife's relief."

Alec let out a sigh. "All I can say is this beats the heck out of having a family thank me for finding a body and giving them closure."

Steve nodded. "Or knocking on a stranger's door to deliver bad news."

"Or being blamed for not doing more," Christine added.

The three of them fell silent for a moment, then Alec lifted his mug. "To happy endings!"

"I'll drink to that." Christine clicked her mug to his and took a deep sip of cold, foamy beer.

All around them, people recapped the events of the day and relived past rescues. Beer and food arrived in a steady stream for the humans, while bowls of water and treats were brought for the dogs.

"Hey, Alec?" Jeff called from his place by the fire. His wife, Linda, had been waiting with the others, and shared his chair much the same way Christine shared Alec's. "Remember the time those two college girls went rock-climbing and decided to stop on a nice, flat ledge to do a little nude sunbathing?"

"Do I ever!" He let out a bark of laughter.

"Oh, really?" Christine shifted to see his face.

"Turns out a snake decided to catch a little sun on that ledge, too," Alec explained. "In the girls' hurry to, um, 'vacate the area,' they left their clothes and gear behind. Then got stuck on the side of the mountain and couldn't get down."

Everyone around the fire laughed and nodded at the memory.

"Care to guess how many male volunteers I had show up for that call out?" Alec asked.

"All of them?" Christine ventured.

"And then some! That one story has done wonders for our recruitment efforts."

"I'll bet." She raised a brow.

As afternoon drifted toward evening, the stories continued to flow. Mellow from the beer and fatigue, she rested her head on Alec's shoulder and watched the fire. His hand moved lazily up and down the outside of her thigh, stirring a low hum of desire deep in her belly. In the corner, someone dropped money in the jukebox and punched in the number for a slow, sexy ballad.

As the song played, he nuzzled her hair. "Hey," he said near her ear. "You're not falling asleep on me, are you?"

"No." She smiled, thinking her body was far from that. Lifting her head, she watched the firelight play over his face and wished they were alone so she could take his mouth in a long, deep kiss. "Dance with me?"

"Ah—" He hesitated, then spoke low so only she could hear his words. "I'm not sure standing up right now is a good idea."

His chagrined expression told her he was more than a little aroused and didn't want to announce his state to the whole group. She smiled, slow and sexy, and let her eyelids lower. "That wasn't a request."

His brows went up. "Are you ordering me?"

"Do you have a problem with that?"

He seemed nonpulssed for a second, then looked down toward his lap and back up into her eyes. "Apparently not."

"Good." Sliding her legs off his lap, she stood with him coming up behind her in one fluid motion. He clamped his hands to her hips to keep her close in front of him as they left the fire pit.

A few of the volunteers glanced up but went right back to their conversations. While vacationers crowded the tables, the dance floor was empty. When he pulled her into his arms, she discovered just how aroused he was. Her eyes widened as her body heated even more.

"I have a question," he said, moving his body against her as they danced.

"Yes?" She shook her hair back, trying to look calm when everything inside her longed to jump him right there on the dance floor.

"How far are we going to take you ordering me around?"

"What do you mean?"

"Well . . ." A line formed between his brows as he considered. "For instance, is there going to be any begging on the evening's agenda?"

That startled her. "I . . . hadn't thought of that."

"Oh." His expression went flat.

She narrowed her eyes. "Do you want there to be?"

"I don't know." Shrugging, he moved her in a circle that had their thighs rubbing together. "I've never, you know . . ."

"Gotten into dominatrices? S and M?"

He shook his head, then raised a brow. "You?"

"No." She laughed at the idea. "I know some people think I'm bossy, but I'm not into ordering people around that way."

"Oh." He frowned.

She studied him. "Do you want me to?"

"I didn't think so." He made another turn, pulling her close enough for her to feel that he'd gone even harder. "But my body sure seems intrigued by the idea."

There was certainly no denying that! She licked her suddenly dry lips. "So, um, if I asked you to beg me for say, the privilege of pleasuring my body, you'd do it?"

His hand slid up her back, sending shivers of desire racing through her. "Are you asking?"

She leaned forward and brushed her lips against his earlobe. "Maybe."

He missed a step and groaned. "Oh God, you're killing me."

"Really?" She rubbed her hips against his. "You feel very much alive to me."

"That could be rigor mortis setting in."

"Do I need to check you for a pulse?"

His face looked intent in the dim light of the bar. "I think you'd better."

She pressed her lips to his throat, licked his skin with the tip of her tongue and felt the rumble of his moan. Pulling back, she smiled. "Patient's pulse is strong but elevated."

"Only because I'm about to have a coronary."

"Good thing I'm a doctor."

"So what does the doctor order?"

"That the patient submit to a thorough examination."

"As a trained paramedic, I must concur." He stopped abruptly and took her hand firmly in his. "Follow me." He tugged her off the dance floor. "Buddy, up! We're going home." Buddy scrambled toward them. "Harvey," he called to the bartender. "I'll catch you tomorrow."

"Okay, man," Harvey called back.

The gang around the fire frowned as they moved passed them. "You're leaving?" Jeff asked.

"Yep." Alec nodded. "I'm going to walk the doc home, then turn in myself."

Steve scowled at him. "Since when are you the first to leave a party?"

"Must be getting old." Alec grinned, then gave Christine a heated look as they pulled on their coats.

Chapter 13

Cold slapped Christine's cheeks as she and Alec hurried from the pub all but tripping over their feet in their eager haste. The sun had slipped behind Silver Mountain, casting a dusk-like shadow over the village.

"This way." Alec jerked his head.

Huddling inside her coat, she followed him around to the side of the building. They stopped at a door between the back of the pub and a ski shop. He held it open for her and Buddy. Rather than a fancy lobby, this space was barely larger than a landing with a row of mailboxes and stairs leading up.

The instant Alec slipped in behind her, he pinned her against the wall. His mouth swept down over hers. Surprise came first, followed by a heady excitement to finally be able to kiss him with no people looking on. Wrapping her arms around his neck, she welcomed the wild play of lips and tongue. Their bodies molded chest to chest, hip to hip. The bulge of his erection against her belly made her eager to get even closer. To get skin to skin.

Somewhere overhead a door slammed.

They jerked apart, glancing up, then sagged with relief when no one appeared at the top of the stairs. Buddy sat halfway up, his head cocked as if asking why they were standing around down there.

"Sorry." Laughing, Alec rested his forehead against hers, breathing hard. "You've had me so hot for so long, I'm pretty much on the edge here. I'll try to slow down."

"Don't you dare." She grabbed the front of his parka and brought them nose to nose. "In fact, if you don't get me somewhere private in the next two seconds, Alec Hunter, I swear I'm going to rip your clothes off right here."

His eyes widened. "My apartment's this way."

He took her hand and dashed up the stairs to a narrow hallway. At the first door on the right, he reached into his pocket. "Dang it!"

"What?"

"I left my keys somewhere."

"What!" She wanted to slug him. How could he get her this revved up, then say they had nowhere to go and do something about it?

"It's okay." He smiled as if reading her mind. Reaching overhead, he retrieved a single key from the top of the doorframe. "I have plenty of spares."

She laughed in relief.

He unlocked the door and herded her and Buddy inside. Even as he closed the door, they came together with greedy hands and hungry mouths. She felt him fumble for a light switch, but he abandoned the effort. Enough light spilled in through a window for them to see each other. They shed their jackets, then tugged at sweaters.

"Bed," she managed between kisses.

"This way." His mouth on hers, he walked backward, leading the way.

They moved across the room, fumbling with clothes, stumbling over God-knew-what. With sweaters gone, they worked at losing their boots without breaking the kiss. They bumped into a coffee table and something thudded to the floor. The arm of a sofa nearly sent them tumbling.

Then finally, finally, they passed through a doorway into a darker room, tripped over objects scattered on the floor, and landed with a bounce on an unmade bed—her favorite kind. She grinned as he came down on top of her.

Eager to touch and be touched, she turned him on to his back and straddled him as she worked the top of his long johns over his head. She ran her hands over his hard chest and taut stomach, enjoying the heat of his smooth skin, but it wasn't enough.

"Hang on." She planted a quick kiss on his mouth, then scrambled off the bed and out of her clothes at record speed. Finally naked, she started to jump back on the bed but came up short at the sight that greeted her. From the light seeping past the blinds she saw he'd shed his clothes as well. He reclined in the middle of the rumpled bed, his weight on his elbows and one leg bent.

"Oh my." She blinked at his erection, which was . . . impressively proportioned to a man of his height. Uncertainty and excitement hit her at once.

Dragging her gaze to his face, she saw the glitter of desire in his eyes as he openly admired her naked body. He looked as if he could devour her in one greedy bite.

Then his eyes lifted to hers and he held out his hand. "Come here."

A thrill raced through her when he tugged her back onto the bed, then rolled on top of her, kissing her deeply. One of his hands swept down her thigh, pulling her leg around his hip. She reveled in the feel of his back muscles moving beneath her hands and the jut of his erection pressing against her stomach. She pushed against his shoulder, protesting the position.

He rolled on to his back, bringing her with him, until she straddled him once more. Sitting up, she drank her fill of his beautiful body as her hands played over his chest, tracing the contours of his muscles, teasing his flat male nipples to hard peaks.

He brushed her hair behind her back so he could touch her as well. She arched into his palms as he cupped her breasts. Lightly pinching her nipples, he smiled up at her, his eyes smoldering. "Is this where you break out the whips and leather and tell me to beg?"

She gave a throaty laugh at the wicked image that popped into her head. "Another time. Maybe." Leaning forward, she kissed him long and hard. Lifting her head, she smiled into his eyes. "Right now, I have other things in mind."

"Oh?" he queried, then sighed another "oh" as she kissed her way down his chest and over his abs. Her hair flowed like silk against his heated skin as she moved lower, teasing him with her tongue.

Oh God, yes, he thought as she took him into her mouth. He buried his hands in her hair and enjoyed. Arousal built and rippled through his body as everything in him focused on the exquisite sensation of having her pleasure him. A part of him wanted it to go on forever. Another part wanted to roll her over and thrust inside her until they both climaxed in a mindless burst.

As she drove him toward the edge, he moved his hands to the sheets and gripped them tight, fighting for control. "Enough!" he panted, seeing spots of light in the air.

With a rumbling laugh, she released him and started her way back up his body, driving him crazy with her tongue. He felt her mumble something against his abdomen. *What was that she'd said? Condom. Oh, um . . . Think!* "Nightstand. Top drawer."

She rose up on her knees with one hand planted beside his head as she reached for the nightstand. The position had her breasts dangling conveniently near his mouth. Cupping them with his hands, he took full advantage, suckling one nipple as his fingers toyed with the other. She whimpered softly, and he grinned with pure carnal satisfaction.

Then he moaned in protest when she sat back on his thighs, taking her breasts with her. Although, the view certainly made up for a lot. She had an incredible body, taut and toned with smooth creamy skin.

He watched, mesmerized as she tore the foil packet open, then slowly, oh God, so slowly, covered him.

His eyes nearly rolled back in his head from the feel of her fingers on his sensitized flesh.

"It fits," she said with surprise, before giving him a look of naughty delight. "I was worried it wouldn't be long enough." The way she said it, and the look in her eyes, made his groin muscles jerk.

"Oh God," he groaned. "If you're trying to make me go off early, you're about to succeed."

She leaned forward, took his lower lip in her mouth, then pulled back, releasing it slowly. "If you do, I'll have to find some way to make you pay penance."

Cupping the back of her head, he held her for a second kiss, then looked into her eyes. "How about I promise to worship your body for an hour however you want to make up for it?"

"That would do it." She smiled against his mouth.

He started to close his eyes when he felt her heat press against him, then forced them back open. This was one sight he didn't want to miss: Christine's face as she sank slowly over him, taking him inside her inch by wonderful inch. A little frown puckered her brow and she stopped. God, she was tight. A spear of panic went through him. He didn't want to hurt her, and this position would have him going deep. Although it gave her the control she seemed to want. She lifted up and sank back down, going a little farther each time.

Thinking he'd die if she didn't take all of him, he moved a hand to her mound and teased her with his thumb to ease her way.

Finally, she had him completely, gloriously embedded inside her. Her head fell back and she moaned as if she'd just swallowed a delicious treat. He stared at her, awed by the sight, not just by her physical beauty, but her open sexuality, her lack of pretension, her eagerness to play. Everything about her drew him to her, made him crave her.

Something clicked inside him, like the final tumbler of a lock that had been steadily falling into place since the moment he'd first met her. And when she tipped her head forward again, opened her eyes, and smiled down at him, he knew—in one lightning bolt, clarifying moment—that he was in love.

This was it. She was it. He'd found the woman he wanted to spend the rest of his life loving.

Thunderstruck by the idea, he went rigidly still as she began to move. His thoughts scattered, but his body had no trouble staying on track. He hardened even more as she drove them both steadily toward a pinnacle of pleasure. What a wild feeling to have joy fill his mind with his body on the verge of exploding.

"You look very happy," she said, making him smile even more.

"Mmm," he managed, wondering how she'd react when he told her. "Come here," he said instead.

Obliging, she leaned forward to kiss him. He tunneled his hands into her hair, holding her head as he took over the kiss, pouring every ounce of crazy emotion rushing through him into the dance of lips and tongue.

His heart hammered as the pace increased and she arched to catch her breath.

His hands swept down her back, soothing and encouraging. When she started to peak, he squeezed her bottom tightly. Her gasp of fulfillment shot him up and over as well. Snapping free of the strange paralysis, he arched upward, thrusting himself deep over and over, welcoming a shattering release more powerful than anything he'd ever experienced.

When his mind cleared, he found her draped over his chest, breathing hard. Struggling to get his heart and lungs to slow down, he wrapped his arms around her, drifted for a moment, then kissed her temple, which was damp at the hairline. *So*, he thought, mentally practicing the words as he stroked her back, *what would you think about marrying me?*

He felt her body jerk in surprise and realized he hadn't thought the words. He'd said them out loud!

Holding his breath, he waited for her reaction.

She lifted her head and stared at him with horrified eyes.

"That is"—he shrugged as casually as he could manage while having a heart attack—"if you don't have other plans for the next couple of days."

She burst out laughing and hugged him tight. "That's what I like about you. You really are crazy sometimes. Don't scare me like that, though. For a second there, I thought you were serious."

I was! he thought with no small amount of shock, but this time kept the words to himself. Good grief, he wanted to marry her! He really was crazy. A woman like Christine Ashton would never marry a guy like him.

Although, why the heck not? They'd both agreed money and status didn't matter. And they were perfect together!

* * *

"You have a tattoo?"

"Hmm?" Christine roused herself enough to glance over her shoulder. Alec stood in the doorway to the bedroom, stark naked, holding the glass of water he'd offered to get her. His incredulous expression as he stared at her bottom made her laugh. "Ah. I see you noticed my little alter ego. Do you like her?"

"Let me have a closer look." He came forward, set the glass on the nightstand, and turned on the lamp. Crawling onto the bed, he straddled her legs.

She propped up on both elbows and watched over her shoulder as he tipped his head, examining the sexy devil wearing a red merry widow with wild blond hair swirling around her. She had tiny horns, dragon wings, a long tail, and a very devious grin.

Alec nodded. "I finally figured out the name thing."

"Name thing?" She frowned.

"Christine, Chris, and Christi. Christine is 'Dr. Ashton's daughter,' " he said in a deep voice. "Chris is a real woman I like hanging out with. And this"— he looked back at the tattoo—"is naughty Christi."

"Maybe." She grinned.

"I like her."

"Do you?"

"Mmm." He planted a smacking kiss on the tattoo before crawling up to lean his back against the headboard. "How long have you had her?"

"Since college." Comfortable with her own nudity, she sat up against the headboard as well to drink her water. "My friend Amy really wanted a tattoo but didn't have the nerve to do it. Plus, she didn't know where to go, and the whole idea of needles and infection scared her. So I agreed to take her, provide moral support, and be sure the place was clean. When we got there, I saw a drawing of this devil on the wall and decided on the spur of the moment that I had to have her."

"Of course you did. She looks just like you."

"The artist did that."

"Have you ever regretted it?" He bent a leg and draped his arm over the knee, looking sexy and rumpled in the lamplight.

"Never." She gave him a quick kiss.

"That's a pretty permanent decision to make on the spot."

"Actually, I think some of my best decisions are made on impulse."

"Same here." He gave her a deep probing look that made her wonder what he was thinking; then he shifted his gaze as he played with her hair. "What did your friend get?"

"A butterfly. Right where I got my little devil, so we're tattoo twins." She smiled, remembering Amy's delight over their mutual brazenness. "We tried to talk Maddy and Jane into joining us, but Maddy said she'd never be able to make up her mind on what to get, so best to just not go there. Plus, Maddy's a fantastic artist. I don't think she'd be happy with someone else's artwork on her body."

"And Jane?"

"Yeah right." Christine snorted. "Like Miss Perfect would get a tattoo."

" 'Miss Perfect'?" Alec lifted a brow at her tone.

"Hmm. That sounded cattier than I meant it." She took a sip of cold water, then set her glass aside. "I liked Jane in college, I really did. I just kept wanting her to let her hair down and stop worrying so much about what other people think. It's sad to let the fear of making a single mistake in front of others control all your actions."

"She seems so confident on TV. You're saying she isn't like that in real life?"

"Sadly, no. But all the rest of her public persona is true. She honestly cares about people, which makes her a great motivational speaker. She's just really hard on herself. Makes me wonder about the subtitle of her book, *Ten Steps to Outrageous Happiness*. Granted, the gist of *How to Have a Perfect Life* is having the life that's perfect for *you*. But outrageous happiness? Give me a break. Do you know anyone who's 'outrageously happy'?"

"Well, I'm pretty outrageously happy at the moment." He leaned over to give her a quick kiss. "How about you?"

"I feel pretty dang good." A smile welled up from inside her as she looked back into his eyes.

"Glad to hear it." He held her gaze.

Feeling almost dizzy, she glanced around the room, really noticing it now that the light was on. He had bookshelves lining the bottom portion of every wall, holding all manner of objects, from clothes and shoes, to duffel bags and backpacks, to medical gear and books. Above the shelves on one wall were hooks holding more clothes. Another wall was covered with colorful bundles of rope and other rock-climbing gear. She frowned at the sight. "You have rather, um, interesting decor."

He glanced about, apparently not seeing anything out of the ordinary. "It's my organizational system. Keep everything out in the open, so I don't lose it. That's the problem with things like wallets and keys. You can't see them, so you assume they're in your pocket, until you reach for them and they're not there."

"And here I thought you were just really into ropes."

"Ah, the rock-climbing gear." He glanced at the wall. "Ever done any climbing?"

"With my fear of heights? No way!"

"Here, I'll show you how it works."

"Now?" The word left her mouth as he plucked her from the bed. "I guess now."

He showed her a variety of gadgets and gizmos, and even got her to step into a harness that went about her thighs and fastened in the front at her crotch, which felt really weird since she was naked. "Gee," she said, looking at the rope he was holding. "This could get kinky."

He looked from the rope to her. His brow lifted. "You're right."

Before she saw it coming, he looped and tied the rope about her wrists. The harness fell to the floor with a clunk.

"Alec!"

"Ha! I've got you now."

She shrieked when he hefted her over his shoulder and tossed her onto the bed. "What are you doing!"

He lifted her arms over her head and secured the

rope to the headboard. A strange thrill shot through her when she tugged on the rope and realized he'd actually tied it. "Alec, this isn't funny. Let me go."

"What if I said no?" Mischief danced in his eyes.

She looked at his face, and her heart raced. In spite of his grin, he looked deadly intent on ravishing her. A primal desire blossomed deep inside her at the thought.

He placed his fingertip on her chin and drew it slowly down her throat to the center of her chest. "I think it's my turn to have my way with you."

"Alec—" Her breath hitched as her nipples tightened. Need raced through her with shocking speed, making her ache for him to touch her however he wanted. "I don't know about this."

"Oh, I do. I let you have fun earlier. Turnabout is fair play."

"I didn't have you tied down!" She pulled at the rope, but it held firm.

"Even so, I feel obliged to, um, return a favor." He settled between her legs, moving her thighs apart as he kissed his way down her belly. Her heart beat wildly as she watched his steady progress, his lips brushing the skin just below her navel, followed by the lick of his tongue. His hands slipped beneath her bottom, tipping her hips to give him better access. With her legs held apart by his upper arms, her hands securely tied, she felt completely vulnerable.

She'd never given anyone this much trust. The fact that her helplessness excited her also frightened her, which seemed to excite her more. "Alec, no, untie me."

He looked up at her. His grin slipped a bit as he studied her. "If you say no—and mean it—I'll stop."

She stared back at him, barely able to catch her breath, her heart hammering as her body begged for erotic adventure. "It's just . . . I've never done this."

"That wasn't no." He flashed a grin before his mouth descended to cover her.

"Oh God!" She arched her back and closed her eyes as he brought her to the point of screaming. When he'd pleasured her to delirium, he turned her onto her knees. She opened her mouth to protest, but gasped instead as he entered her with one swift stroke.

After that, she lost herself in a barrage of pleasure.

When the storm ended, she lay in an exhausted heap, staring at the ceiling. "I can't believe you made me scream."

"Three times." He reached up and untied her hands. He frowned a bit as he rubbed the red marks on her wrists. "You okay? I didn't hurt you, did I?"

"If you did, it was worth it," she insisted, still dazed with pleasure. "And I was going too crazy to even notice. God! Who knew I'd be into getting tied up?"

"Hmm." He studied her face. "It's my theory that a lot of women who like control, also like losing it."

She stared back at him. "You've done this before?"

"I never kiss and tell." He smiled slowly.

She shook her head. "To think when I first met you, I thought you looked like a choir boy."

"Yeah, the face fools a lot of people." He punched the pillow behind his head into a better shape. "That worked really well when I was in school. 'No, sir, Mr. Truant Officer. That wasn't me you saw skipping school yesterday. I was home sick.' " He coughed three times.

"You are so bad."

"I didn't hear you complaining a minute ago. In fact, what was that you were saying? 'Oh yes, oh yes, oh God yes!' "

"Stop it!" She swatted his shoulder, but her laughter took the heat from her words. "So do you have any other kinky ideas?"

"Oh, honey, do I ever."

"Like what?" Her interest peaked.

"Most recently? Doing it on a chairlift."

"You have got to be kidding me!"

"You know, all that time staring into your eyes while we were going up—" He traced a fingertip along her jaw.

"You were thinking about having sex?"

"Yo, Doc, I'm a guy. I'm always thinking of having sex. But hey, maybe that would help you get over your fear of heights. How about we try it tomorrow? Ditch your family and spend the day with me. Better yet, spend the night with me too."

"You know I can't do that. Speaking of, what time is it?" She twisted to see the clock on his nightstand. "Oh man! I need to get home."

"No, stay." He grabbed her arm as she started to rise.

"I can't do that." She slipped free. "What would my family think?"

"Who cares? You're an adult."

"No, really." She searched for her clothes. "I have to get home."

"Oh, all right." He sighed heavily as he sat up. "I'll walk you."

"You don't have to."

He scowled at her. "Okay, let's get one thing straight. There's not much good you can say about my family, but when it comes to manners, we Hunters never shirk. I walk you home. I open your doors. I hold your chairs. Got it?"

She grinned. "May I be politically incorrect and say I like that?"

"You may."

Once they'd dressed, they braved the cold and hurried through the village. In the lobby of her parents' condo, Alec pulled her into his arms and kissed her.

"Will I see you tomorrow?" he asked.

"That depends." With her arms looped about him, she smiled. "What do you have in mind?"

"What are you up for?" he asked suggestively.

She couldn't help but laugh. "A lot of things, apparently."

"How about this? I need to take the snowmobile and check on one of our cabins in the backcountry. Want to go with me?"

"Snowmobiling?"

"Without any stupid stunts like Paul and Ted pulled. We can pack some food, build a fire, and play snowbound pioneers. You know, pretend we're caught in a blizzard, crawl beneath some blankets, and share body heat."

"Ooh, wait." She brightened with an idea of her own. "Can we play lonely widow who finds a wounded mountainman stranded in the high country instead?"

"Do I get to wake up in your bed with both of us naked because you're warming my body?"

"Absolutely."

"You're on."

"Okay." The elevator opened. "Now I have to go. Really."

"Hang on." With one hand holding the elevator doors open, he moved as if to brush something from her nose.

"What?" She held still, wondering what it was.

Rather than a light brush of his finger, he rubbed his whole gloved hand over her face, then studied her. "Nope, didn't help."

Sputtering, she shook her head, then glared at him. "What was that for?"

He grinned. "Just trying to erase the 'Oh boy, I just had sex' look."

After a smirk, she gave him a quick kiss. "Trust me, Alec, you have no room to talk."

Smiling, he stepped back and let the doors close, then stood a while, grinning like a fool.

Later that evening, after the rest of the family finally had gone to bed, Christine opened up her laptop to e-mail Maddy and Amy.

Subject: *I'm in love!*

Message: *Not big love with a capital L, but Alec Hunter is so much FUN!*

She'd already told them yesterday that he was very much employed so she went on to tell them all about their wild first date.

Chapter 14

"Hey, Hunter, where's Chris?" Jeff asked nearly a week later as they stood in the truck bay of the fire station. "I thought she was going to help with this project."

"She is," Alec assured, even though he'd been wondering the same thing for the past hour. Several volunteers, along with a few spouses and kids, had arrived that morning to decorate his truck for the Winterfest Parade. Since the avalanche rescue, Chris seemed as much a part of the team as the others, hanging out at the pub and planning their entry in the parade. The volunteers had welcomed her into the fold, treating her with the same teasing and camaraderie they all shared. "She's probably still rounding up some last-minute items on that list your wife gave her."

"I hope she scores on the wig." Brian laughed as he and Kreiger worked in the bed of the truck to erect a fake ship's mast. "I can't wait to see the lieutenant here sporting long curls."

"Watch it, guppy," Kreiger warned. "I haven't committed to anything."

"Oh, man, ya gotta do it," Brian whined over the banging of hammers and the buzz of a saw. "This is the best float idea we've ever had. We'll stomp everyone for the most kick-butt entry."

"Absolutely," Alec said as he and Jeff carried the ship's bow the team had just finished making to the front of the truck. Search and rescue was sure to outdo all the rest in the ongoing war for the coveted title of Best Entry from the Chamber of Commerce, along with bragging rights for a solid year.

"We've got the firefighters beat by a mile." Jeff sneered in the direction of the yard where the competition was converting the fire engine—affectionately known as Big Red—into a giant Santa's sleigh.

"Santa's sleigh," Brian scoffed. "Talk about no originality. Okay, so their truck is ten times bigger. So they have a louder siren and more lights. So they win more applause every year. This year, we have imagination on our side."

"You got it, kid," Jeff agreed as he and Alec worked to attach the bow to the grill guard. "Thanks to Alec's girlfriend."

Alec smiled with pride as he remembered the day they'd settled on a theme. Inspired by Alec's nickname, Christine had suggested *Christmas in Neverland*. The team had loved it and launched into an all-out effort to pull it off.

Now here they were, down to the wire, and no sign of Christine.

While the others continued to extol the ingenuity

of their float to the discordant noise of construction, Alec's mind drifted to the question that had plagued him constantly for the past few days: how to talk her into moving to Colorado. After the stupid blunder of blurting out a marriage proposal, he'd been too nervous to bring up the less intimidating topic of her moving. He had only one week left, though, before she headed back to Texas.

Should he bring the subject up right away so she'd have time to get used to the idea? Or should he wait, and ask her with some big, romantic gesture after they'd had more time together? How did he know? He'd never cared about a woman enough to contemplate something this terrifying.

Just thinking about a possible rejection had nausea roiling in his stomach. What if she laughed again and thought he was joking? He'd known her for barely two weeks. How could he convince her he was serious?

What he needed was some solid advice. He glanced at Jeff. The two of them were crouched down on their boot heels, out of earshot from most of the other workers. He cleared his throat. "So, um, Jeff, you're married. Can I ask you something?"

"As long as it's not a question about women."

"Well, actually, it is."

"Wait, I need to hear this." Kreiger folded his forearms on the roof of the cab, staring down at them. "Men giving men advice about women is always amusing. Like the blind leading the blind."

Alec glowered at him. "Okay, Kreiger, since you're so wise about everything, maybe you can help."

"I doubt it," Kreiger said. "But fire away, boy."

Alec steadied his nerves with a breath. "First, I guess I should mention I'm serious about Chris—"

"Naw!" Kreiger feigned shock. "None of us would have figured that one out. Hey, troops!" He turned to the group building an island on the trailer. "News flash. This just in. Hunter has a thing for the doc."

That won a round of laughs.

"Would you hold it down!" Alec shot a look over his shoulder to be sure Christine hadn't just walked in.

"So what do you need to know?" Jeff shifted to give his four-year-old daughter more room to help. Actually, Colleen wasn't much help, but she was cute as heck while getting in the way.

"Like this, Daddy?" Colleen scrunched her face as she twisted wire.

"Exactly, baby." Jeff beamed at her.

"Okay, well, here's the deal." Alec struggled for the right way to phrase his dilemma. "I want to talk Chris into moving here, but every time I start to bring it up, my brain freezes and I break out in a cold sweat."

"I know the feeling." Jeff widened his eyes at some memory.

"Well, so . . . ?" Alec forced the words out. "How do you work up to something like that? You know, asking a woman something really . . . *big*?"

Brian's red head popped up over the roof of the truck where he joined Kreiger staring down at them. "You're going to ask Doctor Dish to marry you? First Will, now you? This is like mass desertion."

"No, jeez," Alec lied. "I've only known her two weeks. I'm not going to propose. I'm just going to ask her to move here."

"Sometimes two weeks is all it takes," Jeff said. "Isn't that right, Linda?"

"Hmm, what?" His wife's voice came from the trailer.

Oh great, Alec thought, *let's get everyone in on this conversation.*

Jeff raised his voice. "How long did it take for us to know it was the real deal?"

"Well, let's see," Linda answered. "I fell in lust when you showed up at my office to fix my corrupted hard drive. It wasn't love, though, until you actually did it."

Deciding a woman's take might not be a bad idea, Alec shifted sideways so he could see Jeff's wife. "We're being serious here, Linda."

"So am I." She shrugged as she crinkled cellophane to simulate water. "Men think it's the macho stuff that impresses women. Trust me, though, when my hard drive crashes, I want a man who can get me up and running. Well, the fact that Jeff is a computer nerd with a rock-climber's body doesn't hurt either."

Jeff leaned closer to Alec and wiggled his brows. "Which also gets her 'up and running.' "

"What was that?" Linda narrowed her eyes in her husband's direction.

"Nothing!" Jeff claimed, all innocence.

Alec stood. "You know, as fascinating as all this is, it's not helping me. Anyone have an idea for how I can convince Chris to move here?"

Several of the men and women offered suggestions, from bringing it up on the slopes, since Chris liked skiing, to Brian suggesting Alec give her great sex, then ask her to move. That earned the kid a cuff on the head from Kreiger and an admonishment about children being present.

"Russo's," Jeff finally said, cutting through the chatter.

"What?" Alec frowned.

"Take her to Russo's." Jeff lifted his daughter to his hip. "It's quiet, private, and has great atmosphere. Ply her with good food and a nice bottle of wine. Then point out the view, which is killer from there, and say, 'Now, wouldn't you love to live here?'"

Alec snorted. "Like I can afford Russo's"

Jeff cocked a brow. "Do you want this woman to move here or not?"

Before Alec could answer, Christine burst into the bay from the main part of the fire station, her arms loaded down with costumes. She looked flushed and out of breath. "Guess what?"

Alec flashed a warning look at everyone before going to greet her. "There you are. We were beginning to think you'd forgotten about us."

"Hey, Chris!" the others all greeted her.

She deposited the colorful bundle of clothes on a bench, then gave him a quick kiss. Excitement shone in her eyes. "I have some fabulous news."

"What?" He smiled, thinking anything that made her this happy had to be good.

"My dad called Ken Hutchens this morning, the CEO of St. James Hospital, to wish him a merry

Christmas. Whew, I can't catch my breath." She worked at removing her gloves. "Apparently, on my dad's recommendation from a few days ago, Ken's been asking around about me."

"Oh?" His smile froze. He could think of only one reason for why a hospital CEO would ask around about a soon-to-be certified trauma specialist.

She got her parka unzipped. "Apparently the people at Breckenridge Hospital, where I served my residency, were very generous with their praise."

"Oh?" he said. This was not good.

"St. James has an opening in the ER and . . ." She clasped her hands together below her chin. "Ken Hutchens said he'd like to talk with my head hunter about a contract if I'm interested!" With a shriek, she flung herself against him.

"Wow!" He staggered back a step as the impact of her body and the news hit him. Dazed, he wrapped his arms around her. "That's . . . great."

"It's more than great." Stepping back, she held her arms out and twirled about like a little girl. "It's the best Christmas gift ever!"

"Better than a Barbie Dream House?" Colleen asked. "That's what Santa Claus is bringing me. My daddy promised."

"Way better than a Dream House from Santa." Christine smiled at Colleen.

Alec stood as if turned to stone, watching her bubble over with happiness about a job offer in Austin. He was so screwed.

"Let's see, what can I do?" She looked around, oblivious to the fact that everyone was giving Alec looks of sympathy. "Oh! Costumes! Linda, I found everything on our list." Turning back to the pile, she extracted a long black wig and held it up. "Kreiger, I even found a Captain Hook wig for you, so no getting out of it, okay?"

He grumbled something under his breath and turned his attention to the mast. The others went back to work as well.

Alec cleared his throat, pretending she hadn't just kicked him in the gut. "Sounds like you really want this job."

"More than I can possibly say," she proclaimed.

"Then we should celebrate." He forced a smile. "How about I take you to dinner at Russo's?"

"Oh." That drew her up short. She gave him a startled look. "You don't have to do that. We could just go to the pub."

In other words, she didn't think he could afford Russo's either. "I'd really like to take you somewhere nice to celebrate."

"Are you sure?"

"Very." He managed a smile even as he wondered if he'd lost all hope of getting her to stay. "I'll make reservations for tonight."

"Okay. Sounds wonderful."

"First, though"—he looked around, trying to focus—"we need to finish this."

"You got it, Peter." She pulled a green hat out of her pile and plopped it on his head, then looked at Buddy. "And for you, my furry friend . . ." She tied a white cap to Buddy's head, then clapped her hands together. "What a cute Nanna!"

Buddy gave her a doggy grin, completely unaware his masculinity had just been insulted.

"Did you find a costume for you?" Alec asked.

"Yep." She retrieved a blue ribbon and tied her hair at the nape, then held an old-fashioned nightgown to her shoulders. "How's this?"

He tucked a stray strand of blond hair behind her ear. "You make a very sexy Wendy."

"Thank you. Although, I should have armwrestled Colleen for the part of Tinkerbell. She's a lot more fun."

"Except Wendy's the one Peter loves best."

"Not enough to grow up and be with her in the real world. Not that I blame him." She scrunched up her nose. "Wendy's such a Goody Two-shoes."

He leaned close enough to whisper in her ear, "How do we know that when Wendy got older, she didn't get a naughty pixie tattooed on her butt?"

"Ooh, I like that thought. Okay, I'll be Wendy with an inner Tink." She wiggled her brows and whispered back, "Maybe we can rewrite the story so that Peter does grow up. That way he and Wendy get kinky together."

"Hmm, eternal childhood or kinky adult sex?" Alec weighed the two, then shook his head. "If he'd only known, he probably *would* have grown up. On the spot!"

She laughed and gave him that happy look that went straight to his heart. Fortunately, before he could blurt out anything stupid, she moved away. "Did you get the goodies for the lost boys, pirates, and mermaids to toss to the crowd?"

"I did." He gave himself a mental shake and crossed to the back of the truck. In the bed were buckets of flashlights the same size and shape as credit cards. They had emergency phone numbers printed on one side and safety tips printed on the other. "What do you think?"

"Oh! These are the perfect thing for Peter Pan to hand out."

"They are?" He frowned at the bucket. "I just thought they were the perfect thing for search and rescue to hand out. So what's the Peter Pan connection?"

"You know." She held one up at arm's length and shined it back toward herself. " 'Second star to the right and straight on till morning.' That's how you find your way to Neverland."

"I still say we won," Alec grumbled for the hundredth time since the parade ended.

"I agree." Christine struggled against a smile as they stepped onto the elevator that would take them up to Russo's. Alec sounded as passionate as a sports fan whose team had lost on a questionable call from the officials.

"We were robbed," he insisted, hitting the button for the top floor.

"Absolutely."

"How could the judges pick Steve?"

"Look at it this way." She wrapped both her arms about one of his, admiring how handsome he looked dressed all in black, from the leather jacket and turtleneck to the slacks and boots. "At least the firefighters didn't win."

"True, but *Steve*?"

"Come on, admit it. His entry was clever. The sheriff as 'The Grinch Who Stole Christmas'? That's funny!"

"Maybe." He scowled. "Our float was better."

"I totally agree." She took his face in her hand to get his full attention. "If I told you I wasn't wearing any underwear, would you feel better?"

"Are you serious?" His gaze dropped to the long charcoal-gray coat she wore over an ankle-length dark blue dress. "You're naked under that?"

"No, but I got your mind off the parade for a second, didn't I?"

"Oh man, that bites, Chris. You build my hopes up, then lay me low. Now I'm even more bummed."

Laughing, she laid her lips against his. *I love this man.* Startled by the thought, she jumped back and stared at him.

"What?" He frowned at her expression.

"Nothing," she insisted as the elevator doors opened.

Her mind whirled as they crossed the hall to the maître d' station just outside an ornate doorway. She couldn't be in love. She enjoyed being with Alec, but that didn't mean love. They barely knew each other.

And yet . . . at times she felt as if he knew her, understood her, and accepted her in ways no man ever had.

They lived in completely different states, though. Falling in love with him would be totally impractical.

"This way, please," the maître d' said, and led them into the softly lit restaurant that ran along the top floor. Private booths made of dark wood paneling lined the inside wall, facing a wall of glass. The ambience offered intimacy and old-world charm. The aroma of pasta sauce and freshly baked bread blended with the quiet strains of Italian folk music.

The maître d' stopped at an empty booth. "Will this do?"

"This is perfect." Alec nodded. "Thanks."

"Very good." The man laid menus and a wine list on the table and lit the candle. "Your server will be with you shortly. Enjoy your meal."

"What a wonderful view," Christine said as Alec took her coat.

"It really is," he agreed.

The snow-covered mountains glowed a bluish white beneath a star-filled sky. In the plaza around the skating rink, golden light spilled from shops as people strolled about in their colorful winter clothes. The scene reminded her of a child's snow globe after all the white flakes had gently settled.

After hanging their coats, Alec slid into the booth beside her.

A waiter appeared, wearing a crisp white shirt and apron over black pants. "Will you be having wine this evening?"

Alec reached for the wine list, frowning. "I don't know much about wine. Maybe you should pick one."

Christine didn't have to see the list to know everything on it would be outrageously overpriced. She smiled at the waiter. "Actually, do you have any Italian beer?"

"Moretti," he answered.

"Oh, that sounds good. I'll have that and some water, please."

"Very good. Sir?"

"I'll have the same," Alec answered, looking relieved.

As soon as the waiter moved off, she reached for the menu. "I wonder if they have authentic Italian pizza."

"You don't have to get pizza," he assured her. Then he opened his menu and his eyes bulged ever so slightly.

Oh yes I do, she thought, looking at the prices. "Do you know how long it's been since I've had a real pizza?" She scanned the list and saw that even the pizzas weren't cheap. At least they were better than lobster with linguini at triple the market price. "Aha! They have *quattro stagioni,* four seasons pizza, my favorite kind."

He chuckled. "Bring the woman to a fancy restaurant, and she orders pizza and beer."

"Aren't those two of the four major food groups? So what are you having?"

"Good old-fashioned spaghetti and meatballs, if I can find it." Alec stared at his menu, which had the names of all the dishes in Italian with English descriptions beneath.

"Don't you hate it when restaurants make everything sound so fancy you can't even order?" Christine wrinkled her nose playfully, which would have defused his embarrassment if he'd had any. He actually found the restaurant's pretentiousness more amusing than intimidating. Christine leaned closer to read his menu. She smelled clean and simple, like she always did. No froufrou perfumes or clashing fragrances from too many scented lotions and hair goo. "Here you go." She tapped the menu. "*Spaghetti e polpette.*"

"You speak Italian?"

"No, I speak food, in several languages. When you travel in Europe, you either pick it up or do a lot of pointing and praying. I've wound up with some really strange dishes using the point-and-pray method."

"Okay, then you pick out an appetizer." He held his menu toward her. When she took it, he draped his arm behind her along the back of the bench seat.

"Let's see, I'd go with the *formaggi*, which is a bunch of different cheeses, or fried calamari."

"That's squid, right?" He frowned. "Will I like it?"

"I don't know, but I *love* it." Her eyes sparkled in the candlelight.

"Then order both." He toyed with her hair. "I'm starved."

"You're always starved." She laughed.

He felt an odd mix of arousal and nerves as he remembered why he'd brought her here. But he couldn't very well blurt out "So what would you think about moving here" before they'd even ordered. He needed to bide his time. Wait for the right opening. Then bring it up slowly.

Unfortunately, the nervousness grew during dinner. He could barely even focus on her words as she regaled him with stories about family trips to Europe while she was growing up. Instead, he sat staring at her, thinking about how badly he wanted her to stay with him forever. To live together and grow old together. Good Lord, he sounded as sappy as Will.

When their dessert of tiramisu and cappuccino arrived, he stared at it and realized his time was running out.

"You're awfully quiet," she said, tipping her head to catch his eye. "You're not still brooding over the parade, are you?"

"No. I was . . . thinking about . . . something else."

"Oh?"

"Yeah." This was it. He took a deep breath and laid his hand over hers. "I was thinking about how much I enjoy spending time with you."

She sent him a smile as if she'd just melted inside. That was a good sign. He hoped. "I enjoy spending time with you too. In fact, I've never been so . . . *comfortable* with anyone before."

"Same here."

Her hand turned over beneath his and she squeezed his fingers. "I'm going to miss you when I leave."

"Ah. Well. Hmm." He cleared his throat. "About that, I was wondering . . . how serious is this job offer from the hospital in Austin?"

"Very serious, I hope." Elation made her face even more beautiful.

"The reason I ask is because, well—" A fist of tension squeezed his chest. "The thing is, they have hospitals here."

"I know. But none of them are St. James."

"Yes, but if you found a position somewhere nearby, you wouldn't have to leave." He watched a frown dimple her brow, as if she were trying to decipher his words. He tightened his grip on her hand. "I don't expect you to make a snap decision or anything. You're going to be here another week, but . . .

well, see, I'd like you to consider moving here. So
we can keep seeing each other."

He watched as understanding hit. Her eyes widened in surprise.

"I realize we met only two weeks ago, but the deal
is—" He lifted her hand and kissed her finger. "You
have completely blown me away." He wanted to say
he loved her, to let everything inside him come spilling out in a rush, but the stunned look on her face
stopped him. His heart raced as she continued to sit
there staring.

Then with a breathy laugh she settled back and
stared out the windows. "This is so my life! I can't
believe this." The words sent a streak of fear racing
through him. It mounted toward panic when she
turned back to him with regret in her eyes. "Alec,
I . . . I really will miss you, but this job is important
to me."

"If you need more time to think about it—"

"No," she interrupted. "I don't have to think about
it. Nothing in the world could make me turn this job
down. Please don't take that personally."

"How can I not take it personally?" His voice rose
slightly as he realized she was turning him down,
just like that, without even a second's hesitation. "I
say I want to keep seeing you, and you won't even
consider it? How is that not personal?"

"It's—" She searched for words, then gave up.
"You know, never mind. You wouldn't understand,
so maybe we should just drop it."

"To heck with that!" He leaned forward when she
tried to look away. "Talk to me. Make me understand."

"Alec . . ." She shifted to face him. "If I could pick

one hospital in all the world to work for, it would be St. James."

"Why?"

"Because . . ." Frustration lined her face. "All my life, I've wanted to prove myself to my dad. To make him proud of me." She took his hand in both of hers, her eyes pleading. "If I get this position, I'll have that chance. I'll be working with colleagues Dad respects. I'll have the chance to show them I'm good. Really good. Every bit as good as Robbie."

He stared at her in confusion. "You're going to take a job simply to impress your father?"

She looked away. "I told you you wouldn't understand."

"Christine . . ." He put a finger to her chin to turn her back. "I'm probably overstepping my bounds here, but it sounds like you want the job for the wrong reason. You do know it's never going to change, right? This weird triangle between you and your dad and your brother, it's never going to change."

"It's already changing." Some of her earlier excitement returned. "Don't you see? This morning, after Dad told me about Ken Hutchens and what good things he'd heard about me, he said he was impressed."

" 'Impressed.' " Alec scowled. "Is that enough?"

"Are you kidding? It's huge!"

"So you're going to take a job in Texas rather than even consider looking for one here because it will impress your father? Won't he be impressed no matter where you work?"

"It wouldn't be the same."

"But—"

"No. There is no 'but.' I'm going to get that position no matter what it takes." She turned back to stab at her dessert. "End of discussion."

He stared at her in disbelief. "So I'm just supposed to drop it?"

"Yes."

"But—"

She sent him an irritated look. "Do you really want to fight about it?"

Yes, he thought. He wanted to argue and push and get her to open up to him. Instead, he sat back and stared out the window as he considered his options. They could fight it out now, or he could give her a few days to think about it, then bring it up again. Maybe she needed time for this thing between them to grow.

Time for her to fall in love with him.

But what if that never happened? What if she never returned all the thrilling, frightening things he felt for her?

He had a week to win her over—or lose her completely.

His gut churned as he nodded. "Okay. We'll drop it." *For now.*

Chapter 15

Communication is easier said than done.
—*How to Have a Perfect Life*

Christine felt the awkwardness mount as they walked through the village toward Alec's apartment. They didn't talk, or hold hands, or walk arm in arm as they usually did. Instead, Alec stared straight ahead, his shoulders hunched and his hands thrust into the pockets of his black leather jacket, as if he were freezing. In truth, the night was mild, with people strolling about, admiring the Christmas lights and the displays in shop windows.

She'd hurt his feelings. So now what did she say? How did she explain?

Even when they reached his apartment the awkwardness persisted. Alec mumbled something about taking Buddy out, and left her standing there alone. After hanging her coat on a peg by the door, she plugged in the little Christmas tree they'd bought and decorated together. Alec had said it was his first ever as an adult because he'd never thought of buying one just for him.

Christine had had even more fun decorating this one than the one Natalie and Robbie had snuck in for the kids. She and Alec had made the ornaments themselves by stringing popcorn for garlands and tying red ribbon around candy canes. The origami animals they'd made from aluminum foil reflected the multicolored lights, giving the tree a cheerful sort of magic.

Fingering a foil frog, she remembered how goofy they'd acted that night, how they'd laughed until her sides ached, and how they'd made love afterwards by only the lights of the tree.

The memory faded to the scene at the restaurant, leaving her in a state of semishock. Alec wanted her to move to Colorado. The look in his eyes when he'd said it had made everything inside her expand with joy, then pop like a balloon, leaving her deflated.

She stared numbly about the small living and dining room. His apartment wasn't that much smaller than hers back in Austin, but here was secondhand furniture that didn't match. In lieu of framed art, he'd tacked up snowboarding and skiing posters. Everything about the place was so Alec, she loved spending time here. They'd packed a lot of fun moments into a very short time.

If she moved to Colorado, would he ask her to live with him? Her heart ached with longing at the thought.

Why was life so cruel? Did the Fates enjoy toying with humans? Dangling someone's deepest desire right in front of them, then naming a painful price?

Just that morning she'd learned the one dream she'd had her whole life had a chance of coming true. She'd floated through the entire day—only to have the Fates say, "But wait, there's a catch. That other thing you've always wanted, a good man to love and be loved by? That may or may not be behind curtain number two. The only way to find out is to give up the prize behind curtain number one. Now what will you do? Which will you choose?"

Wrapping her arms about her middle she wondered if the chance for love was worth so large a sacrifice. She had no way of knowing how things with Alec would turn out. What if she threw away the goal of a lifetime, only to find out the Fates had pulled the cruelest trick of all?

A fear rose inside her that she would do precisely that. She wasn't exactly known for making brilliant choices where men were concerned. She could so easily see herself tossing responsibility, her family's respect, and everything else to the wind so she could live here with a man who made her laugh.

Tears welled unexpectedly in her eyes.

At the sound of the door, she turned to the window that overlooked the plaza to keep her back to the room.

She heard Alec come inside and watched him in the reflection of the glass as he stopped and stared at her. Then he turned and headed for the kitchen in the corner.

"I, um, I bought some wine earlier," he said, his voice flat. "Jeff recommended it, so it should be good. I thought we might want some after dinner."

The fist about her heart squeezed tighter when she realized he'd bought it so they could celebrate her agreeing to move.

"Would you like a glass?" he asked.

"That would be nice," she answered without turning. How was she going to dispel this stiffness between them?

When Buddy came over to her, she busied herself petting him as Alec opened the bottle. By the time she straightened, he was moving toward the sofa with two glasses.

She went to join him, accepting the glass as she sat, but not really looking at him.

"Alec, I . . ." She stared at the glass in her hand. "I think I need to explain."

"Oh, so now you are willing to talk about it."

Looking up, she saw the hurt lining his face. "I don't want to, but I need you to understand, because I'm scared to death you'll talk me into doing something I know I'll regret later."

He looked away, and she realized she'd hurt him even more.

"This isn't easy for me to talk about, okay? So if I don't say it neatly, please try—" Her throat started to close, so she sipped at the rich red wine, letting its smoky flavor slide over her tongue. "Okay, I'm going to just say it." She took a deep breath. "They didn't want me."

"What?" He turned back to her.

"My parents," she clarified, gripping the glass. "I was an accident."

"Okay," he said slowly. "How is that connected to you refusing to move here and give us a chance?"

"Because it's the reason I want the position at St. James. I've always had to work harder than most kids to earn their affection and their pride, to not feel like an intrusion in their lives. An uninvited houseguest who moved in and stayed."

He stared at her, clearly stunned.

"I, um—" She took another sip. "I don't think Mom wanted any children, really. I've watched her with my nephews, and it's as if the mommy gene is missing. It's simply not there. I can sort of understand, because, to be honest, I don't have it either." That was equally hard to admit, that she feared being as cold as her mother and that her children would wind up feeling the same simmering cauldron of inadequacy that she felt. "Don't get me wrong, I like kids well enough, and enjoy being around other people's children, but I've never wanted any of my own."

"Something else we have in common."

"Really?" She looked at him, momentarily distracted. "That surprises me. I would have pegged you as someone who loves kids."

"Let me guess. Because I'm still a kid myself, right?"

"Something like that." At any other time, she would have smiled. "So why don't you want children?"

He shrugged. "My brother and sister are doing more than their share to overpopulate the planet. Besides, it's much more fun to play with someone else's kids, then hand them back the second they need a clean diaper."

"Exactly. Which is why I can empathize with my mother and what I imagine happened."

"Which was?"

She sat back, finding the words came easier now that she'd started. "Mom was young, pampered, and perfectly happy in her newly wedded bliss. But here was her husband pressuring her for progeny. I think she agreed without really knowing what to expect. I have this picture of her as a sheltered socialite day-dreaming about baby showers and cute clothes with ribbons and lace and tiny little booties. Then *wham*, here comes morning sickness, water retention, and you know—a *baby*! A screaming, crying baby that spits up and wets."

"They do that," he agreed.

"They also take a lot of attention. Attention she thought would be focused on her, the new mother. Add to that the fact that Dad was very stubborn when they first married. The Ashtons have always been well off and respectable, but mom's father, Grandpa Honeycutt, was a self-made man who achieved a great deal on his own. I think Grandpa said something that tweaked Dad's pride a bit, made Dad want to prove he was man enough to make his own way. So he wouldn't accept any financial help from either of their parents. All that's changed now, but back when Dad was in residency, there was no money or room for a live-in nanny."

"Oh, the horror." He shuddered. "How did she survive?"

"Laugh all you want, but that had to be traumatic for someone like my mom. Frankly, I wonder how their marriage survived it. I can only imagine my mother's relief over getting it right the first time."

"Getting it right?"

"You know, having a boy. Giving her husband a son. She didn't have to go through any of that again. Then, finally, Robbie was old enough to go to school. She was probably thinking, 'Thank God. A halfway normal life again.' And, out of the blue, here I come and ruin everything."

"She told you this?" He stared at her.

She shrugged. "She didn't have to. Contrary to what a lot of people think, children aren't too stupid to understand adult speak."

"That's horrible!" He set his glass down hard on the coffee table. "I can't imagine how much that hurts. Granted, I'm not wild about my family, but I never felt unwanted."

"Well, I did." She stared at her glass, unable to look at him. "There used to be this little girl inside me who wanted desperately to be their pride and joy. I realized early on that would never happen with Mom. I can forgive her that lack of maternal affection, though, because she's equally distant to Robbie as she is to me." She looked up. "But I can't forgive Dad his lack of . . . simple attention." Tears welled up in her eyes. "I can't forgive him for constantly blowing me off simply because I'm a girl. So yes, having him be 'impressed' this morning meant a lot to me."

"Is it enough, though?" he asked gently.

"No," she said. "It's not, which is my point. If I get a job at a hospital halfway across the country, he may hear about my successes, but it's not the same as hearing it from people he knows. It's not the same as him seeing with his own eyes that I'm good." The hurt swelled within her. "One way or another, I'm going to make him notice me and make him admit I'm every bit as worthy of his pride as Robbie is."

He studied her for a long time. "And none of this strikes you as mentally unhealthy? To live your whole life for this one goal?"

"I think it's mentally necessary if I'm ever going to let it go."

"What if that never happens?"

"It will. If I get the position at St. James, I'll make sure it happens." She took his hand in hers. "That's why I'm asking you to not take my decision personally. I would love to go on seeing you, but I'm not willing to give up this chance for anything."

"I see." He looked blindly across the room, clearly struggling to accept her decision.

"You know," she ventured, "the alternative would be for you to move to Austin."

He released a bark of laughter. "Trust me, that ain't gonna happen."

"Why not? They have search and rescue there."

"Not alpine search and rescue. No mountains, no snow, no skiing." He glanced over his shoulder at the posters on the wall, then shook his head. "You might as well ask me to cut off a limb."

Disappointment filled her. "Then I guess we're at an impasse."

"Not yet." He lifted a brow. "I have one more week to change your mind."

"I'm telling you, you won't."

"And I'm saying, we'll see."

She shook her head at him. "Do you ever give up on anything?"

He leaned forward and pressed his lips against hers. "Never."

Alec felt as if a ticking clock floated over his head in the days that followed. After Christine's confession about her family, she closed that part of herself off and hung a big Do Not Disturb sign on it. He ignored the sign as much as he dared and prodded her gently with all the reasons why living in Colorado was better for both of them. He had to. Every day, every hour, every minute brought them closer to her getting on a plane and flying out of his life.

How appropriate that their last night together was New Year's Eve, the night when the whole world counted down the seconds.

Dancing with her at the pub, he held her close as their bodies swayed together. They seemed to exist in a bubble of quiet while all about them people laughed too brightly, wheeled about too gaily, and the music blared too loudly. He swore he could feel her wishing, as he did, that the clock would simply stop.

Someone shouted, and the band stopped playing. When Christine lifted her head off his shoulder, they turned to the TV mounted high on the wall near the bar. A hush fell over the room as they watched a street celebration in Denver—Colorado's version of Times Square. The crowd on TV surged and shouted as the countdown began.

Ten, nine, eight, seven, six, five, four, three, two, one. Happy New Year!

A lump rose in his throat as he looked down at Christine the same instant she looked up at him. Balloons and confetti rained over them as he cradled her face in both hands and lowered his mouth to hers. He kissed her slowly at first, but need built as horns blared and people cheered. A drunken couple bumped into them, reminding him where they were.

He raised his head. When their gazes met, no

words were needed. They turned and made their way through the crowd as the band began to play "Auld Lang Syne." At the door, they gathered their coats and headed outside. The snow muted the sounds of revelry as they walked hand in hand.

Christine was glad he didn't speak. One word might have broken the dam of emotions she'd been holding inside for days. When they reached his apartment, they came together with an aching tenderness that heightened all the senses.

She wanted to remember every touch and every taste as they helped each other undress, then laid together on the bed. His movements held a restrained intensity, as if he too wanted to commit this time, their last time, to memory.

When at last he came over her in the bed, he stared down into her eyes as he joined their bodies, filled her with that sweet, throbbing desire. Need grew touch by touch, thrust by thrust into desperation. Until she arched and gasped beneath him.

The dam holding her emotions threatened to break along with her passion. As if sensing how close she was to giving in to everything he wanted, he covered her mouth and kissed her and kissed her and kissed her as he continued driving inside her.

The dam burst, letting out a shocking rush of pleasure and pain. She sobbed as she came apart in his arms. He held her tightly to him as he surrendered to his own need, his body shuddering over her.

And then, somehow, he was beside her, cradling her to his chest as she sobbed.

"Shh." He soothed her, stroking her hair. "It's okay. I've got you."

"I'm s-sorry. I don't know what's wrong with me."

"It's okay." He murmured the words against her forehead.

"No, it's not. It's not okay." Without thinking, she balled her fist and punched him lightly in the chest. "I'm going to miss you, damn it!"

"You don't have to." He took her fist and brought it to his mouth. "Don't go, Chris. Don't leave. Stay here."

"Stop it!" Sitting up, she wrapped her arms about her legs and cried against her knees. The mattress shifted as he sat up behind her. His hand rubbed against her back, gentling her. When her breathing settled, she rested her cheek on her knees and offered him a watery smile. "I didn't want our last night to be like this. I promised myself I wouldn't get emotional."

"At least I know I'm not the only one hurting over this."

"I wish things could be different."

"They can."

"Don't—" She started to get off the bed, but he drew her back. Shifting to his knees, he faced her, holding both her hands. "Christine, I want you to stay more than I can possibly say. Stay with me." He brought both her hands to his mouth. "Be *my* pride and joy."

"Alec, please don't do this." She felt her heart tearing in two. "I told you I wouldn't change my mind, and I won't. Please don't make it even harder on both of us."

"What am I supposed to do?" Frustration sounded in his voice. "Walk you home tonight, shake your hand and say, 'Well, that was fun. Have a nice flight'? In case you haven't figured this out, I'm in love with you."

Her breath caught at hearing the words from him for the first time. "You're w-what?"

"You heard me." His hands tightened about hers. "I said I love you. And this is what people do when they're in love. They fight to be together. They don't give up and walk away or let go and say.'Oh well.' They find a way to make it work."

"Are you willing to move to Austin?"

"No."

"Then there is no way to make it work."

"At least I have a healthy reason for refusing to move."

"I can't handle this." She climbed from the bed.

"That's it?" he demanded as she gathered her clothes. "I tell you I love you, and you say you can't handle it? Don't you dare tell me this is one-sided."

"I—I don't know! I don't do love well."

"What's that supposed to mean?"

"It means I'm lousy at this." Her insides quivered as she dressed. How could she make him understand? "I make terrible decisions when I fall in love."

"How many times has this happened for you?"

"Too many."

"Great." He gave a self-deprecating laugh. "It's good to know I'm one of many."

"No. God!" She sat in the chair by the window and buried her face in her hands. "Actually, you're not. I've never had a relationship like this before."

"Like what?"

"Where I feel . . ." Happy, terrified, safe, out of control.

"What?"

"I don't know!" She glared at him. How could she tell him any of that, knowing he'd use every word against her to talk her into staying? "Why are we having this discussion? I'm leaving tomorrow. I have a plane ticket. I have my board certification exam scheduled in a few days and a job interview with St. James Hospital. I'm not going to change the plans of a lifetime over two weeks of great sex."

"That's all this was for you?" Temper blazed in his eyes. "Great sex?"

"I didn't mean that. I meant—" The hurt in his eyes frightened her. How could she hurt this wonderful man she loved so much. No, not loved. Cared for. She cared for him. It couldn't be love. She couldn't let it be love. "I don't know what I meant. Why are you doing this?"

"Because I want you to stay."

"Jesus. Alec, I told you . . . I have to go. I *have* to."

"No, you don't." His voice went deadly calm.

"Don't end things like this." She sent him a pleading look, her heart aching for both of them. "I had a great time with you. These have been three of the best weeks of my life. Let's not end it with a fight."

He gave her a level look. "How about we not end it at all?"

She stared right back. "How about you walk me home? If you want."

"No, I don't want!"

"Fine!" She stood. "We'll say good-bye here."

"That's not what I meant, and you know it." He rose and grabbed his clothes off the floor.

"You don't have to walk—" The look he sent her

was so sharp, she closed her mouth and waited for him to dress.

They made the walk to the condo in brittle silence. Alec fumed the whole way about a hundred little things, paramount among them was the way she closed off parts of herself and denied him access to her whole life. Her whole self. In fact, in the two weeks her family had been in Silver Mountain, she'd never once invited him inside her parents' condo, much less to have dinner with her family. That alone should have told him he didn't stand a chance with her. As much as she swore money and status didn't matter to her, he'd bet it mattered to them. And their opinion mattered to her.

When they entered the lobby, his anger swerved back to panic and hurt. This was it. The moment to say good-bye.

"I want you to call me when you get to Austin," he said as she punched the button for the elevator.

"I'm not sure that's a good idea." She didn't even look at him.

"I don't care." He took her arm and turned her to face him. "I want to know you arrived safely."

She searched his eyes a long time, then nodded. "All right. If you want, I'll call you."

"Yes." He cupped her face. "I want." Aching need tore through him as he covered her mouth and poured all his longing into a kiss.

When it ended, she wrapped her arms around him. "Okay," she said against his chest. The elevator dinged as the doors opened. She broke away and hurried inside, where she turned to face him with a tear-streaked face. "Good-bye, Alec Hunter."

The doors closed, leaving him staring at his own cloudy reflection in the brushed metal. He wondered why his image wasn't bleeding when his heart had just been ripped out. "Oh, yes, I definitely want."

Chapter 16

A little distance often brings things into focus.
—How to Have a Perfect Life

"Yo, Hunter here."

"Hello, Alec."

"*Chris?* Is that you? Hang on! Let me get where I can hear you. I thought you were going to call me when you got home. I've been worried out of my mind for two weeks."

"I know. I'm sorry. It's just I started thinking on the flight home that it might be easier for both of us if I didn't call. But then, I don't know, I guess I wanted to hear your voice."

"So how are you? Is everything all right?"

"I'm fine. To be honest, though, I'm still not sure this is a good idea."

"Don't you dare hang up. Fill me in on everything."

"I passed my certification exam."

"Of course you passed. I bet you kicked butt."

"I did actually."

"Does that mean . . . I guess you took the position at St. James."

"They offered me a very generous five-year contract."

"Five years? Yeah, um, well. That's great. Congratulations. I mean that. I'm happy for you. Really. I just—Never mind. Tell me about the job."

"I start next week. You should see their emergency ward. They have awesome equipment and enough staff to actually handle the patient load. I can't wait to get started."

"You know, I really am happy for you. I just . . . miss you."

"I miss you too. I—"

"Oh shoot, my radio just went off. I gotta go. I've got your number on my caller ID, though, so I'll call you back!"

"Chris, hey it's me."

"Hello, Alec, of course it's you. It's five o'clock Mountain Time, which means you're heading to the pub for a cup of joe. Time to call Christine."

"Am I getting that predictable?"

"A little. So what's shaking in your world today?"

"Jeff and Linda are having another baby. Oh and Brian is in *luuuuv*."

"Really? That's wonderful. On both counts. Although, try not to razz poor Brian too much."

"Yo, Doc, that's what guys do."

"You're right. What was I thinking?"

"So how about you? Did you have another wild and woolly day in the ER?"

"Well, let's see . . ."

"Hey, Chris. It's me again."

"Alec? You're calling awfully late."

"Yeah, see I was just lying here in bed, thinking about you."

"I've been thinking about you too."

"Good. That's good. Because I was going to ask . . . you ever had phone sex?"

"Alec! I swear, you're so outrageous sometimes. I never know when you're joking and when you're not."

"Then let me be very clear. I'm not joking."

"Oh my God! Have you ever done it before?"

"No."

"Well, me either!"

"Cool. That makes us both virgins. Let's see, how does this go? I think I'm supposed to ask what you're wearing."

"I can't do this. It feels too weird."

"I'm not wearing anything. Although, there is an impressive tent in the bed sheets. Are you in bed too?"

"Oh God. Give me a minute to stop laughing. And blushing."

"Blushing is good."

"Okay. Okay. Yes, I'm in bed."

"What are you wearing?"

"You know that red corset my little devil wears? What would you say if I told you I have an outfit just like it, and I'm wearing it right now. . . ."

"Hello, Dr. Ashton speaking."

"It's me."

"Alec! Where've you been? I haven't heard from you in three days. I've been worried sick."

"I was on a call. A bad one."

"Oh, Alec. I'm sorry. You want to talk about it?"

"Yeah . . ."

"Hmm, hello? God, what time is it?"

"Alec, it's me. I'm really sorry to call so late."

"Chris? What's wrong? You sound upset. Has something happened?"

"No. It's just, after we talked today, I started thinking. Actually, I've been thinking for a long time."

"I'm not going to like this, am I?"

"We have to stop doing this."

"Doing what? Are you crying?"

"We have to stop calling each other every day. This isn't healthy. We agreed when I left Silver Mountain that our relationship has no future—"

"Whoa, wait. You're the one who came up with that. I'm the one who wants you to move here."

"Which is why this isn't fair to you. We need to move on . . ."

"Alec?"

"I thought you weren't going to call anymore."

"Please don't be mad."

"I'm not mad. I'm confused."

"I know. I shouldn't have called . . ."

"Then why did you?"

"I had a really bad day, and I just—I needed to talk to you. Oh God!"

"Okay, deep breath, baby. It's all right. I'm here. Tell me what happened. Did you lose a patient?"

"Y-yes. A little girl. I've lost patients before, but children always get to me. Then my father saw me crying in the doctors' lounge and told me I needed to 'maintain professional distance,' and . . . and I don't know! I just needed to talk to you! I miss you!"

"Jesus. Chris, what are you doing to me?"

"I'm sorry. I shouldn't have called."

"No, it's okay. You need a friend, and I'm here for you. Tell me what happened."

Silver Mountain, Colorado
Early February

Alec turned his phone off and dropped his hand to his lap. Numbly, he stared at the flames dancing in the fireplace at St. Bernard's Pub. Outside, a blizzard raged, keeping skiers, and everyone else, trapped indoors.

"Yo, dude." Trent came into the pit, stomping snow from his boots. The place rang with voices and music as everyone did their best to make merry while off the slopes. Trent dropped into the chair next to Alec and plopped his feet on the hearth. "We're gonna have powder junkies out in droves when this stops blowing."

"Yeah," Alec answered sourly.

Trent frowned at him. "So what's up with you?"

Alec tossed his phone on the table between the two chairs, where it clattered and spun, then came to a stop. "Nothing, apparently."

"Don't tell me." Trent looked from the phone to him. "Chris called. Again."

"Actually, this time, I called her. To give her a friggin' weather report," he said with self-disgust.

"Jeez, Hunter." Trent rolled his eyes. "I thought you two broke up. Again."

"We did." Alec scrubbed his face and realized he'd forgotten to shave.

"I don't get you two." Sympathy and confusion lined Trent's face. "If you're 'moving on,' then move on. Stop calling each other."

"I don't think we can." Alec gave thanks that the noise in the bar was enough to keep them from being overheard, but not enough to keep them from talking. "It's like an addiction. It's killing me, and I know it's killing her too, but it's like we can't stop."

"Harvey!" Trent straightened enough to call to the bartender. "Bring a beer for Hunter here."

"No, coffee's fine." Alec scowled at the mug and realized his coffee had gone cold.

"Pal, you don't look like a man who needs coffee. You look like a man who needs to get drunk."

"Like that ever solved anything."

"Oh, so you have a better idea? Like actually doing something about your sorry love life? You know, if you two can't break up and stay that way, maybe you should stop trying."

"And do what?" Frustration joined despair. "Have a relationship over the phone?"

"How about find a way to be together?"

"I told you, her moving here isn't even an option since she signed a contract with that hospital."

"Then maybe you should move down there."

"Move away from the mountains and be miserable? Give up the job of *my* dreams?"

"Seems to me you're pretty miserable in the mountains. Besides, what was it Will said the night before he married Lacy and moved to Ohio? When it's for the right woman, it's not a sacrifice."

Alec felt a leftover shudder at the thought of Ohio. Yet here he was, faced with losing Christine or moving back to Texas—the place he'd sworn he'd never return to. "The deal is, search-and-rescue jobs don't exactly grow on trees. What if I give this up, move down there, and things with Chris don't work out?"

Trent cocked a brow. "And yet aren't you asking her to do exactly that for you?"

Alec scowled at the fire while the logs popped and sparks danced upward. Trent was right, damnit.

Austin, Texas
One week later

Christine pulled her silver Mercedes convertible to the curb before Maddy's old house and saw Amy's yellow Beetle sitting in the driveway. The pretty, two-story limestone house sat on a professionally maintained lawn in an upscale neighborhood west of Austin. The for-sale sign in the front yard had a new Sold banner attached to one corner. Next to it stood a sign announcing an estate sale that weekend. Maddy had flown in yesterday to pack up her things, sell off the furniture, and make her move to Santa Fe official.

The end of an era, Christine thought, looking at the house. How many years of laughter and tears had she shared with Maddy and Amy inside that house?

Maddy and her first husband, Nigel, had moved in shortly after their wedding. They'd planned on filling the rooms with children and growing old within those walls. Then Nigel had been diagnosed with cancer two years into their marriage and died five years after that.

Christine and Amy had been there for Maddy through all of that and now couldn't be happier that Maddy had found love a second time. Well, actually, they'd be happier if her getting married didn't involved moving away, but they had to admit that Joe Frazer put a huge smile on Maddy's face, and that was what mattered.

Too bad life hadn't handed her a similar happy ending with Alec.

She looked at her purse sitting in the passenger seat, with the all-too-silent phone inside. He hadn't called since the blizzard last week, and she refused to be the one to give in this time. Even though there was the urge to rub it in that here she was driving around with the top down, enjoying beautiful springlike weather while he was snowed in. Of course, he'd just say, "Are you kidding? This is great!"

But no, she wouldn't do it. She feared he'd add a suggestion that she buy a three-day ski package and come enjoy the snow with him. That thought terrified her, because she wasn't sure she had the strength to say no.

This had to stop. Prolonging the inevitable wasn't making the breakup easier. Especially now that they'd agreed to start seeing other people. Well, actually, she'd brought it up and Alec had gotten mad and hung up on her. When he'd called back the next day, neither of them had mentioned it, which was sort of an agreement.

What would she do, though, if she called him now and he told her he was dating someone?

Since the thought made her physically ill, she

grabbed her purse and headed up the walkway to the front door, needing the distraction of friends. Formal chimes sounded inside when she pushed the bell, followed by bare feet running on tile.

"Christine!" Maddy flung open the front door, a striking contrast to the house, the neighborhood, and even the doorbell with her wild red hair and saucy grin. Her generous curves filled out a pair of ratty jeans and crop-waist tie-dyed T-shirt. With a happy squeal, she pulled Christine into a hug. "It's so good to see you!"

"It's good to see you too." Christine squeezed back, realizing how much she missed her friend. E-mail and phone calls just weren't the same.

Grabbing her hand, Maddy pulled her inside. "Amy's already here."

"Yes, I saw her car in the driveway." Christine glanced around and noted the knickknacks covering the dining room table and price tags dangling from lampshades. "I see you've started without me."

"There's still plenty for you to do, believe me." Plopping her hands on her hips, Maddy considered the cluttered room. "How did Nigel and I acquire so much stuff?"

"By never throwing anything away?"

"That's me." Maddy laughed. "I'm sure getting rid of a bunch now, though."

"Are you really selling everything?"

"Well, not everything, but darn near. Time to start fresh. Joe will be here with the truck in a couple of days to pack up the few things I'm keeping."

"Which leaves you to deal with all of this on your own." Christine frowned.

"Actually, I insisted." Maddy looked around. "I wanted time by myself to say good-bye, if that makes sense."

"It makes perfect sense." Christine gave her another hug. "You holding up okay?"

"Mostly." Maddy smiled, but her eyes looked suspiciously wet.

"Hi, Christine." Amy appeared in the archway that led to the kitchen. Christine bit back a sigh at seeing the baggy Capri pants and oversized T-shirt. Amy had lost forty pounds over the last two years, yet still refused to show off her figure or wear her curly brown hair in anything but a long braid down her back. "You're just in time to help me price the dishes."

"Forget that," Maddy said. "I'm declaring it time for a break. Anyone up for margaritas by the pool?"

"Me!" Amy huffed out a breath and looked to Christine. "The woman is a slave driver."

Minutes later, they sat around the table on Maddy's covered patio, watching the sunlight sparkle off the swimming pool. The lawn company had kept up the grass and trimmed the hedges, but the flower beds no longer burst with vibrant color the way they had a year ago. Another sign of change, Christine thought, and how life was duller without Maddy around.

"I've forgotten how warm it is in Texas even in February," Maddy said, plucking at her T-shirt. "It seems so strange when we have snow on the mountains in New Mexico."

"Yes, I heard about the snowstorm that hit the

Rockies last week," Christine said, then went still, hoping her friends would assume she'd heard it on the news. They'd both scolded her for making the "wrong" decision with Alec, then ragged on her more for staying in touch with him, claiming she was torturing him as well as herself. Since they were right—about the second part at least—she'd stopped confiding in them, which was something she'd never done. The three of them shared everything. "So, um, how are the wedding plans coming?"

"Pretty good, now that Joe took over." Maddy sucked her margarita through a straw. "Can you believe he fired me as our wedding planner?"

"Maddy." Christine laughed. "You have trouble scheduling a hair appointment, so yes, I can believe it."

"I think it's sweet." Amy smiled. "And wonderfully romantic for him to be so eager."

"We'll see how romantic it is when the day arrives. A former Army Ranger planning a wedding?" Maddy made a horrified face. "I have visions of camouflage decorations and the minister barking out vows like a drill sergeant."

"When's the date?" Christine asked.

"The second Saturday in April, right here in Austin so my family can attend. If that works for the two of you to be my bridesmaids."

Christine and Amy looked at each other, then both nodded.

"Great." Maddy beamed. "I really wanted to go with that because it's the one-year mark for our bet."

"You're right." Christine turned to Amy. "And one of us hasn't met her challenge."

"Gee." Maddy also looked at Amy. "I wonder who that could be? Let's see. I got my artwork in a gallery."

"Big-time." Christine nodded.

"And you went skiing," Maddy added.

"I did."

"So who hasn't faced her fear of getting lost to take a trip on her own?" Maddy tapped her chin.

Amy smiled back at them, looking smug. "Before y'all get too righteous, I have an announcement."

"Oh?" Maddy cocked a brow.

A grin spread over Amy's face. "I'm going to the Caribbean!"

"Yea, you!" Christine gave her a high five. "When did this come about?"

"An older couple called just yesterday, looking for a nanny to take care of their grandchildren during a cruise. It's exactly the type of assignment I've been waiting for, so I'm taking it myself."

"Wait a minute." Maddy turned to Christine. "Didn't we decide that a cruise would be cheating, since it's hard to get lost on a ship?"

"We did," Christine agreed.

"But that's just it," Amy went on. "The couple doesn't like to leave the ship, so they want me to take the children to shore for the excursions." Panic widened her eyes. "I'll have to find my way around all the islands with children in tow."

"Hmmm." Christine looked at Maddy. "Sounds scary enough to me. What do you think?"

"As someone now living at a summer camp for girls, I say the children factor alone makes it terrifying."

"Except Amy adores children as much as they adore her."

"True," Maddy conceded. "Even so, I vote we allow it. How about you?"

"Works for me." Christine looked at Amy. "So when do you leave?"

"In one week." Amy looked suddenly horrified. "And I have so much to do! Like go shopping for a swimsuit." She pressed a hand to her breast. "What was I thinking to pick a cruise? I should have picked a trip to the mountains so I could wear bulky sweaters, not show off my fat, dimply thighs on a beach."

"Hey!" Maddy's brows snapped together. "You and I are practically the same size now."

"Except it looks different on you," Amy countered.

"It does not." Maddy struck a diva pose. "Sexy is all about attitude."

"Maddy's right." Christine laid a hand over Amy's forearm. "Besides, I'll take you shopping, and I promise we'll find a swimsuit and a cover-up you're comfortable wearing. Okay?"

"Thank you." Amy gave her a nervous smile. "You guys are the greatest. I don't know what I'd do without you."

"We love you too." Maddy squeezed Amy's other arm, then looked at Christine. "So that covers my wedding and Amy's challenge. How about you Christine? Have you found anyone to help you get over Alec?"

Christine bit her lip before she could stop herself.

"Chris-ti-ne." Maddy plopped her hands on her hips. "Don't tell me y'all are still calling each other."

"Not for a while. Honest."

"How long is 'a while'?" Maddy demanded.

"A whole week. Well, nearly. And he was the one who called me last."

"And you've spent every day since trying to think up a legitimate excuse to call him back." Maddy made a face. "I thought you both agreed to stop doing this."

"We did, but it's just hard, okay?" Loneliness stirred painfully in her chest. "We enjoy talking to each other. Is that really so bad?"

"It is if it keeps you from seeing other people," Maddy insisted.

Amy squeezed Christine's hand. "Isn't there any way you can be together?"

"Not unless he's willing to move back to Texas, which he isn't." The truth of that weighed down her shoulders. "Why do I have to be the one to move? Why can't it be him?"

Maddy gave her a scolding look. "Because there are hospitals in Colorado but no mountains down here."

"Great, take his side," Christine grumbled, even though she knew they were right. "The problem is, I signed a contract with St. James. I can't break it without hurting my professional reputation and putting my father in an awkward situation because he recommended me."

"I'm sorry," Maddy said.

Amy chewed her thumbnail, considering. "Could you visit each other, though? Until your contract is up, then move up there?"

"Fly back and forth for five years?" Christine

asked. "Even longtime married couples have trouble sustaining a relationship like that."

"I know." Sympathy lined Amy's face. "I just hate the thought of you finding this man who seemed so perfect for you, and you having to walk away because you live in two different states."

"I hate it too." The ache in Christine's chest grew. "I didn't realize how much I'd miss him, though. I knew him only three weeks. How can so much change in three weeks? I thought I'd come back here and get on with my life. I didn't have this empty spot inside me before. Why do I have it now?"

Maddy studied her. "What are you going to do?"

"I don't know!" She covered her face. "Stop calling him, I guess. And stop answering the phone when his number shows up on my caller ID." Her breath hitched at the thought.

"Oh, Christine." Maddy opened her arms, and Christine went eagerly into the hug. "I'm so sorry."

"Me too." Amy patted her back.

"Maddy?" Christine held tightly to her friend.

"Yes?"

"The emptiness does go away after a while, right?"

Maddy didn't answer.

Chapter 17

Dwelling on mistakes does no good.
—*How to Have a Perfect Life*

A few days later, Christine sat in one of the doctors' lounges, trying to concentrate on patient files. All she could think about, though, was Alec. The fact that it was Valentine's Day didn't help. Ten days had passed since his last phone call, making her wonder if things really were over. He couldn't possibly have been on a call for that long, could he?

She glanced at her watch and saw it was ten minutes to five in Silver Mountain. If he didn't call today, of all days, she'd have her answer. He wouldn't be calling anymore.

That would be for the best, though, wouldn't it? Maddy and Amy were right; they had to stop torturing each other. Yet the thought of never talking to him again made her feel as if someone were tearing her apart inside.

Maybe she should call him. If for no other reason than to say good-bye. Their last conversation had left things too open-ended. If things truly were over, they should say good-bye, shouldn't they?

She reached into the pocket of her white lab coat and brushed her fingers over her phone.

At the last instant, she grabbed the flashlight she'd started carrying like a talisman, a piece of Alec to hold near. Looking at it now didn't make her smile at the memory of the parade. Instead, the emptiness inside her expanded to an all-consuming ache. She could picture Alec so clearly in her mind, his quick grin and laughing eyes. The way he looked at her when they made love.

The look on his face when he'd pleaded with her to stay.

If she could go back in time, would she choose differently? She couldn't, though. She'd made her decision, and it couldn't be undone. Her eyes prickled with tears.

Lifting her arm, she shone the light back at herself. "Second star to the right and straight on till morning."

Someone knocked on the open door of the lounge.

"Dr. Ashton?" a nurse said.

She startled and schooled her features into a bland expression, praying her eyes weren't red. How embarrassing to be caught talking to herself and crying. "Yes?"

A smile spread slowly across the nurse's face. "There's someone in the waiting room asking to see you."

"Oh?" Something in the nurse's expression peaked her curiosity. "Who is it?"

"Come see." The nurse's smile grew even bigger.

Premonition tingled along the back of her neck as

she headed down the hall past examining rooms. Then she stepped through the double doors into the waiting room, and her heart stopped.

There stood Alec. He leaned against the admittance desk, flirting with the older woman behind it, making her giggle like a young girl. Elation rushed in, filling up all the empty spots inside her until she thought she'd burst. He looked tall and lean and wonderful in faded jeans and a dark blue "Ski Silver" T-shirt. Buddy sat obediently at his feet, wearing his red vest and looking official enough to get in anywhere.

Buddy saw her first and wiggled with glee.

Alec glanced down, then over at her. The world paused as their gazes collided and held. All she could think was *He's here. He's really here.*

Then a slow smile spread across his face, turning into one of his mischievous grins. Happiness clogged her throat, making her fear she would burst into tears.

When she simply stood there, staring, his smile faded. He ducked his head, looking sheepish as he picked up a bouquet of red roses from the counter. "Buddy reminded me Valentine's Day was coming up and he thought we should get you flowers."

Her first impulse was to rush forward, throw her arms around his neck, and cover his face with kisses. Remembering where she was, she stopped herself. A quick glance confirmed several staffers were watching the scene with wide grins.

How quickly would tales of such unprofessional behavior reach Ken Hutchens and the entire hospital board, including her father?

She tucked her hands into the pockets of her lab coat so no one could see them shaking. "Alec." Her voice sounded oddly flat. "This is . . . quite a surprise. Why don't you come back to the lounge and I'll get you a cup of coffee?"

Conscious of every eye following her, she turned and headed back through the swinging double doors.

Alec's stomach dropped at Christine's emotionless reaction. Numbly he followed her down a wide, brightly lit hall with Buddy at his side. He'd spent the entire three-day drive down here wondering if he was making a mistake. Well, now he had his answer.

Huge mistake.

Colossal, idiotic, embarrassing mistake.

At least maybe this would finally end things and let him get over this woman. Jesus, though. A knife to the chest would hurt less than this. The fact that she looked sexy as hell in green scrubs and a lab coat added an extra twist to the blade.

Christine stopped at a door marked Doctors' Lounge. He heard male voices inside. After a quick glance around, she headed toward a different door.

"In here." She opened the door for him and looked up and down the hall before following him and Buddy into an examining room.

"Look," he started before she could light into him for showing up at her workplace. "I guess I should have—"

"Ohmygod!" She launched herself against his chest, her arms going about his neck. He staggered back but managed to catch his balance before he fell. "Alec, Alec, Alec." Kisses rained over his face. "I can't believe—you're here. You're—really—here."

She took his face in both her hands and kissed him more deeply.

His arms went around her as her tongue came into his mouth. Too startled to think, he had the hand holding the roses against her back and the other holding her raised thigh against his hip before his brain caught up with his body. Lifting his head, he stared down at her glowing face.

"Hmm." He cleared his throat. "I take it you're happy to see me."

She planted a hand on the back of his head and pulled him down for a long ravenous kiss. His body responded eagerly as he pressed his instant arousal into the juncture between her thighs. She moved against him, her greedy hands sweeping up under his T-shirt, stroking his heated skin.

A desperate idea involving the exam table sprang to mind just as Buddy whimpered and pawed his leg, trying to squeeze between them so he could greet Chris. Alec tried to nudge him away while nibbling along her neck. "Get your own girl, pal. This one's mine."

Buddy whimpered louder, and Christine started to laugh. Voices sounded out in the hall, along with footsteps passing the door.

"Wait. Stop." She pulled back enough to look at him even though her leg remained twined around his hip. "Buddy's right."

"Buddy's neutered. What does he know?"

She pressed a hand against his chest, leaning back to evade his lips—which put them in dance's dip with her back nearly parallel to the floor. "He has more sense than us at the moment."

He smiled down at her, relishing the feel of her in his arms. "I've missed you."

"I've missed you too." Her eyes smiled up at him. "And don't you dare drop me."

"You mean like this?"

She shrieked as he pretended to let go, then snatched her back against him.

"I'd never drop you." He straightened, releasing her leg so it slid slowly down along his. "Let's go somewhere and get naked."

"I get off duty in an hour." Flushed and breathless, she smoothed her hair.

"An eternity." He presented her with the flowers. "Buddy insisted on roses. He's a traditional kind of guy."

"Thank you." Her expression turned mushy as she buried her nose in the red blossoms.

He wiggled his brows. "Wanna lock the door and play doctor?"

"Tempting." She grinned up at him through her lashes. "But I have work to do."

"Spoilsport."

She shook her head, staring at him in wonder. "I can't believe you're here. Why didn't you tell me you were coming?"

"Because if I had, you'd have given me the whole speech about how our relationship has no future and we need to end things once and for all."

"Probably. So where are you staying? How long will you be here?"

"I don't know, and I don't know. That depends on you."

"Oh?"

"I could get a hotel room near your apartment."

"Or . . . you could stay with me."

"I was hoping you'd say that." He pulled her into his arms.

"You'll wind up sleeping at my place anyway, so why waste time and money?"

"I love a practical woman."

"Opposites attract." She rubbed her nose against his.

"Hey!" He mocked offense. "I resemble that remark."

She gave him a quick, laughing kiss. "Let me get my purse from my locker and give you my key. You can settle in and I'll see you when I get home." She started to step away, then hugged him instead. "I'm glad you came. This is probably a terrible idea, but I don't care. I'm so happy to see you."

Christine thought the last hour of her shift would never end. When it did, she raced home through the gathering dusk. Singing along with the radio, she turned onto the steep road to her hilltop apartment complex on the northwest side of town.

A ridiculously battered Jeep sat in her parking slot. She wondered if he'd borrowed it, or bought it for the trip, since he couldn't very well drive the county vehicle. Although, for all she knew, he'd already owned the ugly thing. Smiling, she parked behind it, then hurried down the breezeway to her front door. The city lights sparkled in the distance as day gave way to night.

Finding the door locked, she gave it a rap. "Alec? Let me in. You have my key."

He opened the door with a playful grin and spoke

in a falsetto. "Hi, honey. Welcome home. How was your day?"

"Who are you? Lucy?"

"No." He scowled. "Laura Petrie. You know, the *Dick Van Dyke Show*?"

"Dang." She gave him a smacking kiss. "Now I can't say, 'Oh, Loo-cy, I'm ho-me.'" Bending over, she ruffled Buddy's ears. "This is much better than coming home to an empty apart—" She stopped abruptly when she saw the main room of her small two-bedroom apartment.

An ice bucket sat on the coffee table in the living area flanked by two lit candles. Beyond that, the small dining table in front of the sliding-glass doors to her balcony had been set with a tablecloth, more candles, and the roses he'd brought, which she'd asked him to put in water for her.

"Oh, Alec." She moved over to admire the flowers. "You've been busy."

"I hope you don't mind me snooping around your kitchen."

"Not at all." She noticed he'd also changed into a white dress shirt even though he still wore his jeans, and his face looked freshly shaved. The scent of something cooking drifted from the kitchen, which opened on to the main room with a granite-top breakfast bar. "Are you cooking?"

"I'm not sure I'd call it cooking. I stopped by the market and got a rotisserie chicken, Caesar salad in a bag, a jar of Alfredo sauce to pour over pasta, and chocolate-covered strawberries for dessert." He lifted a bottle of champagne from the ice bucket. "And since it's Valentine's, I also got this."

Her eyes widened. "Boy, you really know how to spoil a girl."

"I see you're onto my nefarious plan." He wiggled his brows. "Shall I go ahead and pop this so we can have a glass before dinner?"

"Let me change first. If we're going to have a Valentine's dinner, I'd like to enjoy it in something nicer than scrubs."

"Need any help?" he asked eagerly.

Laughing, she gave him a quick kiss. "How about I let you help me undress later?"

"You are so on."

Ducking into the bedroom, she noted the suitcase sitting in the corner and smiled again, as she'd been smiling for the past hour, at the idea that Alec had driven all the way from Silver Mountain to see her. She slipped into a short black tank dress, fastened on pearl earrings and a diamond drop necklace, freshened her makeup, but left her feet and legs bare.

When she emerged from the bedroom, she found Alec sitting on the sofa, staring out the sliding-glass door. A rare frown wrinkled his brow, as if he wrestled with a mental dilemma. Her heart swelled at the mere sight of him. "I can't believe you're really here."

He turned at the sound of her voice, and the frown instantly vanished. His gaze roamed down and back up as he rose from the sofa. "Wow, you look great."

"Thanks." A warm thrill went through her at the gleam of desire in his eyes. "Do I get that glass of champagne now?"

"You bet." They both stood as he removed the foil

and untwisted the wire cage. The cork popped out on its own, startling a laugh from both of them.

She dove for the glasses as champagne bubbled out. "Here, quick, pour."

"Got it." He managed to fill the tall Waterford flutes with remarkably little spillage. "See, all those years of opening sodas at high altitude pay off."

"Should we make a toast?"

He looked steadily into her eyes. "To following your heart, not your head?"

She touched her glass to his. "If that's what brought you here, I'll drink to it. Mmm, very nice. I love champagne. Nearly as much as I love a good cold beer."

He chuckled as they took a seat on the sofa. She let him pull her feet into his lap and nearly melted in pleasure when he started massaging them. "Oh, man, you really are trying to spoil me."

"Just getting you mellow before I tell you my news."

"News?" She tipped her head, noticing his frown was back.

"Drink a little more wine first." He nudged the glass toward her mouth.

"I hope it's not bad news." She sipped.

"I hope not either." He studied her so hard, her stomach tightened.

"You're starting to scare me a little."

"I'm scaring myself a little too." The line between his brows deepened. "I was going to wait until after dinner, but the suspense is killing me, so I'm just going to go ahead and tell you now." He took a deep

breath. "You know the day of the parade when we
both said the end of Peter Pan was bunk? That a
better ending would be for Peter to grow up and live
with Wendy in the real world?"

"Yes." Her body started to shake as hope blossomed inside her.

"Well . . . what would you say to me moving back
to Texas?"

"Are you serious?" Happiness squeezed her
throat, making the words hard to force out. "You'd
give up search and rescue?"

"Hopefully not. I'm on two weeks of vacation right
now. So with driving time, that gives me eight days
to look for a job down here. I'm hoping one of the
counties around Austin has a paid position open. It
won't be alpine search and rescue, but it'll be close
enough."

"Yes, but the mountains. Skiing. Snow. Your
friends. You love living in Silver Mountain."

His gaze held hers. "I love you more."

"Oh my God. I can't think." Her mind whirled
with the realization that for once life was handing
her what she wanted without a huge price tag. She
could have everything she wanted and give up nothing. Her breath hitched as she tried to take it all in.
"I can't—I can't—believe—this."

"Hey." Concern lined his face as he took the glass
from her. "Here, lean forward." He moved her feet
to the floor and urged her to put her head between
her knees. "Are you okay?" His hand rubbed circles
on her back. "I thought you'd like the idea"

"I do!" Tears filled her eyes as she laughed and
cried at the same time. "I love the idea!"

"Take a deep breath." He massaged her neck.

"I'm okay." She sat up and smiled at him. "Oh, Alec . . . are you sure about this? That's a lot to give up just so we can date."

"Ah, well, here's the catch." His words made her freeze in fear. "I don't want to date you."

"Y-you what?"

He smiled slowly. "I want to marry you."

"Oh my God!"

He frowned. "I hope that's a good 'oh my God.' "

"It's a very good 'oh my God.' I can't believe this." She squeezed his hand. "Are you really, really sure?"

"About wanting to marry you? Absolutely sure."

"But you're giving up so much. What if it doesn't work out? What if I'm not enough to make you happy? What if you come to resent me?"

"Stop." He placed a hand over her mouth, and she realized he was laughing. "It's going to work out, because I love you. And even though you've never said it, I know you love me too." Doubt flicked through the amusement. "You do, don't you?"

She sagged as he lifted his hand. "Oh, Alec. Yes, I love you."

"Thank goodness." This time, he covered her mouth with his. She wound her arms about his neck and kissed him back with all the wonder and happiness filling her to overflowing. When he lifted his head, she saw all those emotions shining in his eyes. "Then it's settled," he said. "Now all you have to do is say yes."

"But what if—"

He cut off his words with another kiss, this one brief. "That wasn't yes."

"But—"

He kissed her again, then gave her a stern look. "You're supposed to say yes. Now let's try it again." He held her hand against his heart. "Christine, will you marry me?"

She smiled into his eyes. "Yes, Alec, I would love to marry you."

"Thank God." He pulled her to him for a very long kiss.

Chapter 18

Once you set a goal, stay true to your course.
—*How to Have a Perfect Life*

"I can't believe how nervous I am," Christine said as she turned into the insanely crowded parking lot for the Tex-Mex restaurant near Zilker Park.

"Well, I wish you'd cut it out, because you're making me even more nervous." Alec stared at her in the darkness of the car. "I mean, jeez, at least you know these people. I'm the one who has to pass the Friend Test."

"You're right. I'm sorry." She tried to reassure him as she circled around to the front. As usual, Chuy's appeared to be packed, but this was where Amy had wanted to go for her send-off party before she left for her cruise. "I'll try to calm down."

"Do you mind if I ask why you're so nervous?" Alec shifted in the passenger seat to face her as she snagged a rare space near the front door. "If there's a serious chance they're not going to like me and you're going to call off the engagement based on their opinion, I'd like to know."

"Of course they'll like you, Alec. Everyone likes you. It's just—" Turning off the car, she faced him.

The colored lights strung along the front of the old-house-turned-restaurant revealed the worry wrinkling his brow. "Okay, not to make you even more nervous, but you know I've always had really poor judgment where men are concerned. That's made my friends extra critical."

"Great." He exhaled in a rush. "I always enjoy a little anxiety with my dinner. It aids the digestion so nicely."

"It'll be okay, though. They're going to love you. They will."

Alec tried not to panic as he followed Christine into the restaurant. He remembered the place from his high school days and was glad to see they still had the Elvis shrine at the front door. Inside was an explosion of clashing colors, music from the jukebox, and voices from the press of people waiting at the bar for a table.

Christine waved at three people seated on the far side of the bar. They headed that way, passing beneath hundreds of wildly painted wooden fish hanging from the ceiling.

"Sorry we're late." Christine hugged a redhead sitting on a stool. "I had trouble getting away from the hospital, and the parking lot's a zoo, as always."

"Not a problem." The redhead eyed him with a smile. "I assume this is Alec."

"Yes." Christine slipped her arm about his waist, drawing him close enough that the group could talk over the noise. "Alec, my college roommates, Maddy Mills and Amy Baker."

Maddy, the redhead, offered a friendly finger

wave, while Amy, a plump but pretty brunette, gave him a shy smile.

"And this is Maddy's fiancé, Joe Frazer." Christine gestured to a formidable-looking man with jet-black hair, deeply tanned skin, and the rock-solid body of a Special Forces soldier.

"Pleased to meet you." Alec shook hands with Joe, then eyed the two women warily. "I think it best to tell you up-front, I'm absolutely terrified."

Maddy laughed while Joe excused himself to tell the hostess their party was complete. They were seated a short time later in the intentionally tacky dining area. On the wall opposite a painting of Elvis on black velvet hung the quarter panels of three vintage Chevys.

"Well, Amy," Maddy asked after they'd placed their orders, "are you nervous or excited about leaving tomorrow?"

"Both." Amy laughed. "I'm all packed and ready to go, though, so I guess there's no turning back."

"Then we'll wish you bon voyage." Maddy lifted her margarita and they all followed suit and drank. Then she lifted her glass toward Christine. "And a second toast to Christine and Alec on their engagement."

Alec breathed a small sigh of relief at that. A toast had to be a good sign. He hoped. His sigh came a bit soon, though, he realized, as Maddy and Amy started grilling him about growing up in Elgin and his work with search and rescue. He barely tasted his food as he answered every question.

Finally, in a desperate attempt to get the heat off

of him, Alec turned to Joe. "Tell me about this civilian boot camp of yours."

"Oh no." Maddy rolled her eyes. "That will keep Joe talking for hours. I think I'll go to the ladies' room. Christine?"

"Yes, I need to go too." Christine scrambled out of the booth.

"Me too." Amy rose as well and the three women hurried off.

When they disappeared around a corner, Alec slumped in his seat. "Oh crap. There goes the jury." His heart beat painfully as he eyed the man across from him. "How long do you think they'll deliberate before coming back with a verdict?"

"Not long." Joe dredged a chip through salsa. "And relax. You passed."

"Really?" Alec straightened. "How do you know?"

"Maddy wiggled her brows and smiled at me about ten minutes ago. You're in."

"Jesus." Alec pressed the heel of his hand to his heart to slow it down. "I hope you're right. They're really tight, aren't they?"

"Yeah, they are, which has given me an idea. Did Christine mention that I'm handling all the plans for our wedding?"

"She did. Which has me wondering if you're incredibly brave or totally insane."

"Sometimes a man has to take things into his own hands if he wants action." Joe's expression was every inch the tough Army Ranger. "And since the women are off having their powwow I'll run my idea by you first. I'd like to ask Maddy what she and Christine would think about a double wedding. They may hate the idea, since women are completely unpredictable on these issues, but I thought it would be worth bringing up."

"What's the date?"

"Second weekend in April, here in Austin, since Maddy's family lives here."

"Works for me. Actually, anything that gets Christine to the altar before she changes her mind works for me."

"Okay, then we'll ask them when they come back."

"Assuming Amy and your fiancée aren't telling my fiancée to ditch me right now."

"I'm telling you, you're in."

"Well?" Christine asked the instant the restroom door closed behind them.

"Oh, Christine!" Maddy pulled her into a hug. "He's wonderful!"

"Really?"

"Yes!" Maddy stepped back so Amy could hug her too.

"He's absolutely perfect for you," Amy proclaimed.

"Oh, thank God." Closing her eyes, she tightened her arms around her friend. "I was so scared you wouldn't approve. Like him, yes, everyone likes Alec, but I worried you would think he wasn't right for me. He's younger, he comes from a really different background, and he's so . . ." She tried to think of the right words and couldn't. "So Alec!"

Maddy tipped her head. "Actually, I thought he was quite reserved compared to what you've told us."

"Only because you two had him sweating bullets."
Christine laughed. "I kept expecting one of you to
break out a bare lightbulb."

"We weren't that bad." Maddy laughed.

Christine rolled her eyes.

"Has your family met him yet?" Amy asked with
a worried frown.

"No." That let some of the air out of her elation.
"Well, they sort of met him in Colorado, but I
haven't told them we're engaged."

Maddy frowned at her. "You've been engaged two
days and you haven't told your family."

"To be honest"—she took both their hands—"I
wanted to see what you thought first and get some
advice on how to handle it. I'm really worried they
won't approve. At least not at first."

Maddy snorted. "I can promise you they won't
approve—at all. I think you need to trust your heart
on this one, though, and go for it. Don't let your
family ruin this for you, because they're going to
try."

"I don't know if I'd go that far."

Maddy gave her a "get real" look.

"Okay, so what do I do?" Christine asked. "How
do I get them to approve?"

"You don't," Maddy answered. "You ignore
them."

"I can't do that."

Amy squeezed her hand. "Do you want my
advice?"

"Are you kidding?" Christine laughed. Amy always had wise insights on everything, as if she were

an old soul who had wisdom beyond this lifetime. "I'd love your advice."

"Okay, here goes." Amy turned so serious, she looked almost stern. "The very things that make Alec perfect for you, his youthful attitude and lack of polish, are the things that are going to drive you crazy at times. Don't let them, Christine. Don't obsess over little things and pick fights over nothing just because you're wound up and worried over what your family thinks. If you love him, love him just the way he is. The way he loves you just the way you are."

"You really think he loves me?" Her heart fluttered at the words. "I mean, he certainly seems to, and he says he does."

"Oh, honey." Amy smiled at her. "That man lights up every time he looks at you."

"But I didn't do anything to make him love me."

Maddy laughed. "If Mama Frazer were here, she'd tell you love doesn't have to be earned. It either is or it isn't. And it doesn't come with a list of conditions that say 'I'll only love you if . . .' "

"What scares me most, though, is all the things he's sacrificing to be with me," Christine admitted. "I keep waiting for him to look at me and think, 'Am I crazy? I'm giving up everything for *her*?' "

Maddy plopped her fists on her hips in disgust. "Okay, that right there deserves about an hour-long lecture. We don't have time, though, so I'll leave it to Alec to explain why you're worth any sacrifice. For now, let's get back to the table, before your fiancé has a nervous breakdown wondering what we're saying about him."

When they returned to the table, she saw Alec and Joe talking. The mere sight of him set off a warm glow inside her. Then he looked up, saw her smiling at him, and he visibly relaxed. The worry was still there, the questioning look in his eyes, but as Maddy had said, he lit up at the sight of her.

"Hi," she said as she slid back into the booth beside him. What had she done to deserve this wonderful man who so clearly loved her?

"Hi." He smiled back at her.

Across the table Joe turned to Maddy. "Alec and I were just talking about the wedding."

"You were?" Maddy looked baffled by the thought of two men sitting around discussing wedding plans.

"Yep." Joe nodded. "And we have an idea to toss out. If you hate it, no problem."

"Okay . . ." Maddy looked wary. "What's your idea?"

"What would you two think about a double wedding?"

"A double wedding?" Maddy tipped her head, then brightened. "I think that's a fabulous idea! Christine?"

Christine tried to absorb it. She'd only agreed to marry Alec a couple of days ago, and now they were talking actual plans. "I—I don't know." She looked at Maddy. "You wouldn't feel like I was horning in on your special day?"

"Actually," Maddy said, "I'd feel like you were sharing it. What about you?"

"Yes, I suppose. Can I think about it?"

"Of course," Maddy assured.

Joe snorted. "You two women think about it all you want. Alec and I will get started planning it."

Maddy rolled her eyes, laughing. "Never get between Joe and a plan."

"Well, one hurtle down." Alec sighed in relief as they climbed into Christine's car to leave the restaurant. "Two more to go."

"Two more?"

"You meeting my family, and me meeting yours."

"Oh, yes." Her stomach tensed as she tried to imagine how her family would react to Alec. Surely they wouldn't be as disapproving as Maddy feared.

Alec seemed equally thoughtful as she drove through Zilker Park toward the highway. "I don't suppose we could skip over that first one."

"Hmm?" She glanced at him in the dark. "You think your family won't like me?"

"I have no idea what they'll think, and frankly I don't care. I'm much more worried about what you'll think of them."

"Oh, come on, Alec." She managed a teasing smile. "Do you think I'm such a snob that I'll break up with you because your family is . . ."

"Poor white trash?"

"Culturally challenged."

He laughed. "They have a politically correct term for everything these days."

She glanced over again and saw the worry in his eyes. "Are you really that ashamed of them?"

"In a word?" He arched his brow. "Hell yes!"

"That's two words, and I thought you didn't cuss."

"I stand corrected, and I was showing my roots."

"Hey, I cuss."

"When you do it, it's a funny quirk of character. When they do it, it's a basic form of communication."

"You know, if you're serious about us getting married, I'll have to meet them eventually. Wouldn't it be better to find out how I'll react now?"

"Good point." He let out a loud sigh. "I'll call Mom and tell her to expect us for lunch on Saturday. I assume you like barbecue."

"I love barbecue."

Chapter 19

There are no easy roads in life.
—*How to Have a Perfect Life*

"Okay, Buddy, go boy!" Alec removed the leash and watched Buddy take off across the open field behind his parents' mobile home. The dog bounded over tall weeds and zipped around a rusted-out car on cinder blocks before heading toward the creek that ran along the back of the five acres. His happy barks filled the air. "Well, at least one of us is having fun."

"He does love to run," Christine said, laughing as Buddy made a wide circle, his golden coat rippling in the sunlight.

Following at a slower pace, Alec sent Christine a sideways glance, trying to read her expression. Her face held nothing but pleasure as she watched Buddy's antics. "You know, it's okay if you say it."

"Say what?" She gave him a puzzled look.

Alec glanced over his shoulder at his parents' trailer house with its sagging porch and rusty streaks running down metal sides that he believed had been white once upon a time. "That they're every bit as bad as you imagined. Worse, probably."

The day had been a giant flashback to all the reasons he'd wanted to escape this place. He rolled his shoulders in a vain attempt to loosen the knotted muscles.

"Actually"—she slipped her hand into his as they walked—"they're not as bad as you described them. And you forgot to mention your brother and sister were *so* good looking. My goodness!" She glanced back at the mobile home, her eyes wide. "Your brother could charm the pants off a woman at twenty paces with that smile of his."

He laughed a bit at that and thickened his Texas accent. "Yep, that's one thing you sure can say about them Hunters. They may be as useless as tits on a boar hog, but they know how to breed some good-lookin' kids."

"Stop that." She gave him a playful swat.

"It's true," he insisted. "You saw my sister's three kids."

"They are beautiful," Christine said.

He rolled his eyes when she tactfully left off that they were also undisciplined brats who'd screamed all through lunch. Of course his sister screamed back, which did no good because she never followed through on any of her ridiculous threats.

Watching Christine and his sister seated at the same table in the cramped and cluttered dining room had brought the contrast between them into sharp relief. Both were tall, blond, and beautiful, but his sister was strident, crude, bigoted, and vain.

The fact that Christine had been gracious to every-one since they arrived made him realize her physical beauty wasn't what pulled him nearly as much as who she was: a woman of intelligence, tolerance, and refinement, with a wicked wit that constantly surprised and delighted him. Then there were those glimpses of self-doubt that went straight to his heart. How could he not love this woman?

"Didn't you tell me your brother also has children?"

"Oh yeah." He snorted. "From the pictures Mom sends me, I can attest that Dwight's kids are five of the best-looking brats you've ever seen. And probably every bit as obnoxious as Carla's."

"Five?" That stopped her. Standing in the sun-drenched field, she faced him.

"And two ex-wives," he added. "Kids two and three are only six months apart."

"Oops." She raised her brow.

"Yeah." He shook his head in disgust. " 'Not his fault,' of course. When a man has women throwing themselves at him every time he walks into a bar, 'what's he supposed to do?' "

She tapped a finger to her lips. "This is just a suggestion, but he might try not going to bars when he has a pregnant wife and a child at home."

"Ya think?" he asked dryly.

Buddy zoomed back to them, barking for them to keep moving. Obliging, they continued to the cool shade of the trees that grew along the lazy, muddy creek. Alec scowled as he looked about. "This used to be my favorite place to hang out when I was a kid. I remember it as being a lot prettier, though."

"You've been living in the mountains for eleven years. That's bound to dim a lot of places by comparison."

"True." He watched Buddy wade into the water

and put the word "bath" on the evening's agenda. "Plus, I picked up the trash that gathers along the banks after every rain. Clearly, no one's bothered with that task since I left."

Looking back toward the trailer, he felt irritation mount. "But why am I even surprised? If Dad can't get off his lazy rear end long enough to fix the leak in the roof, why would he bother cleaning up trash? Oh, excuse me. Dad's not lazy. He has a 'bad back.' That's why he hasn't worked a real construction job in twenty years. Jeez, though, my brother's in construction. Why can't he find an afternoon to fix the stupid roof?"

"The cobbler's wife has no shoes?" Christine ventured.

"Dang it." He looked at the porch with the same moldy sofa that had been sitting there for as long as he could remember. It had permanent dents in the cushion from years of conforming to people's backsides while they sat drinking beer and watching cars pass on the highway. "I guess once I get moved down here I'll have to come out and fix a few things myself. For Mom. If it were just Dad, I'd let him lay in bed and get rained on, but as hard as Mom works at the diner, she deserves to come home to a house that doesn't leak."

Christine tipped her head, studying him. "You seem closest to her."

He shrugged and rested his back against an oak tree. "She's the only one who didn't make fun of me when I started studying hard and doing well in school."

"When was that?" Christine stepped between his

boots and looped her arms about his neck, eager to learn more about him. How had he turned out so different from his siblings?

"When I was twelve, I discovered search and rescue, and everything changed for me." He circled his arms about her hips. "We had a tornado rip through here. You can probably still make out its path if you walk up in those trees."

"It came that close?" She twisted her head to look in the direction he nodded. "That must have been terrifying."

"Especially living in a mobile home. I swear the things are tornado magnets." Buddy came and flopped down beside them, panting from his run. "The twister missed us, but tore apart several houses not far from here. Killed eight of our neighbors and left several families homeless."

"Oh, Alec. That must have been tough."

"It was. For the whole community." He widened his stance to settle her more fully against him. "That's the only time I think I've ever been really proud of my dad. He and Dwight worked a lot of volunteer hours rebuilding homes. They also ridiculed me to no end for not helping."

"You didn't help?" She frowned. "That doesn't sound like you."

"I didn't help with the construction," he clarified. "At least not at first. The day after the storm, a search-and-rescue team arrived with FEMA to look for bodies. I knew some of the people who were missing. In a community this size, how could you not? So when the coordinator asked for volunteers, I jumped at the chance, thinking . . . I don't know, that I'd be helping, yes, but also that it would be exciting. Boy was I wrong there."

"Oh?"

He cocked a brow. "Have you ever watched a team search a wooded area?"

"The only search I've seen was the day of the avalanche."

"Well, it's similar on flat land, but not as physically grueling. You line up, no more than an arm's length apart, and walk very slowly, staring at the ground right in front of your feet the whole time. The sheer tedium is enough to bore most people to tears. We did that for days." He stretched the last word out. "To my dad's way of thinking, here he and my brother were doing real men's work, while his youngest boy was off walking around in the woods like some pantywaist sissy."

Christine felt a twist of empathy on Alec's behalf. She knew how much a put down from a father could hurt. "What'd you do?"

"Ignored him." Alec shrugged. "At the end of the day, though, who do you think I was going to hang out with? My dad and his foul-talking drinking buddies? Or this fascinating group of men and women who were like . . . aliens to my world?"

Christine tried to picture a young Alec meeting search-and-rescue volunteers for the first time. Most of the ones she'd met were extremely dedicated and well trained at what they did. They came from all walks of life, frequently had college educations and white-collar jobs. They made tremendous sacrifices and took personal risks to help people in trouble.

She'd come to admire them greatly working in ER. "My guess is the search-and-rescue guys."

"I could listen to their stories for hours," Alec said. "That search might have been boring, but clearly some were very exciting. Plus, every call is important, so there's that sense of doing something that matters. I decided then and there that that's what I was going to do. That's what I was going to be.

"Even after the team left and I was driving nails with the rest of the construction workers, I knew the whole course of my life had changed. Search and rescue was an escape route from this dead-end way of life. I worked my butt off to make it happen."

"You know what?" She felt her heart expand as she fell in love with him all over again. Framing his face in both her hands, she kissed him briefly on the lips. "You impress the heck out of me. You already did when we were in Colorado and I saw you in action. But to know that this is where you started, now I'm really impressed."

"Thanks." He hugged her.

"And you thought meeting your family would drive me away." She rested her head on his shoulder, enjoying the intimacy of the simple embrace.

"Do you blame me?" His hand rubbed up and down on her back.

"No. Because the shoe's about to be on the other foot."

"Oh?"

She lifted her head as restlessness replaced peace in the blink of an eye. "Mom's pressuring me to bring you to dinner tomorrow evening."

"I'm up for it."

"I know." She stepped back, out of his arms. "I was just hoping to have you to myself a little longer." And hoping he would have a new job before she introduced him to her family. She studied the slow-moving water. "Are you still planning to head back for Silver Mountain on Tuesday?"

"Weekends are always prime time for accidents in the backcountry, so I didn't want to be gone for more than one. If I leave Tuesday, I'll be back at work Friday. Plus, I have a lot of stuff to settle. Like turning in my resignation."

"Oh?" She glanced back to him. "I thought you were going to wait until you had a new position nailed down."

"Yeah, well . . . Hmm."

She tipped her head. "What are you not telling me?"

"I was going to wait until later, when we were back at your place, but I had an interview yesterday."

"You did?" She brightened, then noticed he wasn't smiling. "What is it? Why aren't you excited?"

"Mostly because I've been in denial." He sighed heavily. "Oh man, this is going to be even harder after everything I just said."

"What?"

He let out a heavy sigh. "The job isn't with search and rescue. There flat aren't any paid positions open within reasonable driving distance, and no one expects that to change anytime in the near future."

"Than who was the interview with?"

"The Austin Fire Department. They offered me a

job as a paramedic. And . . ." He took a deep breath, as if bracing himself. "On Monday, I'm going to accept."

"Alec . . . no. With a schedule like that, you'll barely be able to do search and rescue as a volunteer, if at all."

He came off the tree trunk, his jaw tight as he paced the bank. "What else am I going to do? Work some flunky job and do search and rescue on the side? That was fine when I was twenty, but I'm about to turn thirty, and I'm getting married. I owe it to you to be a professional and pull my weight."

"Alec, with what I make you don't have to work—"

"Don't!" His face went instantly hard. "Don't even say that. First, I'm not my dad."

"I'm sorry. I didn't mean to imply—"

"And second, isn't that exactly the kind of thing your past boyfriends have tried to do to you? How would I be any better than them if I mooched off of you."

"None of them ever wanted to marry me."

"I fail to see the difference." His eyes blazed, letting her know she truly had insulted him. "Besides, I enjoy working, and I'm actually okay with the paramedic job. Really."

"Really?"

He subsided. "Mostly."

"Then why do you look so unhappy about it?"

"Because . . . I just— Oh man!" To her surprise, he turned his back to her. Sensing something was wrong, Buddy let out a questioning whine.

"Alec?" She laid a hand on his back and felt the tension bunching his muscles. Concern raced through her. "What is it?"

"It's going to kill me to give up Buddy."

"What!" She hurried around so she could face him. Hearing his name, Buddy sat up, looking back and forth between the humans. "Why would you have to give up Buddy?"

"He's not a pet, Chris. He doesn't even belong to me." Looking down at the dog, Alec's eyes grew damp. "He's a trained rescue dog who belongs to the county. If I'd landed a paid position down here, I probably could have talked my new county manager into buying him so I could still be his handler, but if I take the paramedic job, I'll have to turn him over to whoever replaces me in Silver Mountain. There's no way I could afford to buy a dog worth thirty thousand dollars."

She blinked at the figure he named. Even knowing rescue dogs were valuable, she hadn't known they cost that much. "I'll buy him for you."

"God, do you know how tempting that is?" He laughed dryly. "But no. Absolutely not. And not because of the money, but because it would be wrong. Just because I'm giving up search and rescue is no reason for the world to lose a great rescue dog who can save lives. Plus, it wouldn't be fair to Buddy." When the dog whined, Alec squatted down and ruffled his ears. "I can't ask this guy to give up something he loves."

"What about you?" She watched them together, feeling as if someone had just reached inside her chest and pulled her heart out. How much more was Alec hurting? "How is any of this fair to you?"

"Because I'm doing it by choice." Looking up, he gave her a sad smile. "And I get you to compensate."

"Alec, I don't know about this." She wrapped her arms about her middle. "It's asking you to sacrifice too much. First you have to move away from the mountains. Now you have to give up Buddy? How long before you resent me for it?"

"What is the alternative?" He rose and cupped her face in one hand. "Not get married?"

"It just . . . doesn't seem fair." Dangerously near tears, she twined her arms about his neck and buried her face against his chest. "Why does everything have to have a price?"

"Because that's how life works." He rubbed her back, soothing her when she should have been soothing him. "It'll work, honey. Honest. We'll make it work." They clung to each other a long time before he lifted his head. "Now, come on. Let's go back to the trailer. My mom promised cobbler and ice cream for dessert. I can't say much for the company around here, but you can't beat the food."

"Okay," she agreed, even though nothing seemed remotely okay.

Chapter 20

"I can't believe we're running so late."

"We're not that late." Alec tried to relax as Christine drove through her parents' neighborhood. The houses ranged in size and style from quaint bungalows to imposing mansions. He knew even the smaller ones went for a bundle. "It's not like we have to get there right at the stroke of six, is it?"

Her only answer was a shaky laugh.

"Ah, come on, it's your family, not a firing squad," he teased in an effort to lighten the tension that had been mounting all day. He couldn't believe she'd dragged him to a department store earlier to buy a sport coat and tie, then changed her own clothes three times before leaving the apartment. "What's the worst that will happen when we arrive fifteen minutes late?"

"Twenty," she corrected, glancing at her diamond watch. "But at least we're here."

He glanced out the side window and felt some relief at the sight of a moderately sized house. Except she drove past that and turned into what looked like a small park. Then he saw the house and blinked.

Holy moly. He stared at the rock castle complete with a turret. The flower beds surrounding it would take an army to maintain. So much for relaxing.

"You grew up here?" His voice went up in pitch as she followed the drive around to a covered motor court on the side.

"No. Mom and Dad didn't move here until I was in high school. We lived in several houses before that, starting with the little place they lived in when I was born and gradually moving up."

He looked at her. "Define little."

"Crap," she swore. "My brother is already here. Of course. Why can't he ever be late?" She pulled in beside a black BMW, then sat staring at the house. With a muttered curse, she opened her purse and dug through it.

"Chris, one question before we go any further."

"What?"

"You know I can't afford to live like this, ever, right? And that even if I could, I wouldn't want to?"

"Actually, that's not true, but at least we agree on the last part."

"What's that supposed to mean?"

"Alec." Impatience tinged her voice. "The minute we marry, what's mine is yours and vice versa."

It hit him suddenly that she probably could afford to live like this. If not now, sometime in the future. He'd known she came from money, but knowing and seeing were not the same thing. Good grief, she probably had trust funds and mutual funds and all kinds of dollars tucked in accounts multiplying like rabbits.

Even if she didn't want to live like this, she'd want a much nicer house than a paramedic could afford.

She pulled a prescription bottle out of her purse and shook a small white pill into her hand.

"What is that?" He frowned.

She tossed the pill back and swallowed it dry. "Just a little something to help me get through the evening without hyperventilating."

"A tranquilizer?" The knots in his stomach tightened even more. "You need a tranquilizer to introduce me to your parents?"

"Alec—" She sighed heavily. "I'm on the verge of an all-out panic attack here, so please, don't take it personally. It's hardly the first time I've needed help getting through an evening with my family."

"Hey." Concern rose as he took her hand. "Look at me." When she did, he saw the same wide-eyed look she'd worn those first few rides on the lift. "Why don't we sit here for a minute?"

"Because we're already late."

"I know, but talk to me." He shifted toward her. "Are you embarrassed to have your family meet me?"

"No," she insisted a little too strongly.

"Truth, Chris. Please."

"I don't know." She rubbed her forehead. "Maybe, but it's not you. It's hard to explain. I just . . ."

"What?"

"I want them to respect my decision and be happy for me." Her eyes searched his. "For them to see that you make me happy. That you're perfect for me, even if—" She broke off.

"Even if I don't measure up to their standards."

"I didn't say that." She looked away. "Let's not

have this conversation, okay? Anything I say is going to come out wrong. Let's just go in and get this over with."

"All right. But first—" He slipped his free hand around the back of her neck and covered her mouth in a long, deep kiss. Pulling back, he stared hard into her eyes. "I love you. You got that?"

She sagged a bit as worry lined her brow. "I love you too."

Why did he hear an ominous "but" on the end of that statement? He squeezed her neck. "I'm marrying you, not them. So I only care what you think."

"You really do make me happy." Another silent "but" hung between them.

He decided to ignore it. For now. "Okay, then. Let's go brave the lion's den."

He stepped from the car and waited for her to come around to his side. She tugged at her pearl-gray cocktail dress and smoothed the hair she'd twisted up in back. Bypassing the side door, they headed down a flower-lined path to the imposing front entrance. He frowned when she rang the bell, rather than going straight in. "You ring the bell at your parents' house?"

"Alec, this isn't a casual visit." That was the third time in the past five minutes she'd started a sentence by saying his name in that exasperated tone. She was nervous, though, so he would cut her some slack. Or not, he thought as she tightened his tie and smoothed his lapels. "This is our engagement dinner and we need it to go well."

"Of course." He resisted the urge to loosen the tie back to where he'd had it.

A small, dark-hared woman wearing a maid's uniform opened the door, bobbing her head and motioning for them to enter.

"Good evening, Rosa."

While Christine greeted the woman, Alec glanced discreetly about the foyer. Walls soared upward from an acre of marble. Stone columns held up archways, and a staircase with a fancy railing curved up to the second floor. He felt as if he'd stepped into some Italian villa that dated back to the Whatever Century, when Prince Whosit summered there. That's how the wealthy said it. They didn't visit places, they summered.

"Are my parents in the den?"

"*Sí.*" The woman nodded, eying Alec with open curiosity.

"Oh, Rosa, this is Alec Hunter, my fiancé. Alec, this is Rosa."

"Pleased to meet you." He moved his hands restlessly, not sure if they were supposed to shake. What was proper protocol for meeting someone's maid?

The woman smiled back broadly, saying nothing but looking pleased. Well she, at least, approved of him.

"Ready?" Christine slipped her arm through his.

"Lead the way." They headed through a formal dining room, where the table had been set for their engagement dinner. The place settings sparkled and gleamed white, gold, and silver against the dark, massive table. He heard the rumble of male voices and classical music playing softly as they crossed another acre of marble. They finally reached the archway to "the den."

Alec held back as Christine hurried forward to greet the two women seated on a red and gold sofa. Christine's father and brother stood before a large window that offered a view of the gardens out back. They looked like matched bookends, both wearing gray suits and facing each other with highball glasses in hand.

"Hello, Mother."

"Ah, Christine. There you are."

While Alec had met the others, this was his first glimpse of Christine's mother. The woman rose gracefully, wearing a silk pantsuit that looked like fancy pajamas but probably cost a fortune.

Christine kissed her mother's cheek. "Sorry we're late."

"You always are." Mrs. Ashton turned to him. Her face held all of Christine's beauty: the same gray eyes, fine bones, and even the same haughty expression that Christine could summon so well. Here, though, was none of the underlying humor that made the look amusing. "This must be Alec, the young man you spent so much time with during our skiing trip."

"Yes." Christine held out her hand, beckoning him to her. When she took his hand, she clung to it, squeezing his fingers as she made the introductions, first to her mother, then her father and brother as the men came forward, and finally to her sister-in-law.

With Natalie came the only genuine warmth in the room. She was petite and pretty in a sleeveless red dress that looked more classy than sexy. She smiled broadly. "We met the day of the snowboard competition."

"Yes." He nodded. "It's good to see you again." She'd been friendly that day too.

"Christine's ski instructor, right?" The brother lifted a brow, then looked at his father. "You remember, right, Dad?"

"Vaguely." Robert Ashton studied Alec with cool blue eyes.

"I told you," Christine corrected with a stiff smile. "Alec isn't actually a ski instructor. He was helping out a friend. He's Silver Mountain's search-and-rescue coordinator. Although he'll be working as a paramedic here."

"Search and rescue. Now there's an . . . interesting job." Robbie's hesitation was brief but telling. His subtle hostility surprised Alec since the man had been cordial the one and only time they'd met.

Natalie slipped an arm about her husband's waist, and if Alec had to guess, pinched him in the side. "We're all delighted over the engagement and eager to get to know you."

"Thank you." Alec felt the tie cutting off his air.

"Can I get you two a drink?" the senior Dr. Ashton asked. "Christine, I assume you want a glass of chardonnay."

"That will be fine."

"Alec?" Dr. Ashton moved to a wet bar with lighted shelves that held a variety of liquor bottles.

Alec stared at them, having no idea what to request, since this sort of quality would be lost on him. What was that stuff Kreiger drank when he was feeling extravagant? "Do you have any single malt Scotch?"

Dr. Ashton gave him a bland look. "I assume Glenfiddich will do?"

"Sure." Alec shrugged casually. No big deal. Drink it every day. For all he knew, Christine's father was about to serve him something that was a hundred years old and cost a hundred bucks a shot.

"My son and I were just discussing long-range stock planning," Dr. Ashton said as he poured amber liquid into a fancy glass and handed it to Alec. "What are your thoughts on the subject?"

Alec sniffed at the potent liquid in his glass, wondering if it was Scotch or paint remover. Dr. Ashton watched him expectantly, and Alec knew no matter what he said, he was screwed. Christine's parents had made up their minds before he'd even walked in the door. Well, if they were going to disapprove, it might as well be of the real him and not this dressed-up version Christine was trying to present.

"Long-range stock planning?" He looked Dr. Ashton straight in the eye. "Yes, I think everyone should have a good breeding schedule for their prize bull."

The brother choked on his drink, then laughed. "Oh, that's good. Bull as in bull and bear. I get it."

Alec remembered vaguely that people used the term bull and bear to describe the stock market, even though he'd been referring to the question as bullshit. Here he was, in the door five seconds, and they were asking him about money?

Dr. Ashton gave him a steely look, letting Alec know he'd understood and was not amused.

Natalie frowned at the men. "Financial talk is so boring. I'd much rather hear about the wedding plans. Christine, have you set a date?"

"The second weekend in April."

"So soon?" Mrs. Ashton frowned. "That barely

gives us seven weeks. Although the country club has a superb staff for handling a reception."

"Actually . . ." Christine looked at him. "It's going to be a double wedding with my friend Maddy. Alec and Joe are handling the plans."

"How romantic!" Natalie exclaimed.

"You can't possibly be serious." Mrs. Ashton gave her daughter a chilly stare.

Christine squirmed. "Well, nothing's set. Exactly." She sent Alec a pleading look. "We could think about the country club."

He stared at her, stunned to see someone as strong willed as Christine cave so instantly. "Is that what you want?"

She dropped her gaze. "I guess we can talk about it later."

"Of course." He fixed a smile on his face and kept it there the rest of the evening.

"Do you mind driving?" Christine asked as they left the house. Her head felt ready to explode.

"Not at all," Alec answered in the same bland voice he'd used for the past three hours.

After digging through her purse, she handed him her keys and prayed he didn't notice how badly her hands were shaking. Anxiety had burned straight through the Xanax and wine, leaving her entirely too sober. Even so, she had no business getting behind a wheel.

She stared out the window as he drove through Tarrytown, past elegant houses and manicured lawns.

"It wasn't that bad," she said as they reached the

highway. "Robbie and Natalie liked you. Dad always takes time to warm up to people, so his stiff manner tonight really isn't a big deal. As for Mom . . . She may get used to the idea of you planning the wedding. If not, we'll let her do it. She lives for things like that, and she's really good at it. Everything will be okay."

Alec didn't say anything.

"The wedding itself isn't that important," she said as her nerves tangled even more. "What matters is us getting married. So if she wants something fancy and formal, that'll be okay, right?"

Silence reigned from Alec's side of the car.

She watched the scenery slip by for a few minutes, then started the litany at the top, repeating it in various versions all the way to the apartment. None of it helped. Nausea churned in her stomach. Her parents couldn't have made it more clear that they disapproved of Alec. Surely that would change, though. Surely. In time.

When they reached the apartment, Buddy greeted them at the door, then whimpered in confusion when Alec walked past him with barely more than a pat on the head. Shadows filled the room even though she'd left the lamp by the sofa on. Without bothering to turn on any more lights, Alec went to stand at the sliding-glass door, staring out at the Austin skyline. She stayed by the front door, watching as he removed his tie.

Why wouldn't he say something?

"I'm sorry Mom and Dad weren't warmer." She laid her purse on the table by the door. "That's just how they are, though. It'll be all right."

He turned to face her. "Actually, Chris, no it's not going to be all right."

"It will." She sorted blindly through some junk mail, then curled her fingers into her palm when her hands wouldn't stop shaking. "They just need time to get to know you."

"No." His flat tone made her look at him again, but she couldn't read his face in the darkness. "It's not going to be all right, because not once on the drive home did you say, 'Fuck them. I don't care what they think.'"

She jolted at hearing that word come from Alec. "They're my parents. Of course I care what they think."

"A little too much. Have you ever once told them 'Fuck you. I'm going to do what I want'?"

"Don't be absurd. I don't cuss at my parents." Nerves turned to anger as she headed for the bedroom, taking off her earrings as she went.

"Of course not." He followed but stopped in the doorway. "If you cussed in front of them, or heaven forbid, acted like yourself, you wouldn't be the perfect daughter anymore, and they might never come to love you the way you want them to."

"I told you why they don't. It's not their fault."

"That's such bullshit. For one thing, children shouldn't have to earn their parents' love. What I saw tonight was the equivalent of your mother saying 'Sit up straight, eat your vegetables, mind your manners, and we'll tolerate your presence.' While your father ignored you to fawn all over your asshole of a brother."

She whirled to face him. "Robbie is not an asshole!"

"Oh, yeah?" He jerked off his jacket and tossed it onto the chair by the window. "What do you call Robbie's suggestion that I 'bop by the club some Saturday for a set of tennis so he can introduce me around'?"

"He was trying to be friendly." She kicked her shoes toward the closet and unzipped her dress.

"He was rubbing my nose in the fact that I don't fit into your social circle and I never will." Alec sat on the bed and removed his shoes. "At least him I can forgive, because I think he was trying to protect you. Your parents, though, Jesus."

"Don't you dare insult them." She stepped into the bathroom, wearing only her panties and bra as she took down her hair.

"Christine—" He came to stand in the doorway, unbuttoning his shirt. "How can you care so much what they think when they don't care about you at all? They only care about how they'll look if their daughter marries a hick."

"You're not a hick!" Her voice rose in anger on his behalf.

"I am!" he shouted back. "You saw what I come from."

"I've also seen where you've gone. What you've made of yourself." Taking up a brush, she jerked it through her hair, fearing any minute all the emotions of the evening would break free in a torrent of tears. "I'm proud of who you are and what you've become."

In the mirror, she saw him come to stand behind her. "That's not going to matter to them." Putting his hands on her shoulders, he turned her to face him. "I thought I could live with that, but . . ."

"But what?" Fear knifed through her. "Are you saying you can't?"

"No." He looked straight into her eyes. "I'm saying I'm not sure you can."

"Alec—" She moved past him, back into the bedroom. "Why are you talking like this? You sound like you think we should break up."

When he didn't answer, she turned to face him.

He stood staring at her a long time, his shirt hanging open over his bare chest. "Maybe we should."

"What?" The floor tilted beneath her feet. "What do you mean? You're the one who said we were perfect together, and now you're doing a complete about-face?"

"Until tonight, I didn't realize what I was asking you to give up. I was too busy concentrating on what I was sacrificing, giving up the mountains and a job that meant everything to me before I met you. Giving up my dog!"

"And now you're changing your mind?" She pulled her silk nightgown from the closet, but simply held it as her vision blurred. "Oh, that's great. That's just great!"

"No." He came to stand beside her, lowering his voice. "Now I'm asking you the same questions you've asked me. If you marry me, Chris, you will lose your father's approval and you'll never get it back. How long before you come to resent me for that?"

Her throat grew too tight for her to speak.

He tucked her hair behind her ear, speaking in a soothing voice, as if she were a child. "You know what's sad is you're throwing us away for something that shouldn't have to be earned. Your parents' love should be given, no strings attached."

"I'm not throwing us away." She looked up into his eyes. "You're the one who's suddenly having doubts."

"I'm the one facing reality. As long as you put impressing your father before us, we don't stand a chance."

"So you want me to tell him off? Sever all ties with him? Not care what he thinks?"

"Christine, listen to me." His hands closed about hers. "You're throwing your life away over something you'll never get, and you're asking me to throw my life away too. And for what? A marriage that I'm starting to see doesn't stand a chance? I can't fit into your family's world any more than you'd fit in with mine. But we both fit in fine in Silver Mountain. Let's go back."

"I can't." She closed her eyes as his words tore at her. "If I break my contract with the hospital, I'll hurt my career and embarrass my father. I can't do it! Goddamn it! I can't!"

"You can! Just as you can accept the truth. Christine—"

She felt his hands cup her face and opened her eyes to find him staring intently at her, as if he could will her to accept his opinion.

"Your father is never going to love you as much as he loves your brother. Never. Nothing you do will change that. You could fly to the moon and back on your own power and your father will still think Robbie hung it. That's what you're afraid of. You aren't afraid of heights. You're afraid to face the truth."

The room wheeled about her as she pulled away. "What in the world does my fear of heights have to do with this?"

"You've known in the back of your mind for years that you could outski your brother and it wouldn't make a bit of difference, so you created a convenient excuse not to ski at all."

"That's ridiculous." With her back to him, she removed her bra and jerked on her nightgown. "You're saying my phobia isn't real?"

"I watched you have the same panic attack tonight that you had on the slopes the day you realized that what I'm saying is true, because you knew what was going to happen once your parents met me. Just as you know, right now, that we don't stand a chance if we live here. Give up, Christine, and put us first. Put yourself first."

"How very convenient for you that me putting myself first saves you from having to give up anything."

He studied her a long time, as a strange calm seemed to settle over him. When he spoke, it was with quiet conviction. "I love you without limits. Do you honestly think you will ever hear your father say that?"

"He's proud of me!" she insisted as tears flooded her eyes. "I've made him proud of me."

"That's not the same thing."

"Yet you would have me destroy even that?" She

swiped angrily at her wet cheeks. "I can't do that, Alec. I can't!"

He turned away, as if to study the wall. Finally his shoulders dropped. "Then we don't stand a chance."

"No, I guess we don't!" she fired back, hurting so much she couldn't think straight. "But then I tried to tell you that all along. This relationship is utterly hopeless and always has been." She turned her back to him as tears coursed down her cheeks.

"Well," he said after a very long silence, "I guess there's nothing else to say." Another long silence followed. "Do you want me to sleep on the sofa?"

"No," she managed to choke out. Turning around she flung her arms about him. "I'm sorry, Alec. I'm sorry."

"Shh." He hugged her to him, his lips racing over her face. "Don't cry, baby. Don't cry."

Somehow they wound up on the bed, his hands stroking and soothing. She touched him back, desperate and demanding.

"Love me, Alec." She looked up at him as fear tore at her. "Love me."

"I do." His eyes burned into hers. "I will. Always."

He stripped her bare and put action to words, not merely pleasuring her body, but making her feel wanted inside as well. The latter left her feeling exposed and raw as he brought her body release. When it was over, when they were both spent, he held her as she wept herself into a fitful sleep.

Chapter 21

Sometimes winning means knowing when to throw in the towel.

—*How to Have a Perfect Life*

Alec heard Christine getting ready for work before dawn, moving quietly around the bedroom as she had on other mornings when she'd had a shift. Sometimes he woke enough to visit with her while she dressed. He'd sit up in bed while they talked about the coming day and what they'd do that evening.

This morning, he kept his back toward the closet and bathroom, feigning sleep while everything inside him ached. Last night's fight kept going though his mind. He had no idea what to say to make things right. Or if things could be right.

The light in the bathroom clicked off, and he sensed her standing near the door to the main room, looking at him. Would she tiptoe around to his side and kiss his forehead as she sometimes did? Whisper for him to go back to sleep, that she'd see him later?

He wanted her to. Even more, he wanted the chance to hold her close and kiss her without saying anything more than "I love you. Have a good day. See you when you get home."

He rolled onto his back to let her know he was

awake, to call her over to the bed, to say something. Anything.

She'd already turned away, though. He caught only a glimpse of her retreating back, then heard the closing of the front door.

Lying in the dark, he stared at the ceiling as the emptiness of the apartment descended around him. Buddy came over to nudge his hand with his wet nose.

"Yeah, I know." Alec hauled himself upright, swung his legs over the edge of the bed, and scrubbed his face. Apparently some things in life didn't care if you'd just been kicked in the heart. "Time for a visit with nature, eh, boy?"

The dog danced with glee as Alec pulled on jeans and a T-shirt. When the morning ritual was done, Alec dragged himself to the kitchen. Christine had left half a pot of coffee in a thermos on the bar as she'd done before. No note this morning, though. No silly or sentimental words to make him smile. Just the coffee.

He poured a cup and sat on the sofa, slumped forward with his forearms braced on his thighs. Buddy came to sit before him, whining as he sensed something was wrong. Rubbing the dog's head, his heart ached even more as he remembered his plan to give this guy up. Buddy had been a constant part of his life for three years. How was he going to explain to him he'd have to be someone else's dog now?

He'd have to, though, if he stayed in Austin, gave up search and rescue, married Christine.

If he stayed.

Yesterday that hadn't even been a question. Well,

perhaps it had been a small nagging one in the back of his mind he'd been trying to ignore.

Last night, he'd asked Christine when she was going to give up chasing the impossible. Maybe he needed to ask himself that same question. He'd willingly sacrifice anything for her, but did he have the right to make her sacrifice the one thing she cared about most: her father's pride and approval? He wanted her to be happy, but if she married him, she wouldn't be, not for long.

He could see them a few short years from now at some country club party, Christine introducing him to friends of the family, all of them thinking: So this is the hick who's living off his wife. As for that, *where* would they live? A house in Tarrytown where he'd have more in common with the yard workers than his neighbors?

Why hadn't he seen up-front how impossible this was?

Because in Silver Mountain, they'd fit together. His friends couldn't care less that she was rich. In Silver Mountain, they could be happy. But not here.

A tearing pain ripped down his chest and settled in his gut.

He looked into Buddy's brown eyes and had to swallow hard to speak. "So, boy, what do you think? Is it time to go home?"

Hearing the word home, Buddy dashed for the door, twirling and barking with joy.

Alec gave up fighting and let himself cry.

"You wanted to see me?" Christine asked from the doorway of the doctors' lounge. The room was outfitted with a narrow bed, small table, and one chair. Her father had just come from surgery and stood in his scrubs, pouring coffee.

"Yes, come in." Her father took the chair, crossing his legs as he sipped from the Styrofoam cup. A patient file lay open on the table before him. "Close the door."

A familiar dread settled in her stomach as she closed the door, then went to perch, back straight, on the bed. Exhausted from a twelve-hour shift and emotionally frayed from last night's fight, all she wanted was to get home and make things right with Alec.

Her father studied her a long time. "So you and Alec met during our recent ski trip."

"Yes." She smoothed the legs of her scrubs over her knees as her palms started to sweat. "I know that doesn't sound like much time to get to know each other, but I'm very much in love with him. He's honest, hardworking, dependable. And he makes me very happy."

"I see." Her father picked up a silver pen and turned it end over end, tapping it on the file he'd been reading. "What do you know of his family?"

"I—" She hesitated, sensing a trap, but not sure which way to step to avoid it. "They're very down-to-earth people."

He tapped and turned the pen a few more times. "Did you know his brother has been on probation for DWI? His sister is on welfare, and his parents have drawn unemployment and workmen's comp several times over the last twenty years?"

Shock punched the breath from her lungs. "You ran a check on them?"

"Did you think I wouldn't?"

"Before you even met Alec?" Her voice rose as her mind spun at the notion. "My God! He didn't stand a chance last night, did he? You'd decided he wasn't suitable before he even walked through the door."

Her father set the pen aside. "I'll be honest with you, Christine. He's not the type of man I'd hoped you'd marry. But then, you've always been a willful child."

"A willful child?" She stared blindly about. "When was I ever willful?"

He frowned at her as if confused. "You never behaved properly for a girl. You were always tagging along after your brother and his friends, getting in their way."

"Robbie never minded having me around." *Unlike you. Robbie knew how starved I was for love, and he didn't mind giving it.* Tears threatened, but she battled them back.

"Even your choice of specialty was a puzzlement," her father went on. "I'm pleased that you decided to go into medicine, but I expected you to choose something more appropriate, like a private OB-GYN practice."

" 'More appropriate'? How is that more appropriate? Because I'm a woman?" Something deep inside her that had been pulled taut all her life, snapped. "That's what it all boils down to, doesn't it? My lack of a dick."

"Christine!" He straightened with shock at her language.

The dam broke, and years of anguish came gushing out. "Alec is right. You're never going to love me the way you love Robbie because I don't have a penis. What do I have to do, grow one? Have a sex-change operation? Dress like a man so your friends won't know your sperm produced a girl?"

"You will not talk to me in that manner."

"Or is it because he was planned and I was an accident? If Mother was so against having another baby, why couldn't you have kept your pants zipped?"

"That's enough!" He set his cup down so hard coffee sloshed out.

"No, it's not enough!" Her whole body started shaking as if electrical currents flowed through it. "I have a right to know. Why can't you love me?"

"You're being absurd. Of course we love you."

"You tolerate me. But only if I do what I'm told. Only if I behave properly." She remembered everything Alec had said last night. "Well, I'm God-dammed tired of being proper. Yes, that's right, I said Goddammed. I'm Goddammed tired of worrying that if I do something wrong, if I displease you, if I'm less than perfect, you'll send me back."

The last words stunned her—a fear that had never been voiced. The shaking intensified as tears streamed down her face. "I thought if I wasn't perfect, you'd send me away. Well, guess what, Dr. Ashton, your daughter isn't perfect. She drinks beer and cusses and sleeps with 'inappropriate' men. She even has a tattoo on her ass. And you know what? Alec Hunter loves me in spite of—or maybe because of—my flaws. He doesn't expect me to be perfect. He only expects me to be me. So if you want to tell me you'll disown me if I marry him, fine. Maybe it's time you did disown me, since I'm such a disappointment to you."

"You are not a disappointment. And if you would simply calm down, I'll tell you why I called you in here."

"To tell me not to marry Alec. Yeah, I got that already."

"No. Granted I'd prefer it if you didn't make such an abominable mistake. But since you seem bent on marrying someone so utterly beneath you, your mother and I think you should talk to a lawyer about a prenuptial agreement."

She laughed bitterly as a strange calmness descended over her. Rising, she crossed to the door. "You know, Dad, there's something I've always wanted to say but never had the guts."

"And that is?"

"Fuck. You."

She sailed through the door, slamming it behind her so hard, the wall shook. Staff members stared as she marched past the nurses' station onto the elevator and punched the button for the parking garage.

Thank God she'd already finished for the day. It was time to go home.

Power sang in her veins during the drive. Even as her body still shook and her stomach burned, she felt . . . triumphant.

Tomorrow she would talk to Ken Hutchens about getting out of her contract. She'd call her head hunter and tell him to find her a position near Silver Mountain.

For now, though, she only wanted to reach her apartment and tell Alec she loved him. No, more than that. She wanted to thank him for giving her the courage to set herself free.

Reaching her parking slot, she found it empty, which surprised her. Maybe Alec was out buying groceries for a makeup dinner. Pleased for the chance to spruce herself up, she strode to her apartment and breezed through the door.

A sense of foreboding niggled her mind when Buddy didn't bound forward to greet her. Could Alec have taken Buddy to the park for a workout this late in the day?

Moving into the room, she noticed the envelope on the bar. Her name was written on the outside. Too many emotions were already coursing through her body for her to feel anything other than curiosity as she opened it and unfolded the handwritten letter from Alec.

A numbness grew inside her as she read every line, until, by the end, she couldn't even feel the fingers holding the paper. She couldn't feel anything.

He'd left her.

She scanned back over the words in disbelief, catching snatches and phrases.

. . . decided to give up pursuing the impossible . . . no right to ask you to sacrifice . . . your happiness is what matters to me . . . I will always love you . . . wish you well . . . a clean break . . . too painful . . . don't . . . call . . .

Don't call? *Don't call?* Through the numbness, anger began to build. After everything they'd been through, after agonizing all day about their fight, after standing up to her father so she could have a life with Alec, she comes home to a Dear Jane letter that ends with "I don't think we should call each other anymore"?

"Oh no, you don't, Alec Hunter." She pulled out her mobile phone and hit speed dial for his mobile number. His voice mail answered. She was about to leave a scathing, tear-filled message, but hung up instead.

This was not the time for rash words. With her emotions ping-ponging all over the place, Lord alone knew what might fly out of her mouth. She needed to think this through. Pacing off adrenaline, she began to form a plan.

So, you don't want me to call, huh? Okay, I won't!

Chapter 22

The key to having a perfect life is having the life that's perfect for you.

—How to Have a Perfect Life

By the time Alec realized he was making an enormous mistake, he was halfway to Colorado. He'd told Christine that when you love someone, you fight to be together. You find a way to make it work.

So what was he doing giving up and walking away?

He thought about turning the Jeep around and heading back to Austin to argue and plead until Christine realized that what they had was a lot more important than the shallow, conditional love she'd been trying all her life to win from her father.

Was that possible, though? Would she ever accept the truth and find a way to let it go?

Maybe not. But was he willing to give up?

Fighting would mean risking everything on the hope that Christine would come around. If she didn't, they'd probably wind up in divorce court, because he wasn't sure he could live with only half her love while watching her jump through hoops to impress her father.

Was he willing to take that gamble?

Yes! he decided and felt conviction rush in. He'd return to Silver Mountain and fight his campaign from there, though. He'd do everything in his power to talk Christine into joining him, because that was the only hope he saw of their relationship working.

The chances of success, however, were slim enough to have his stomach churning as he pulled into the Central Village parking lot.

God, he'd missed the mountains, he thought as he climbed out of the Jeep. He stretched his tired back and took a deep breath of cold air, drawing in the scent of snow and pine trees and wood smoke from chimneys. Sunlight sparkled off the fresh blanket of white, making the village look like a picture-perfect postcard.

"Come on, Buddy," he called as he grabbed his suitcase. "We're home."

Buddy bounded from the Jeep and shook hard, then danced with delight at being back in the land of snow.

Glancing at his watch, Alec saw it was midafternoon. Christine would still be at the hospital. He'd called her during her shift many times, but this was not the kind of conversation for her to have at work. He needed to wait until she was home. Rather than sit alone in his apartment and stare at the clock, he dropped off his things and headed for the pub.

Trying to decide what he'd say when she picked up the phone filled his whole brain. He had no idea how she'd reacted when she returned home and found that note he'd left. In retrospect, he saw that was a cowardly and stupid way to end things. Even if he hadn't decided to fight for her, he realized that he would have had to call her anyway to apologize and end things properly.

Entering the pub, he found Trent, Steve, and Kreiger sitting around the fire pit enjoying a midafternoon break to warm their feet. They all looked up as he approached.

"Surprise, surprise." Trent smiled as Alec dropped into the chair beside him. "Look who's home a day early."

"You know me." Alec propped his feet on the hearth as Buddy settled beside his chair. "Never can wait to get back to work."

"Oh, is that why you left Austin before you planned?" Steve arched a brow.

Alec frowned at the sheriff, puzzled by his tone. Steve sounded almost like he already knew about the breakup with Christine. When the waitress cruised by he ordered a cup of coffee.

Kreiger nodded at him. "Congratulations on your engagement, by the way."

"Actually . . ." Alec squirmed. "That may be a bit premature."

"Oh?" Steve gave him another strangely knowing look. In fact, they all looked a bit smug over something.

Alec frowned at the sheriff. "I, um, hope you haven't started looking for my replacement, since I've decided to stay. Hopefully with Christine, but things are sort of up in the air right now."

"Well, that's good news," Steve said.

Alec's confusion grew. "That my engagement might be on the skids?"

"No, that you're staying in Silver Mountain. I was hoping you'd talk Christine into moving up here."

"After the stupid thing I did, I'm not sure I can, but I'm going to try."

"What stupid thing is that?" Steve asked as he pulled out his mobile phone and a scrap of paper. He glanced at the paper, then punched in a number. Whomever he called must have picked up right away because Steve held up his hand, asking that Alec wait to answer his question. "Hey, it's Steve. I thought you might like to know that Alec is with us at the pub. Yes, he just got in and looks like ten miles of bad road. Great. See you in a minute."

"Who was that?" Alec asked as Steve disconnected.

The sheriff grinned broadly. "Just someone I thought might want to join us."

"Great." Alec rolled his eyes. "That's exactly what I need right now, to share my pain and suffering with even more people."

"That's what friends are for." Trent smiled.

"What's going on?" Alec scowled at all three of them.

"Nothing," Steve insisted. "Speaking of sharing your pain, you were about to tell us what stupid thing you did to piss off Christine."

He sighed heavily. "Actually, I don't know if she's pissed or relieved."

"What do you mean, you don't know?" Steve frowned at him.

Alec rubbed his forehead to partially shield his face. "I, um, left a note telling her I wanted to call things off. So now I have to call her and explain that I've changed my mind."

"You broke up by leaving her a note?" Trent laughed.

"I know." He squeezed his eyes shut in embarrassment. "It was a chickenshit thing to do, but I wasn't thinking straight."

"Man." Steve let out a low whistle. "No wonder she's so pissed."

"I told you, I don't know if she's pissed or not about me leaving. We'd had a really big fight the night before, so for all I know, she was glad to come home and find me gone."

"Well, son," Kreiger said as he rose, "one way or the other, I'd say you're about to find out."

"What?" Alec frowned. Seeing Kreiger glance toward the door, he twisted around and felt his heart jolt.

Christine stood by the hostess stand, the hood of her parka thrown back, fire blazing in her eyes.

"Alec Hunter," she called in a loud voice. The noise in the bar dimmed as the afternoon crowd turned her way. "How dare you give up on me!"

"I'm no expert on women," Steve muttered as he stood, "but I'd say that's pissed."

"Mega pissed," Trent added as all three men went to sit at the bar and watch the show.

Alec's mind blanked of everything but one thought as Christine started toward him: She'd come after him. For the past two days, he'd been terrified she wouldn't take him back—but she'd come after him!

That first wild leap of relief wavered, though, when he saw her shaking with fury.

"You don't do that when you love someone," she

informed him at full volume while Alec scrambled to his feet. "You don't run out on them when they need you most."

A quick look about confirmed everyone within earshot had turned to watch. "Uuuh . . . Hi, Chris. Maybe we should go upstairs."

"Why?" She demanded as she stomped down into the pit, coming to face him toe-to-toe. "Because fighting in public isn't proper? Because my mother might be horrified at my behavior? Because my father might not approve? Aren't you the one who said I should stop caring so much what they think—what everyone thinks? That I should be myself, and do what I want? Well, right now, I want to tell you some things and I don't care who hears, so screw what's proper!"

"Okay," he conceded warily.

Christine balled her hands into fists. A part of her was so mad, she wanted to punch him. Another part wanted to weep with joy at seeing him again. "Do you have any idea how I felt when I got home, eager to tell you my news, and found out that you'd run out on me?"

"I'm sorry." Color darkened his cheeks. "I swear, though, I was trying to do what I thought was best for you."

"Yes, I read your note," she railed at him. "You decided on your own that I shouldn't have to sacrifice anything to be with you. That I deserve to have what I want."

"Exactly."

"Except you took away the one thing I want most." Her vision blurred with tears. "You ripped it away without giving me a choice. What is that if not a sacrifice? An unwilling sacrifice?"

"Christine . . ." He held his hands palm out, as if afraid she really would hit him. "I—"

"No, you let me finish!" She swiped at her wet cheeks. "You said that if my father's respect was what mattered I shouldn't have to sacrifice that to be with you. Well I can't sacrifice something I never had. And what you took away from me means more than something I've been begging for, pathetically, my whole life."

"What are you saying? I didn't take anything."

"You took you! *You* are what makes me happy. *You* are want I want. And *you* are the one thing I refuse to give up."

"Really?" Pleasure lit his face.

"Yes, dammit! How dare you give up on me!"

"I didn't—"

"I'm not finished!" she shouted.

"Okay." A smile flirted with his mouth, as if he found this whole thing funny while she was dying inside. "Continue."

"I know what I said after the dinner party. I was upset. And I was wrong. After I had a chance to think about it, I realized you were right. We can never be happy living in my parents' world, and I have no right to ask you to give all this up." She gestured about the room. "Not when I want it too. I was trying not to see that, but when my father asked me to get a prenuptial agreement, it all became blindingly clear."

Alec's smile vanished. "Your father asked you to get a prenuptial agreement?"

"He did."

"All right. I'll sign one if you want me to."

"The hell you will!"

He frowned. "I don't understand. Did you tell him no?"

Now it was her turn to smile. "Actually, my precise words were 'Fuck you.'"

"Really?" His brows went up.

"Yes, really."

"Good for you." Alec laughed. "That's a good first step."

"What do you mean, first step?"

He took her fists in his hands. "Remember when you said you've never been able to forgive your father for not loving you the way he should?"

"Yes."

Lifting her fists, he kissed each set of knuckles. "It occurred to me that you need to do that."

She frowned. "I'm not sure I can."

"You have to, baby." He coaxed her fists to open so they were holding hands. "For your sake. Otherwise you'll never stop hurting over it, and I can't stand to see you hurting."

She considered it a moment. "If I promise to work on that, will you forgive me for being a blind idiot for so long?"

"Chris, I would forgive you anything except leaving me."

"Good, because I don't like the way we tried to rewrite the end of Peter Pan."

"Oh?"

"No. I don't like the idea of Peter and Wendy growing up and living in the real world. What kind of happy ever after is that? I think they should live in Neverland together forever. What do you have to say to that?"

"I'd say 'Thank God!'" He pulled her against him, held her tight. "Welcome home, Wendy."

The Lost Boys seated at the bar cheered as he spun her about.

Christine threw back her head and laughed. She was home, finally home with a man who was just perfect for her. And that was the best happy-ever-after of all.

Epilogue

Christine woke the following morning to an empty bed in a room filled with sunshine. She had a vague memory of Alec kissing her good-bye before he left for work; then the exhaustion from days of emotional overload had dragged her back under.

Now, though, she grinned as she sat up and stretched her arms over her head. A glance out the window of Alec's bedroom let her know it was a beautiful day outside. They'd spent all of last evening making love and talking about the future. Today she planned to move her clothes from her family's condo to his apartment.

But that didn't mean she couldn't hit the slopes and hopefully bump into Alec.

Dressing quickly, she bundled up against the cold and headed outside. As she walked through the village, she could hardly believe that this wonderful place would now be her home. A lot of loose ends waited for her back in Austin, but Ken Hutchens had been remarkably understanding about her need to take a few days of personal time. The thought of telling her family about her decision made her wince, but that was a problem to deal with later. A big problem that she'd learn to grapple with—slowly—with help from Alec. Her friends, at least, would be happy for her.

Letting herself into the condo, she opened her laptop and fired off an e-mail to Maddy and Amy.

Subject: *Big Announcement*

Message: *The wedding's back on! Alec finally got here, and I told him how much I love him and that I want to live here in Silver Mountain. I think I can safely say, he was "quite pleased" with the idea. Actually, he's ecstatic. The big kid I know and love.*

The best news, though, is we learned the village is definitely adding on to their triage center. I think I have an excellent chance of landing a job right here in Silver Mountain.

So, Maddy, I hope the men do a good job planning this wedding. I'm ready to float down the aisle. How about you?

Maddy: *Congratulations! I'm so glad everything worked out. And of course I'm eager for the wedding. My one concern, though, is that we didn't hear from Amy yesterday. I can't imagine that the ship is out of a satellite area. Do you think something has happened to her?*

Christine: *Oh, hell, I've been so wrapped up in my crisis, I didn't even notice. What did she say in her last e-mail?*

Maddy: *She was taking the kids to a beach on St. Bart's. She hasn't reported in since.*

Christine: *That definitely isn't like Amy. Do you think she got left behind on the island?*

Maddy: *I'm starting to think so. Oh my God, though, can you imagine? Being stranded on a tropical island is most women's fantasy. But for Amy, it's her worst nightmare.*

Kahlúa Recipe

Since Christine and Alec are so fond of coffee, I thought I'd share my favorite recipe for homemade Kahlúa. My husband and I like to make this in early fall, so it has time to age, then give it away as Christmas gifts. It's great in a lot of hot and cold drinks. As a simple warm-me-up, try a shot of it in coffee topped with whipped cream. Yum!

Ingredients:

> 4 cups sugar
> 2 cups water
> ⅔ cup instant coffee
> 1 vanilla bean cut into ½" pieces (2 tsp vanilla extract can be used as a less expensive option)
> 750 milliliters vodka

Directions:

Combine water, sugar, coffee, and vanilla bean pieces in a saucepan and bring to a full boil. (If using vanilla extract, wait and add that when you add the vodka.) Remove from heat and skim froth. Allow to cool *thoroughly*. Remove vanilla beans and add vodka. Pour into a glass container—be sure the container isn't too big, or you'll lose some of the vanilla flavor. Store in a dark place for three weeks. If you choose, divide into smaller bottles and give as gifts.

The adventures continue!
Read on for a sneak peek of

Too Perfect

the next novel in
Julie Ortolon's hilarious
and heartwarming new series,
coming in November 2005.

Big things often begin with a simple dream.
—*How to Have a Perfect Life*

Amy Baker's worst nightmare had come true. She was stranded. Left behind on a tropical island with no money and no way to get home. At least not a way that wouldn't prove humiliating.

Yesterday, after watching the cruise ship she'd been on literally sail off into the sunset without her, she'd agonized over what to do. Being stranded was only half her problem. She'd been traveling with an elderly couple as a nanny to their three grandchildren, and just before being left behind, she'd been fired.

It was all her fault, of course. She'd taken the children ashore on the French island of St. Bartholomew and hired a taxi to get to one of the beaches. As had happened on other shore excursions, she and the children became wrapped up in one of her games of make-believe. They were pirates searching for buried treasure. After a mock sword fight that ranged up and down the white sand beach, she'd glanced at her watch and realized she'd lost track of time. Again! She was an hour late getting the children back to the ship for afternoon snack time with their grandparents.

With the grandfather's health failing, that was the one time of day set aside for him to spend with the children.

Amy had arrived at the landing frazzled and frantic to find a very angry grandmother standing on the dock tapping her foot with impatience. Naturally, the three children—who'd been having a blast all day—picked that moment to break into a full chorus of, "We're tired. We're hungry. We hate this trip."

If Amy hadn't committed several other similar transgressions, perhaps the incident would have been forgiven. As it was, the grandmother had had every right to chew Amy out right there in front of several passengers while loading the children on the tender boat that ferried people back and forth from ship to shore. Embarrassment had swamped Amy down to the soles of her tennis shoes. She'd turned and headed blindly away from the dock—and succeeded in getting lost.

Considering the tiny size of Gustavia, the island's capital, she was sure only she could accomplish such a feat.

By the time she found her way back to the landing, the last tender had come and gone. She'd stood there at the end of the harbor watching in disbelief as the sun sank into the sea and ship grew steadily smaller on the horizon. As much as she'd been dreading getting back onboard, getting left behind was a thousand times worse.

All she had on her was a beach bag containing a few U.S. dollars, a half-empty tube of sunblock, snacks for the kids, her autographed copy of *How to Have a Perfect Life*, and a wet, sandy beach towel. She didn't even have a change of clothes, or underwear so she could take off the swimsuit she wore beneath her T-shirt and shorts. Everything else she'd brought on the trip, including her credit cards and passport, were on their way to St. Thomas.

Calling her grandmother to wire her funds would only earn her a lecture about her absentmindedness, but the thought of turning to her friends Maddy and Christine was out of the question. They'd move mountains to help her, but then she'd lose the bet that had sent her on this trip in the first place.

She refused to be the only one of the three who failed to fulfill the challenge they'd made nearly a year ago. Maddy had faced her fear of rejection to get her art in a gallery, and Christine had faced her fear of heights to go skiing. Now it was Amy's turn to face her fear of strange places to take a trip by herself. So far, she'd only accomplished half of that feat. She'd gone somewhere on her own. Now she had to get back—on her own.

And the more she thought about it, the more she realized that turning to her friends for help wasn't the only thing that would make her a failure. Arriving home a week early with her tail between her legs would do it too. She had to figure out a way to finish her full vacation time. Okay, so it had been a working vacation, but it was still a two-week break from her regular life and everything familiar and safe.

That was the real challenge, wasn't it? Staying away from home for the full two weeks. Facing her fears and dealing with them. She had to do this or lose her self-respect.

That night, though, as she'd lain awake in a hotel room that had wiped out most of her cash, her options had looked bleak. Not only was she stranded on an island, but she was stranded on St. Bart's—one of the most expensive islands in the Caribbean. Even when she sorted out the problems of getting replacement credit cards, how could she afford a week here? Why couldn't she have done something reasonable, like get stranded on an island that had a budget beach hotel and a discount department store for her to buy some clothes? No, she has to get stranded on a chichi island—where the locals spoke French, no less!

Tears started to fill her eyes until she remembered her mother insisting that giving into despair never accomplished anything. "There's a bright side to everything," he mother had said more times than she could count. "You just have to find it."

Swallowing the lump in her throat, she closed her eyes and prayed for an answer.

The following morning, she found a travel agency to help her contact the ship and arrange to have her things packed up and shipped home. That seemed wiser than having them sent to St. Bart's, since she didn't know how long she'd be on the island. They also solved her credit card problem, and within minutes she was picking up a cash advance at a local bank.

Next on her list was the enormous problem of finding a place to stay that she could actually afford. That was when she found the answer to her prayers.

As she stood on the street contemplating her options, her gaze fell on a sign in the window of an employment agency: IMMEDIATE OPENING FOR A LIVE-IN HOUSEKEEPER.

Her breath caught at seeing the perfect solution. Okay, maybe it was wrong to apply for a job when she knew she'd be quitting days later, but, as the idea took root, she realized she actually had four weeks before she absolutely had to be home.

Four weeks. In the Caribbean.

It was terrifying. It was thrilling.

Four weeks. Could she really do that?

The worrywart inside her battled with the part of her that had always longed for freedom to go and do and see.

Yes, she realized. She had things organized enough back home; she could stay away that long. She would work for two weeks—assuming they hired her—give two weeks notice, and be home a whole week before the bridal shower she was throwing for Maddy's and Christine's double wedding on the one-year anniversary of their challenge.

She entered the employment agency shaking with both excitement and doubt. An hour later, she was heading for an interview.

Her spirits lifted with every step as she climbed the footpath that led from Gustavia to the mansion perched on the cliffs overlooking the bay. Her mother was right, she decided. Rather than a catastrophe, life had given her an adventure. A real, live adventure, not the imaginary kind she usually took.

Needing to catch her breath, she stopped and shaded her eyes to take in the view. And oh, what a view!

Dozens of sailboats and yachts bobbed at their anchors in the bay while their owners explored the tropical paradise. Farther out, a cruise ship sat like an enormous luxury hotel floating on the sparkling water of the Caribbean Sea. The sky and water held every shade of blue from azure to indigo, and a light breeze sang through the palm trees around her.

As she'd done so often during the trip, she wished her mother could have seen this. The Caribbean was one of many places they'd visited a thousand times in the stories they made up together, traveling on the ocean or through the air on their magical flying ship. *Do you see it, Momma? It's even more beautiful than we imagined.*

The sweet pain of memories filled her heart in a rush.

Fearing she'd cry if she stood there much longer, she resumed her climb, catching glimpses of a stone structure through the dense, tropical growth. As she got nearer, though, a new worry edged aside some of her enthusiasm. The structure at the top of the trail didn't look like a house. It looked like an old fort, the type that would have guarded the island during the time of pirates.

Before her mind could take off on some flight of fancy

about swashbuckling buccaneers, she wondered if she'd taken a wrong turn. She glanced at the cover sheet to the application she'd filled out. The job description and directions were written in French, but the woman at the employment agency had definitely pointed to this path and told her in English to follow it to the top. As talented as Amy was at taking wrong turns, even she couldn't have messed this up. Could she?

Fighting back doubt, she ducked past the last curtain of palm fronds and found herself facing a very tall bracken-covered rock wall. Staring up at the crenellated battlement that lined the top of the wall made her almost dizzy. On the corner facing the sea, a square tower jutted up even higher.

How wonderfully fascinating. Like ancient ruins in some secluded rain forest far away from civilization.

The path split in two directions, one heading uphill and around to the inland side. The other path headed to the side of the hill that faced the sea. Choosing the seaside path, she let her imagination conjure a story of exploring forgotten ruins: *The intrepid archeologist Amelia Baker battles her way through the jungle to unravel the secrets of a mysterious fortress. What has become of the soldiers who once walked the battlement? Do their ghosts still haunt the old stone walls?*

A delicious shiver ran down her spine at the thought.

She found a door in the base of the tower, but it definitely didn't strike her as the main entrance, so she continued along the edge of the cliff with the bay far below. The moment she cleared the tower, her eyes widened with delight. One whole section of the outer wall had been removed, exposing an inner courtyard to the view of the sea.

Inside lay a garden gone wild. Tropical flowers exploded with color, struggling for space and spilling past their borders. Bougainvilleas climbed the trunks of giant palm trees while bromeliads and orchids dripped down to meet them. Small songbirds and butterflies added a kaleidoscope of music and life. Through the dense tangle, she glimpsed a second-floor gallery with louvered shutters bracketing dozens of doors. Apparently someone had converted the old bastion into a private residence some years back, but the place looked abandoned now.

As she ventured forth through a tunnel of vegetation, the perfume of flowers and damp earth nearly overwhelmed her senses. Very little sunlight reached the ground, and the darkness added an eerie layer to the garden's atmosphere.

Reaching out, she moved the leaf of a banana tree. A small monkey shrieked in her face. She screamed as well, which sent the long-tailed monkey scurrying up a tree trunk where it frightened a red macaw into flight. The ruckus echoed about her in a chain reaction of bird cries.

"Oh, my goodness." She pressed both hands over her racing heart and laughed at herself. "Sorry," she called to the brown-and-white monkey who scowled down at her from his—or her—perch high in the trees.

When Amy's pulse settled, she resumed her search until she found another door. This one didn't look any more welcoming than the one to the tower. The solid panel of aged wood hung from massive wrought iron hinges. At eye level, a snarling gargoyle—who looked a great deal like the vexed monkey overhead—held a large round knocker in its mouth. Its lifeless eyes dared her to knock.

What sort of person would live in such a strange place?

In spite of her fascination, a sense of foreboding crept up the back of her neck. She had plenty of experience dealing with wealthy eccentrics, but this place went beyond odd into the realm of the bizarre. Maybe she should toss her pride to the wind and buy a plane ticket home. Thinking of the challenge, though, stopped her from retreating. If Maddy and Christine could complete their challenges, she could do the same.

She ran a quick hand over her hair to be sure her riot of brown corkscrew curls was still neatly confined in a braid down her back. As for her attire, there wasn't a thing she could do. She was stuck with the white shorts and striped "crew shirt" she'd purchased from the ship's store. It was neat enough, even if this was her second day wearing it.

Okay, no more stalling. Squaring her shoulders, she lifted the circle of gnarled iron and knocked three times. The banging echoed through what sounded like a vast, empty space, evoking visions of gothic mansions from old horror movies.

No sound followed.

She stood in uncertainty, wondering again if she'd taken a wrong turn. An eternity later, the panel began to creak open on rusty hinges. She braced herself, half expecting to see Frankenstein's Igor smiling evilly and bidding her to enter.

For Amy, the reality proved nearly as frightening. The man who answered the door was quite possibly the sexiest man she'd ever seen in her life.